KRIS

SN❄W COUNTRY

A Copper Island Novel
❧ *One* ☙

THE
CHRISTMAS TREE
HOUSE

Acknowledgments

Todd, my husband and best friend, with you I have learned much about love, romance, and writing. Thank you for helping me brainstorm plot ideas and come up with quirky lines. Most of all, thank you for loving me so well.

Sara, my amazing daughter, when you were nine, you caught typos and helped bring scenes to life. For one church scene, you told me, "Have the characters look around at each other. That's what they do in *The Sugar Creek Gang*."

Isaac, my awesome son, I loved hearing your ideas for the book. As a six-year-old, you came up with many exciting police adventures for Danny.

Andrea, my friend, thank you for plowing through my rough drafts and believing this dream would go somewhere.

Cyndi, my colleague, thank you for the big-picture edits. I appreciate your feedback and enthusiasm for the series.

Susan, Stephen, Nathan, Jana, Dan, Alexandra, and Mom, thank you for your help on the home stretch.

God, my Savior, thank you for taking me on this new adventure.

Glossary
of Finnish and Yooper Words

apteekki — Finnish for pharmacy

chook— Yooper for a knitted stocking cap

bush— woods; forest

downstate— the Lower Peninsula of Michigan, below the Mackinac Bridge

hey— also *eh*, a word used at the end of sentences to elicit an affirmative response, similar to the Canadian *eh*

hyvää päivää— Finnish for good day

Kuparisaari— Finnish for Copper Island

makkara— Finnish for sausage, generally summer sausage

nisu— Finnish for sweet cardamom bread

onneksi olkoon— Finnish for congratulations

oofta— Scandinavian-American expression of surprise, astonishment, relief, or dismay

pank— Yooper word meaning to pat snow down to make it more compact

pannukakku—	Finnish for oven pancake; a bready, custard-like dish baked in a pan, similar to Mexican flan but with flour
pasty—	a regional dish of cubed potatoes, carrots, rutabaga, beef, and pork stuffed in a flour shell and baked—ingredients vary, but always includes potatoes and usually some type of meat
puuro—	Finnish for porridge, generally oatmeal—in the UP, Finnish Americans often add an *a, puuroa*
riisipuuro—	Finnish for creamy rice porridge; rice simmered in milk and sweetened with sugar—it is often sprinkled with a cinnamon/sugar mixture and sometimes served with raisins, similar to Mexican *arroz con leche*
sisu—	the Finnish spirit of resilience and determination in the face of adversity; a word with deep cultural significance to Finns and Finnish Americans
suomalainen—	Finnish for "Finnish," such as *suomalainen apteekki*, a Finnish pharmacy
swampers—	rubber boots, typically with leather uppers
UP—	the Upper Peninsula of Michigan, spoken as each letter *U - P*
Yooper—	a resident of the Upper Peninsula of Michigan
yous—	plural of *you*, found in some Northern US dialects, also spelled *youse*, rhymes with *news*

for Todd

Prologue

*B*eth Dawson checked her email. *Can we do lunch today? We need to talk.*

It must be important. Her fiancé knew how busy she was. Maybe Alan had found a vacation rental for their honeymoon. They would drive down to San Diego. Not exotic, but relaxing. She smiled at the thought and typed a reply. *I'll pick up food. Love you.*

She'd always dreamed of a Christmas Eve wedding, but now the timing seemed crazy. Between planning for that and the Family Resource Center's Christmas festivities, she'd barely seen him the last couple of weeks, except for dinner with his mom over Thanksgiving. It would be good to connect today. She turned her attention back to the flyer she was creating. The Christmas party was always fun for the tutors and kids. Christmas cookies. A Nativity play. Angel Tree gifts for all the kids. She clicked print and checked off another item on a long to-do list. She grabbed her purse.

"I'm glad I caught you." Her boss stood in the doorway. "I know you're busy, but would you mind driving the van tonight? Mark went home sick."

Beth grimaced at the thought, but caught herself. "Sure,

Gary."

She stepped out into a 70-degree day in the parking lot. Through the gate, she walked beside a fence topped with barbed wire. The neighborhood was a concrete jungle, except for a few palm trees next to an overpass. Beth wouldn't venture out by herself after dark, but during the day it was safe. Down the sidewalk of the busy street, she passed the Resource Center's thrift store where graffiti covered its metal donation bin. At the bus stop, she chatted briefly with a mother of two kids who came to the tutoring program. She ventured on to Restaurant *El Corredor* and purchased burritos.

She met Alan in his office where she pulled up a chair across from him.

"We've got to call off the wedding." He pushed papers off his desk into a drawer.

"It'll come together." She laughed as she took the burritos out of the bag and set them on the desk. She pulled the foil wrapper off her burrito. "I know it's hectic, but you know how much I wanted a Christmas Eve wedding, and we don't want to wait another year." She shot him a flirtatious smile.

He looked at her blank-faced. "You don't understand. We need to call it off permanently."

Was he serious? She sat frozen, blinking. "Why?" She barely got the word out.

Alan unwrapped his burrito.

"Why, Alan?" She couldn't believe this was happening. Three weeks before the wedding.

He met her gaze for a moment and then looked past her at the wall. "It's not you. It's me." He mumbled the words.

So cliché. Her mind raced with so many thoughts. The non-refundable deposits. The apartment lease they had signed. Gifts they had already received. What would she tell the teen girls she mentored? She had talked about her engagement with them, using it as a model of how life works when you wait on God. What had gone wrong?

Something clicked. The dinner. "It's your mother, isn't it?"

"It's not her. It's not you. It's me." He squeezed a packet of hot sauce on his burrito.

Of course it's you, you spineless weasel. She didn't say it. Instead, she clenched her teeth. She had done everything right.

He bit into the burrito, and his jaw worked as he stared at her dumbly.

Why were they having this conversation in the middle of the day? At work? He couldn't wait until the end of the day or the weekend or better yet, why not months ago? Her chin quivered. Anger rose in Beth's throat. "You think this is a conversation to have over lunch?" She spit out the words and slapped her burrito on his desk.

"We can still be friends." He wiped his desk with a napkin.

Well, I like my friends so that's not going to work, she thought. "Let me help you clean that up." She swept both burritos into the garbage can.

"Hey, I was going to eat that."

"I was going to marry you." She plunked the can down next to him. "Go ahead. Eat it." She twisted the engagement ring off her finger and was about to throw it at him, but then thought better of it. She stuffed it in her pocket and left.

Chapter 1

Five Weeks Later

*B*eth strained to see beyond flashing red lights into the dark past an ambulance parked on the shoulder. A car lay upside down in the snow-filled ditch. She gasped. *God, help them.*

Intermittent wiper blades swept melted snow from her windshield. Her headlights illuminated the side of a sheriff's car, and on the other side of the accident, another vehicle blocked the road. No other cars on the road for over an hour, and now this.

She'd witnessed many accidents in LA, but somehow this one unsettled her. She shivered. She had never seen such darkness as on those country roads on the way to the Upper Peninsula of Michigan.

She checked her phone. Two bars. She'd call Mother.

"Hello, this is Rebecca Dawson."

"Hi, it's me."

"You made it. How's Grandma?"

Beth moistened her lips. "I'm not quite there. There's been an accident—"

"Oh, no. I told you it was too dangerous to drive across the country," Mother scolded.

Beth sighed. Why had she even called? "I didn't get into an

accident. I'm just stopped at one."

"They probably hit a deer. Why are you still on the road? I told you to get an early start from Minneapolis so you wouldn't be driving at night. What took you so long to leave?"

"I don't know." She scrambled for an excuse that would satisfy Mother but came up empty. "I guess it just took a while to get going."

"You must learn to keep better track of time. It was bad enough you drove across the country, but the roads are dreadful there in the winter. It's dangerous driving with all that snow."

The drive had been pretty in the daylight, but it got dark quickly. Mother was right. She should've left earlier.

"How much farther do you have to drive?"

"My GPS says I'll be at Grandma's in a half hour."

EMTs appeared from the ditch, bright reflective stripes and patches on their jackets. They were pulling something. A sled with somebody on it. They lifted the person up and onto a gurney.

That looked rough. *God, I pray he's alive.*

"When you get in, be sure to talk to Grandma about coming to California. Show her the pictures I sent with you."

"Yes, Mother." How many times had she said that phrase? She might have called her *Mom* when she was a young child, but for as long as Beth could remember, her mom was *Mother.*

"It's not safe for her to be in that house by herself out in the country. I want you to talk to her about it tonight."

"Yes, Mother."

Mother droned on about her battle to get Grandma to move.

Grandma had fallen a week before the wedding—well, a week before the canceled wedding. She had still planned to fly out to LA for Christmas, but with the fall wasn't up for traveling. Beth decided to visit her instead. Besides, she needed time away to pick up the pieces. When Mother finally came around to the idea of her driving to Michigan, it was clear she had another agenda. She wanted her to convince Grandma to return with her to LA.

The EMTs loaded the patient into the back of the ambulance.

Beth straightened in her seat, put her foot on the brake, and shifted the car into drive. "I've got to let you go now."

"Call me tonight after you talk to Grandma."

The ambulance sped off with sirens blazing. The cops left, and Beth drove on—the sole car on the road—even slower than before the accident.

She gripped the steering wheel and leaned forward as she struggled to see the snow-covered centerline. She made her way across the Lift Bridge and onto Copper Island. As she drove down Main Street in Quincy, Douglass's twin town, cars passed her. Another driver tapped his horn.

Red lights reflected onto her dashboard, and a siren chirped. He couldn't be pulling her over. Her speedometer read fifteen miles per hour. She slowed to ten, hoping the vehicle would go around. Sirens blared as she drove through town in a slow-speed chase.

In the rearview mirror, headlights blinded her. A truck? She looked for a lit parking lot. Men had been impersonating cops and raping women. That was LA. *This is small-town America, but you never know.* She pulled into a gas station and parked in full view of the cashier. A blue SUV parked behind her. Instead of a bar of lights on the roof, there was one large, old-fashioned, red light. It looked like something anybody could rig up.

A man approached her Toyota Corolla and, with a thick knuckle, rapped on the window.

She cracked it open. "Who are you?" She looked for an actual metal badge, instead of the embroidered emblems on his jacket and tight, black stocking cap.

"Who am I?" he barked. "I'm a trooper with the Michigan State Police. Why didn't you stop?"

She gathered her courage. "How do I know you're a real cop?"

"Ma'am, you can't fake being a cop in a town this small."

He unzipped his jacket to reveal his badge. "Call 911 if you want. They can verify."

She looked in her rearview mirror. "But you're not driving a real cop car."

"We drive trucks. I need to see your driver's license, registration, and proof of insurance."

She rifled through the glove box and slipped the documents through the crack.

"Los Angeles, California, hey."

Beth was silent.

"Ma'am, that was a question. You from Los Angeles, California?"

"Oh, yes, I didn't know that was a question. You didn't up-speak."

"Huh?"

"You didn't use upward inflection of the end of your sentence so I would know it was a question."

"You're a schoolteacher, too, hey."

"Was that a question?" She frowned. "No, I'm not a schoolteacher. I'm a youth worker. Well, I'm nothing, now. Are you going to give me a ticket? I wasn't speeding."

"You were obstructing the flow of traffic, going too slow. How many drinks have you had?"

Beth gasped. "Drinks? None. I'm accounting for road conditions, sir."

"This fluff? This is a dry, January snow. These are not dangerous road conditions."

"I just passed an accident on the way into town." Mother was right. She shouldn't have come here.

"I was there. She didn't go off the road because of the conditions. She was drunk." He shook his head. "What are you doing in Michigan?"

"Visiting…" Tears stung her eyes and she blinked them away.

"Oh, now don't cry." The trooper's tone softened.

"I'm not," Beth snapped. She just wanted the whole ordeal to be over so she could get to Grandma's. "Just give me the ticket."

"I'm not gonna give you a ticket."

"Why? Because you thought I was going to cry?" Instead of holding back like usual, she let loose. "What kind of cop are you if you don't follow through on your threats?"

"I'm a trooper, not a parent. I'm not even married."

"What did you mean by that? Why would you think I'd care about your marital status?" She scowled. "That's so unprofessional."

The trooper cocked his head. "Are you okay?" He stared into her eyes.

She seethed. "You are *not* my therapist."

He shrugged and chuckled. "You might need a better one. Look, ma'am, pick up the pace, or at least stay in your lane."

She clenched her jaw.

"And welcome to God's country." After handing the documents back to her, he walked back to his truck.

Beth regretted her terseness. He was just doing his job, and he had gentle eyes. He didn't deserve that. She put her head down on the steering wheel and sobbed, stress overcoming her. It had been a rough five weeks. Get a grip, she told herself as she pulled a package of tissue from her purse and blew her nose.

Up Quincy Hill and a few miles past town, a pickup truck passed heading the opposite direction, leaving in its wake a short-lived blizzard that both mesmerized and frightened her. She turned down a country road flanked with trees. Even with the snow, it looked the same as it did on her many childhood visits, every summer with her parents. She hadn't been back for years, not since Grandpa Sam's funeral. When was that? He had died the summer after her freshman year of college. Had it been seven years?

Past red pines that lined the driveway, the headlights flashed on a woodshed, sauna, and on banks of snow as she turned her car toward an old, gray stucco farmhouse. She drove through a few inches of fresh powder and parked near the front steps. The porch light was off, but a light inside the house burned brightly.

She turned off the car and sat in silence for a minute, composing herself. As she got out, she slipped and grabbed the car door to steady herself. Beth walked with short strides to the house. She locked the car behind her, and the Corolla chirped.

Inside the enclosed porch, a few pieces of firewood were stacked in a hopper to the right of the main door. Two rocking chairs sat to the left of the door with a small table between them. Beth had played at the feet of her grandparents who sat in those chairs, her grandma drinking tea and reading a book and her grandpa drinking coffee and reading the newspaper.

"Grandma," she called, as she entered the warm house. Hit with the scent of cardamom bread, she inhaled, closed her eyes, and tilted her head back. Ahh, *nisu.* The scent brought her back to her childhood. Eating the sweet, hearty bread in Grandma's kitchen. "It's me."

"Coming," Grandma called. Moments later, she enveloped Beth in a tight squeeze. She was a small woman, not frail, just petite. She had gained a bit of weight since Beth last saw her, but she carried it well. "I'm so glad to see you. I guess I fell asleep waiting for you. How are you, dear?"

"It's good to get away." She bit her lip. Away from all the drama—seeing Alan every day at work, returning wedding gifts, canceling reservations—while he went on as if nothing happened.

"I can't believe that boy. Three weeks before the wedding. So fickle." Grandma shook her head. "Now, don't just stand there. Come have something to eat."

Beth kicked off her boots, hung her jacket, and followed Grandma down the hall. A fire was burning in an antique kitchen stove, and a pot simmered atop a modern cooking range.

"How was your trip?" Grandma pulled a bowl from the cupboard. "Such a long drive from California. Good thing the snow was light tonight."

Beth thought sheepishly about her encounter with the police officer. She brushed it off. It didn't matter. The important thing was that she had made it. Safe and sound.

"Come sit down. I have stew on the range, and I made *nisu*."

"I'd love that." Beth sat at the oak table that stood against the wall under a window. A floodlight lit up the snow-filled back yard. The cardamom bread lay sliced in the center of the table. Next to it, a knife rested on the edge of a saucer beside a stick of butter. She buttered a slice of the bread.

Grandma set a bowl of stew in front of her. "Would you like tea, dear?"

"Please."

"Tea tastes better when it's heated by a wood fire." Grandma set a ceramic teakettle on the old stove.

Beth put a spoonful of stew in her mouth and closed her eyes, savoring the garlic, basil, and vegetables. Happy memories from summer visits at the farm flooded her mind. Helping Grandma weed and water the garden. Digging fresh carrots and eating peas and beans right off the vine. The Upper Peninsula—or the UP as the locals called it—was earthy, real. Like Mother, she was concerned about Grandma living alone in the country, but she wasn't convinced she should leave. "This is delicious. Thank you for having me."

"I'm glad to have you. With Sam gone, this house is too big for me." Grandma leaned against the counter.

"I'm sure it's a lot of work to keep up the farm." Beth tried to get a sense if their concerns were justified.

"There's nothing left of the farm, other than my garden. I kept the goats and chickens for a while because your grandpa liked to watch them, but I got rid of them after he died."

"Are you doing okay here by yourself?" She asked the question tentatively. She didn't want to be in the middle of things between her mother and Grandma. She had come here to escape drama.

"I do just fine on my own," Grandma said sharply. "I didn't give up the farm because I'm incapable of managing it. I gave it up because I'm too busy. But if your mother is worried, tell her Danny, my neighbor boy, checks in on me most nights.

He makes sure my wood hopper's full. I have petroleum, of course, but with the cost, I try to use wood as much as possible, at least during the day."

"I can haul your firewood," Beth offered.

"So can I. I like doing it, in fact, but I also like Danny's company. While you're here, I want you to relax. Get some rest." The teakettle whistled, and Grandma picked it up by its bamboo handle and set it on a woven reed trivet on the table. "I'll make us chamomile tea, if that's all right with you. I dried flowers from the garden last summer. It's so calming before bed."

"That sounds great."

While Grandma stuffed the tea ball and dropped it into the kettle to steep, Beth finished her stew. She pushed the bowl aside. Grandma served two cups of tea and sat across the kitchen table from Beth, who dipped the bread in her tea—something she hadn't done since she was a kid. That's how Grandma taught her to eat it.

"Hello?" A call came from the front hallway, and Beth jumped in alarm.

"That's Danny."

"He doesn't knock?"

"That's the Yooper doorbell—open the door and yell. I'm glad you'll get to meet him. He's about your age. Come on in, Danny." Grandma went to greet him. "Don't worry about your boots just yet. I'll get a towel you can stand on."

Danny stepped into the kitchen still dressed in his State Police uniform. He pulled off his stocking cap revealing short, dark hair. A smile emerged on his angular face.

Beth wanted to hide under the table.

Chapter 2

"*I* see you have company." Danny looked past Grandma at Beth, who glanced at him and then turned to sip her tea and hide her face.

"I'm so glad you get to meet." Grandma Lou's voice sang with enthusiasm. "Danny, this is my granddaughter, Beth."

Beth squinted as she met his gaze, her eyes pleading.

No, I won't tell on you, he tried to communicate with a smile as he offered his hand.

She grasped it, and her face relaxed. "It's nice to meet you."

Grandma retrieved a towel from the kitchen drawer and threw it on the maple floor at Danny's feet. "Do you want a slice of *nisu*, Danny?"

Danny couldn't stop himself from staring into Beth's soft blue eyes. And she wasn't looking away.

"Danny?" Grandma Lou looked at him quizzically.

"Oh, right." He let go of Beth's hand and stood on the towel. "You know the answer to that, Grandma Lou."

"First, would you mind helping Beth haul in her bags?"

"No problem."

"I'll slice you some *nisu* while you do that."

"I'll get my keys." Beth put on her jacket and cowgirl boots and followed him out of the kitchen.

Too bad they had started off on the wrong foot. He flipped a switch, turning on the lights in the enclosed porch. As he held the door open for her, crisp, clean air filled his lungs. It had stopped snowing, and the nearly full moon illuminated the field.

As she made her way down the snow-covered steps, she slipped. He grabbed her from behind, under her arms, and righted her. She was light, youthful. He knew she must be older than she looked, because Grandma Lou talked about her work as a missionary. The cutest missionary he had ever met.

"Thank you." She tilted her face up to his and tucked a strand of blonde hair behind an ear.

She seemed sweet now. She had probably just been stressed when he pulled her over. He kept a hand on her arm. She smelled good, too, like flowers or vanilla or something.

"You can let go now." She tugged her elbow away and held her key fob in front of her as she led the way. The car chirped twice.

"You lock your car?" he asked with a chuckle.

"You up-speak?" she countered. She tossed her hair as she popped the trunk.

Danny hoisted her suitcase onto his shoulder.

"It has wheels." She smirked.

She was feisty, but he could dish it back. "It's not four-wheel drive. The wheels won't do much good."

Beth looked down at the snow. "Oh, right." She grabbed her duffel bag, and they started for the house.

"What do you have in here? Bricks?"

"Books." Beth laughed.

He grunted.

"It's how I relax."

The Corolla chirped again, and Danny raised an eyebrow. "City girl," he teased.

She scrunched her nose.

In the porch, they stomped the snow off their boots and then stepped back into the house.

Grandma had set a few slices of *nisu* on the table "Come and sit with us after you put her luggage upstairs in the larger room."

Beth followed him up the stairs to the guest bedroom, where he placed her suitcase on top of the dresser.

"Your grandma told me you were coming, but I didn't make the connection. I feel bad about your welcome into town." He was just doing his job, but still.

"It's okay. It was a long drive."

He was going to go out on a limb and ask her out. What did he have to lose? Since she was just visiting, he might not have another chance. "Could I make it up to you by taking you out to dinner tomorrow night?"

Beth gasped. She looked horrified.

He had a sinking feeling in his stomach. "With your grandma," he added. "Dinner with you and your grandma."

"I'm sure she already has plans for us."

"Then I'll ask her." He spun on his heel and left the room before she could object. Back downstairs in the kitchen, he went for it. "Grandma Lou, I'd like to take you and your grand-daughter out for dinner. Someplace nice, like the Cornucopia, tomorrow night."

"That sounds delightful." Grandma nodded decisively. She turned to Beth. "Is that all right with you, dear?"

Beth looked at the floor and exhaled slowly. "Okay."

She didn't look thrilled, and it wasn't like him to go on a date with someone who didn't want his company, but there was something between them. Something that made him think they'd connect. He wanted to at least give it a shot. "Grandma Lou, you've been saying you want to try that new restaurant ever since it opened two years ago. We should go now that Aimee's working there. I'll pick you ladies up at six o'clock. I'll take a rain check on the visiting." He wanted to leave before Beth could change her mind. "I'll grab that *nisu* to go, if you don't mind. Maribel called again today. I said I'd stop by tonight after work. Goodnight, Grandma Lou. Nice to meet you, Beth."

After Danny left, Beth and Grandma sat at the table with their tea. "Are you trying to set me up?" Beth asked. "I shouldn't date anyone, not yet. It's too soon. Dr. Benley said no dating for at least six months after a breakup."

"Who's Dr. Benley?"

"He's an author. We need to cancel. Do you have Danny's number?"

"Oh, it's just Danny. It's not a date. It's dinner. And if it were a date, why would you think it's a date with you? Maybe he was asking *me* out." Grandma chuckled.

Beth managed a smile. "I'll give him this—he's smooth." Danny was handsome in a rugged sort of way with broad shoulders and a five o'clock shadow. He seemed the direct opposite of Alan, who was rail-thin and timid. Alan never made her skin tingle the way it just had when Danny shook her hand and when he had kept her from slipping. The connection was magnetic. Now he wanted to go out. He was probably just being hospitable, but what twenty-something guy takes out his seventy-four-year-old neighbor lady and her granddaughter?

She buttered another piece of *nisu* and lifted it to her mouth. Out the window, snow fell in large flakes on a bird feeder. "It's snowing again. It was clear fifteen minutes ago when Danny and I got the bags from the car."

"That's lake effect for you." Grandma sipped her tea. "It snows one minute, and it's clear the next, depending on which way the wind blows."

Beth ate the sweet bread, tasting the cardamom's subtle, unique flavor—like cinnamon mixed with licorice. She sliced off a third piece. "This stuff's addictive."

"It is. That's why I make it for special people."

"Danny seemed familiar with it."

"Danny *is* special." Grandma buttered a piece of bread.

"Mother sent pictures of Cora and Tate. I'll go get them." Beth wasn't sure the pictures of her brother's kids would be the best approach to convince Grandma to move, but her mother would ask about them tonight, and she didn't want to disappoint her. Beth brought the envelope to Grandma. "She made me promise I'd give them to you as soon as I got here."

Grandma fumbled as she tried to pull out the pictures.

"Are you okay?" Beth frowned. The envelope wasn't even sealed.

"I'm just so excited. I can't get them out. You do it."

Beth pulled the pictures out and handed them to her.

"They have grown so much." Grandma studied each picture, tracing their faces with her finger.

Beth sighed. "Cora was heart-broken when she found out she wasn't going to be a flower girl." She had cried and begged until Beth told her there couldn't be a flower girl without a wedding. Beth had cried, too, so the little darling hugged her. "Cora told me she didn't want him for an uncle anyway because he didn't even pretend to like dolls." Beth laughed uneasily.

"It's just as well that I never got to meet him." Grandma laid her hand on Beth's arm. "So fickle."

A lump rose in her throat, and Beth swallowed hard. "How are you feeling after your fall?"

"I feel fine." Grandma set the pictures down on the table. "Let's get you off to bed. I washed the sheets in your mom's old room and turned on the space heater today so it'll be nice and cozy. You need to rest up so you can enjoy your date." Grandma's eyes twinkled. "I mean, so you can chaperone my date tomorrow."

Beth shook her head. The last thing she needed was a rebound relationship.

She crossed the shiny hardwood floors in her mother's old room and sat on the edge of the bed covered with a handcrafted quilt. The reflection in the vanity mirror on the antique oak dresser showed her smudged mascara. Circles under her eyes. Tangled hair. Ugh. So much for first impressions. Danny must be desperate.

She called Mother.

"Did you talk to your grandma about moving to LA?"

"I don't think she's receptive to it."

"Of course not, that's why I need you to talk to her. She won't listen to me. She just keeps thanking me for the offer. So infuriating."

"Sorry, Mother. We got to visiting, and then the neigh… It just wasn't the right time."

"Did you show her the pictures?"

"Yes, Mother."

"Did you—"

"I have to go. Goodnight, Mother."

Chapter 3

*A*t the State Police Post, Danny sat in front of his locker and laced his boots.

"Morning, man." Rich opened his locker and pulled out a black duffel bag. "You responded to the accident on M-26 last night, hey."

"The sheriff was already on the scene by the time I got there, so I just blocked traffic. Another DWI." Danny yanked the laces tight and tied a knot. "Happens way too often."

"Didn't you graduate with her?"

"Kristine Smith? I don't think so. Was she from around here?"

"She was Kristine Hiltunen." Rich studied him, as if waiting for a reaction.

Danny shook his head in disbelief.

"I heard you used to date her."

Danny gulped. There were no secrets on Copper Island. "Yeah, in high school. We were kids." Kristine was popular. He was too, he supposed, though he never really thought of himself as part of that crowd until they started dating. He always liked her. Everyone liked her. She was cute and fun. She surprised him by stopping by the hardware store where he worked. They ended up talking in an aisle for half an hour. She suggested he meet her at a party out on the canal that night. He did, and afterward, they ended up back at her house, in her bedroom. Her parents were out of town.

"I heard she was a drinker back in high school, too."

Danny grimaced. "Yeah, she never could stop at one or two beers." At parties on the weekend, she drank until Danny had to carry her back to the car and bring her home. For the rest of the week, she was a good student and athlete. They had fun together, he loved her, and she loved him. Back then, she had said they'd get married someday. He thought so too, right up until the day she cheated on him.

Hurt from nearly a decade ago worked its way to the surface. It still stung.

During their senior year, they were both taking classes at Douglass State. He brought her to a frat party but had to work the next morning. She didn't want to leave early and said she'd find a ride home from someone else. That someone else ended up being a carrot-topped fraternity guy, but not until after they had disappeared into an upstairs bedroom. Danny heard about it and broke up with her. She pleaded with him, excusing her behavior on intoxication. But it hurt too bad.

The breakup was the beginning of his wild years. He made sure she knew how easily he moved on. They graduated from high school a few weeks later, and he moved downstate.

"You okay, man?" Rich brought him back to the present.

"Yeah." Danny traced a tile square with the toe of his boot. "Haven't heard from her in years." He saw Kristine's mother in town on occasion but didn't make a point to talk to her. He prayed the woman who had broken his heart and sent him into a tailspin was okay.

"You stay safe." Rich threw his duffel bag over his shoulder and left.

Danny shut his locker with a thud. That chapter in life closed a decade ago. Anyway, he had a date, if dinner with his elderly neighbor and her hot granddaughter counted as a date.

Beth woke with a start to the sound of a man's voice coming from downstairs. Was it Danny? Maybe she could sneak down into the bathroom at the bottom of the stairs. As rough as she looked the night before, she must look even worse in the morning.

As Beth descended the stairs, she could hear the voice was deeper and older than Danny's. The man had an easy laugh—a belly laugh—and a thick, UP accent.

Before she could close the bathroom door, Grandma called to her, "Beth, come out as soon as you can. I'd like you to meet somebody."

As she brushed her teeth, she thought of Grandpa Sam. He was proud of being a Yooper, as they call residents of the UP. Before the stroke, he played up his Yooper accent in a sing-songy voice with exaggerated vowels and dropped consonants, and sometimes whole words—a cross between an old-world European and a modern Canadian accent. Grandpa Sam laid it on thick when he told jokes about two old Finlanders, Heiki and Toivo, and when he talked about the mining history of the Copper Country.

After washing her face and brushing her hair, Beth joined Grandma and her friend.

"Mak, this is my granddaughter, Beth. Beth, this is Mak." Grandma's face beamed as she gave Beth a side-squeeze.

Mak filled the doorframe. He was big, at least his top half, but his thin, denim-covered legs stuck out of clunky boots and terminated under a big belly. He smiled. His yellowed, coffee-stained teeth matched his bushy blond beard. He wore a flannel jacket and a fur-lined, orange hat, which covered his ears.

A lumberjack, Beth thought.

"*Hyvää päivää,*" he bellowed. "Am I seeing a ghost from da past? You look just like your mom. Same nose. Same eyes. Even da same hair."

Beth smiled. "Her hairstyle has changed since then." She

had to admit even she sometimes did a double take when she looked at photos of her mother when she was younger. At least she knew what she would look like at age fifty-four.

"I haven't seen Becky for…" Mak stroked his beard.

"Becky?" Beth raised her eyebrows and looked at Grandma.

"Your mother was Becky—until she went to California," Grandma explained.

"Now Lou, when was that she moved away?"

"Thirty-six years ago."

"Thirty-six years. Unbelievable." Mak grunted.

Grandma pulled small plates from the cupboard. "Can I talk you into having a piece of *nisu* and maybe some hot tea? I'll slice up some *makkara* for you."

"I think you could. Yous have coffee made?"

"No. Sam was the coffee drinker. I don't even keep the coffee maker out anymore. I could get it out and make you some."

"That's all right. I'll try da tea." He removed his hat and kicked off his boots. "It's a good time for a break. Beth, I's gonna move your car, but it was locked. I's plowin'. Most people keep their keys on da visor." Mak's *T-H*'es sounded like *D*'s. "I came in to see if I could get da keys, but then got to visiting. You move your car later, and I'll catch that part tonight."

"Mak brought me more firewood, too." Grandma smiled at him.

"Yah, made wood from my old shade tree."

"A big wind last week blew over a tree near his house and he didn't waste any time getting it all chopped up. Mak's got *sisu*."

"It's cold, so it's a good time for makin' wood. Even green wood splits good. I'll miss that tree. Was my writin' tree, but Lorna got 'er wish—wanted an open view from da kitchen window. Your grandma told me God sided with her because she washes da dishes." Mak laughed again, snorting. "I'll have to find a new place to write in da summer." He shook his head.

Beth's mouth opened in surprise. This backwoods lumberjack she could barely understand was a writer?

"I cleared a spot in da woodshed and put all da green wood in da back corner there, so yous ought to save that for next year."

"What do you write?" Beth asked when they were sitting around the kitchen table with tea, cardamom bread, and summer sausage.

"I'm working on a romantic Western."

Beth started to laugh, almost spitting her tea back into the cup, but held it in.

"I know. Not my first choice in genre. I'd like to be da next John Grisham. My first novel was a suspense—hunters found dead in their tree stands. Da fresh snow covered everything up so there warn't no clues. I took it to a writer's conference downstate, but no takers. One of da speakers there said that when he was startin' out, publishers wanted romantic Westerns, so he wrote romantic Westerns. Don't know if they still want romantic Westerns, but writin's writin'. I'm still learning, but some day..." Mak's voice trailed off. He bit into a piece of sausage.

"I thought Mak's novel was excellent." Grandma's enthusiasm showed on her face. "It was a page turner, and clean, too. I stayed up late to finish it."

"Yah, thank you, Lou." Mak pulled from his jacket pocket a bound journal with the word *Inspire* embossed on its cover. "And for this new novel, I don't wan' it to be like all da other chick lit, either. I'll write chick lit if I have to, but it won' be no cheesy chick lit. Lorna has me watch those movies with her." Mak shook his head. "Unrealistic expectations for relationships. It ain't healthy." He set the journal on the table with a thump.

"You write chick lit." Beth stared.

"I don't advertise it much. Don't know if folks'll want to read a Romance written by an old Finn like me. Iris MacDowell. That's my pen name."

"You have a woman's name for a pen name? So Mac is short for MacDowell?"

"No. Mak is short for Maki. Toivo Maki. I don't care for

Toivo, too old fashioned—and too many of those dumb-Finn jokes about Toivo—and Maki is too common, so I go by Mak. That is Mak with a K. You probably picked up on da two degrees of separation with MacDowell. I picked Iris 'cause it's a flowery name and women like flowers. I's gonna call myself Chrysanthemum, but Lorna said nobody'd know how to spell it to find me on Amazon." Mak snorted and smiled broadly.

"Beth's a writer, too," Grandma offered.

"Not really. I haven't written stories. I keep a journal and I've written Bible curriculum to use with kids."

Mak shrugged. "Writin' is writin'. I tell Lorna it's as cheap a hobby as you can find. Don't cost nothin' but pen an' paper—'though that can cost a bit. Yous been in Robin's Nest downtown, eh."

Grandma nodded and Beth shook her head.

"They've got some fancy pens in there." Mak pulled a silver pen from his breast pocket. "This one here is worth a face cord of hardwood. Lorna warn't too happy when I told 'er that. Not that she minds me spendin' money, but she likes somethin' to show for it. More than a pen. But it's some pen." He handed it to Beth. "You're another Becky. Brings me back in time. I used to hire that boy she went with. He was a good worker. What's his name, Lou?"

"That was a long time ago. What's Lorna been up to, Mak?"

"My mother had a boyfriend?" Beth interrupted. Mother had never mentioned dating anybody other than Dad.

Grandma stood, and her chair screeched as it slid on the hardwood floor. "What's Lorna's latest business venture?"

"Now her idea's cupcakes. Gluten-free."

"A bakery?" Grandma refilled Mak's teacup.

"Yep. She wants to open a gluten-free bakeshop and sell cupcakes. She's been baking up a storm. Vanilla cream, Strawberry, German Chocolate." He patted his belly. "And I've been doing da tastin'."

Grandma pulled her chair back to the table and sat.

"Can't say I mind," Mak continued. "It's better than when she was into da herbs. I's da guinea pig then, too, but those herbs... Well, some of them give you da runs. Lorna don't mind da runs, not since we got our bidet. She says da runs is a sign da herbs are working, cleanin' you out. No matter what happens to you, they're workin'. They make you feel better, they're workin'. They make you feel worse, you havin' a Herxheimer reaction, and they're workin'."

"What was my mother's boyfriend like?" Beth asked.

"That was a long time ago." Grandma changed the subject. "You have a bidet, Mak?"

"Yah, a mechanical bidet toilet seat. Turn a knob and it sprays you clean. Saves on TP, too. Pays for itself."

"I've been having problems with my arm lately, maybe carpal tunnel, and I wonder..." Grandma frowned and straightened her right arm across the table.

Mak nodded. "Yah, I had carpal tunnel once when I was workin' construction. Swinging too many hammers. The numbness and tinglin' is da worst."

"I don't have numbness or tingling. Just weakness. Sometimes my hand doesn't work." Grandma shrugged.

"I'm sure it's nothin'. Whatever it is, a bidet'll help. They're highly recommended for da elderly and disabled. You should come over and try ours, both of yous. I love it. Everyone should have one." Mak slapped the table.

"Maybe I'll do that," Grandma said.

Beth stared, hardly believing the conversation.

"You can try da cupcakes while you're at it. Lorna's been bakin' dozens of cupcakes and sendin' them here and there with surveys. She gets feedback on what people like. Is this one too dry? Would yous know it's gluten-free?"

Grandma laughed. "Tell her I'll be over sometime to do taste testing, and maybe to use the bathroom."

"I'll do that. It sure beats da herbs."

After Mak left, Beth called her mother while Grandma took a shower.

"Hi, Elizabeth. Did you talk to Grandma about moving?"

"No, but I did talk to a man named Toivo Maki. Remember him?"

"The name's vaguely familiar."

"He said your boyfriend used to work for him." Beth knew so little about her mother's childhood. "Are you still there?"

"I'm driving now, so I'll let you go."

Mother's abrupt tone surprised Beth. She was usually glad to talk on her long commute to the insurance agency where she worked.

"The next time you talk to somebody, talk about them or you. Good-bye, Elizabeth."

Chapter 4

*B*eth and Grandma sipped tea and watched chickadees out the window snatch seeds and fly away. Beth's phone dinged, and she pulled it out of her pocket.

The text message was from Alan. *Gary told me you left the Center for good.*

Beth seethed but didn't respond. "I don't get it," she told Grandma. "I followed all the rules." She had been careful not to let passion get ahead of reason. She and Alan didn't even kiss until they were engaged. They had followed Dr. Benley's rules for Christian courtship. They dated for a year, were engaged for six months, and stayed out of bed. Dr. Benley said a marriage could work between any two Christians because love is a verb, not a feeling. She was intent on doing it right, having an authentic love that would last. Besides, she was attractive enough. Slender. Silky hair. She had inherited her mother's delicate Finnish nose that turned up slightly at the tip. She had her flaws. Her teeth were too big and she often ran late, but that's not reason to call off a wedding. "I prayed about our relationship. What went wrong?"

"Oh, honey, you're only part of the equation. As hard as this is for you, I'm glad it didn't happen after the wedding."

"I've told myself that, too." Beth shook her head. "I just feel so stupid."

The phone dinged again. *I hope it wasn't because of me.*

"It's the weasel texting me." She frowned.

"Was it difficult to leave your job, dear? I know you love those kids."

"Yeah." Sorrow filled Beth's heart. "But it was time." She missed the kids, but how could she serve in ministry when all she wanted to do was slam Alan's head against a wall? "He broke up with me at work over lunch, like it wasn't a big deal. I thought he was joking at first." She bit her lip. "I don't know what I should do now. What I want isn't an option."

"I know, sweetheart. I know." Grandma stood and put her arm on Beth's shoulder. "It takes time, dear. Give yourself time. You'll figure it out."

Beth stared blankly out the window, her eyes swimming with tears.

"Sweetie, people say that when God closes one door he opens another and I believe that, but sometimes there's a long, dark hallway before the next door."

"Yes, Grandma, that's how I feel." Beth's voice cracked.

"The burden of grief is heavy, like the snow that crushed that old barn out in the field, but spring will come and the snow will melt."

"But the barn will still be broken." Beth sniffed. She and her brother, Jeremy, had played in it when they were children.

"Danny offered to take it apart and haul it away, but I like having it there. Sam built that barn, and when I see that weathered barnwood, I think of him. It's still beautiful, even in its brokenness."

Beth sobbed.

"Cry it out. There's a reason God made tears." Grandma squeezed her tightly.

Beth's shoulders shook.

Finally, she was silent. She wiped her tears with the back of her sleeve.

Another ding from her phone. *My mom wants me to get*

the ring back. Could I stop by to pick it up?

"Unbelievable." Sadness turned back to anger. "His mom wants the ring back. She probably paid for it. It was a lot more than two months of his salary."

"Are you going to give it to him?"

"No, I sold it." She laughed. "That's how I'm funding my trip."

"Good for you. Is he going to stay at the Family Resource Center?"

"I guess, but it's not his dream job. His mom wants him to get a job with a real company. I hadn't met her until a month before the wedding. Ms. Zananski lives on the other coast. She travels a lot, even internationally. When she finally came to visit—to meet me—it was Thanksgiving weekend." Beth set her cup on the table and then retrieved the kettle from the old kitchen stove and refreshed hers and Grandma's cups. She put the kettle on the trivet and sat with her knees pulled up to her chest, holding the warm cup with both hands. "That night was the beginning of the end. We went to an LA restaurant called Isabella's. Formal attire required. White tablecloths. Utensils for each course. Pricey."

"That doesn't sound like your style."

"It wasn't. I was out of my element. Ms. Z went on and on about her work," Beth continued. "When she finally took interest in me, she asked about my long-term goals. I told her I wanted to be a stay-at-home mom. Maybe foster or adopt kids. She rolled her eyes and said, 'That's very noble. And you'll do all that on one income with Alan working IT at a nonprofit?' She was so condescending, and Alan didn't say a thing. He just twirled fettuccine noodles with his fork. He called off the wedding a week later."

"She doesn't sound like a very nice person."

"She told him I lack confidence."

"Lack confidence?" Grandma's forehead furrowed. "My Beth who drove around inner-city neighborhoods in LA ministering to hurting children, facing street thugs with guns and knives?"

"Oh Grandma, I never even saw a gun or knife."

"Well you saved that girl from her abusive father."

"It was her mom's boyfriend." Beth shuddered. She could still picture the drunk man leering at Gloria.

"Your mother said you stood up to him."

"When I dropped Gloria off after tutoring, he stumbled off the stoop and slapped her across the face. I yelled for her to get back in the van." Tears welled up in Beth's eyes. "On the way back to the Center, she told me the man had done more than slap her, so I called CPS and Gloria was placed in protective custody." Beth's tears spilled over. Her problems were miniscule in comparison. Yet, she couldn't shake her own grief, her out-of-control emotions. She took another sip of tea.

"Alan's mom doesn't know what she's talking about. Lack confidence. Humph. You just drove across the country by yourself." Grandma set her jaw.

"I don't know." Beth shrugged. "I think she hoped Alan would marry someone like her."

A ding. *I know you're reading this. My phone tells me when you read the message.*

Beth pounded out a reply with her thumbs. *You can pick the ring up at Sunset Pawn and I'll send you a bill for the lost deposit for the photographer. Now leave me alone.*

She put her phone down and leaned back in her chair. Grandma looked at her curiously. "That was closure." Beth grinned.

"Good. Then we'll have a good time tonight."

Beth winced. "Oh Grandma, we should cancel tonight. Do you have Danny's number?"

Chapter 5

"*N*ow Beth, why would you want to cancel?" Grandma asked.

"Because it's a bad idea. It breaks every rule."

"Whose rules?" Grandma stood and cleared the dishes.

"Dr. Benley's. God's." Beth wiped the table with a dishrag. She couldn't... She shouldn't. She squared her shoulders. "What's his number?"

"I think I might have misplaced it." Grandma smiled. "What size shoe do you wear?"

"Six and a half."

"Close enough." Grandma stepped into the hallway.

"Close enough for what? Listen, Grandma, I appreciate your efforts, whatever you're up to, but I shouldn't be going out with that man."

"You need to get out of the house and get some fresh air." Grandma opened the closet door. As she squatted, she fell to the side and landed on her bottom. "*Oofta*, lost my balance there. At least I didn't fall far."

"Are you okay?"

"I'm fine." Grandma righted herself and knelt in front of the closet.

"Maybe Mother is right. You shouldn't be living by your-self."

"I don't want to talk about it. Here are my ski boots." Grandma pulled them out of the closet. "You should trek around the field. My cross country skis are in the garage against the wall."

"I don't know, Grandma. Maybe I should stay with you."

"You're wound too tightly. You need to get out of the house. Have you ever been skiing?"

"Not cross-country. I went downhill skiing once. It didn't go so well." It was a decade ago but she hadn't forgotten her humiliation at Mammoth Mountain with the church youth group. She had fallen getting off the chairlift, tumbled halfway down the mountain, and spent the rest of the day in the chalet. "I'll go if you promise to get me Danny's number."

"Cross country skiing's like walking—at least the way I do it. Kids these days skate ski, but I don't see sense in that because you can only do it on groomed trails. Half the purpose of cross-country skiing is to cross the country. You can get a nice glide across the field if you make a track. Ski across the field, turn around, and retrace your steps. The fresh air will do you good, and I'd like to live vicariously through you. Ahh, to be young again."

"You're filibustering."

Grandma pulled herself up. "Here's my snow pants. There's warm gloves and a *chook* under the bench."

"Chook?"

"A knitted stocking cap."

"Is chook a Finnish word?" Beth asked.

"No, it's Yooper."

"Okay, I'll try it." She was up for the challenge. She was a different person than that girl who tumbled down Mammoth.

Beth dressed and headed out. It was snowing again, al-ready an inch since Mak had plowed that morning. She moved her car and parked it near the garage where she retrieved the skis.

She latched her toes into the bindings and then made her way across the frozen drive. Snow fell in large flakes. The sun shone through thin lake-effect cloud cover. When she reached the edge of the plowed area, she sidestepped up the bank. Her skis crossed and she fell to the ground. It was much harder than walking. Beth leaned on a pole and stood.

She breathed in the fresh clean air, clearing her mind. She got the hang of it as she skied across the field past the crumpled barn. Weathered barnwood on each gable bowed to the heavy burden of snow that filled a rusted sheet-metal valley of the collapsed roof. It was a sad sight, the passing of an era.

Out of the wind and into the woods, Beth skied between snow-laden firs into a clearing. Ice crystals hung from the branches, lit by the diffused sun. She stopped and stared in wonder at the splendor before looking up at the sky. A God who could create that tree could have prevented her heartbreak.

Why didn't you stop me from getting engaged to Alan? I was trying so hard to follow your will. Don't you care about me? Why, God? There was no answer.

Beth snapped a picture with her phone.

Heading back to the farmhouse, she could see a newer, small, blue house far across the field. She felt drawn to the simple, cozy home—the opposite of the crazy-busy LA life with clustered houses and sprawling apartment complexes.

When Beth got back into the house, she found Grandma sitting at the kitchen table sipping tea. Steam rose from bowls of leftover stew on the table.

"I saw the most beautiful tree." Beth put her phone on the table and showed Grandma the picture of the sparkling fir. "This doesn't do it justice. It was magical."

"I'm so glad you see the beauty in it. Your mother didn't. Well, she did until she didn't. She keeps bugging me to move out to California, but I like the seasons here."

"Mother says you have two seasons—winter and August."

"That's not true. We have a long beautiful winter, a short spring, a spectacular summer, and a breathtaking fall. I wouldn't trade it for the world."

"Did you find his number?" Beth joined Grandma at the

table.

"Who's that?" Grandma took a spoonful of stew.

"Danny. Did you find Danny's number?"

"Sorry, I didn't have a chance to look."

"You said you'd get it for me while I went skiing."

"No I didn't."

Tightness gripped her chest. It was too soon. She didn't want to jump into a new relationship, nor did she want to experience rejection if he didn't like her. "Where's your phone book?"

Grandma nodded to the hutch.

Beth found the phone book in the top drawer. "What's his last name?"

"Johnson."

"You've got to be kidding me." She opened the book. Even in a small town, there were a dozen Johnsons, but no Danny or Daniel or Dan. "There's a Dale and Evelyn who live near here."

"They're his folks. But he doesn't live there. He lives in that little blue house between here and his parents."

Beth sighed and put the phone book away. She joined Grandma at the table and tasted the stew, which was even better than the night before. "So, Grandma, who's this neighbor boy, Danny Johnson? And did you put him up to it?"

"No, dearie, I did not." Grandma's eyes sparkled. "You find it difficult to believe that a nice young man like Danny would want to spend time with an old lady like me?"

"That's not what I'm saying."

Grandma laughed. "I like to get out. That's why we're going."

"I can't date anyone now." Beth looked out the window at the feeding birds, little gray and black chickadees. "After Alan, I should take time to figure out what I'm supposed to be doing with my life." She felt rage rising within her again. "I do better if I don't think about that weasel."

"Let's make pasties. Chopping's a good way to work out emotions." Grandma pulled ingredients out of the pantry and fridge. "I'd like to get these pasties baked before Danny comes so I can give him one for his lunch tomorrow."

Beth washed her hands and found a cutting board and a knife.

They chopped vegetables in rhythm. "This arm's not co-operating again." Grandma stopped for a few seconds to shake out her right arm. "I can still manage the potatoes, onions, and carrots, but you're going to have to cut up the rutabaga. That's one tough root. That's my way—rutabaga. Everybody's got her own way of making pasties. Some Yoopers substitute carrot for rutabaga, but I say it's not a pasty without rutabaga. Some people put in turnips. That's close enough to rutabaga. Some people put in broccoli." Grandma wrinkled her nose. "Yuck."

"Mother made pasties, too, and I've helped her. She uses your recipe, so I know all about cutting up rutabaga. I guess that's one thing she liked about the UP."

"It's almost the same recipe. I changed one thing. I got a new recipe for my crust from Lorna, after she abandoned her plan to open a pasty shop. I think that one would have flown. She makes the lightest, flakiest crust I've ever tasted and she told me the secret."

"Are you going to tell me?"

"I'll tell you, but keep it hush-hush."

"My lips are sealed."

"Lard."

"Eww."

"Vegetable shortening doesn't cut it."

"As long as I don't have to touch it."

"My arm's getting tired." Grandma set down her knife and shook her right hand again. She massaged it. "You're going to have to finish up. I'll coach you." Grandma washed her hands and then sat at the table. "Sorry, sweetheart. My hand is done for today."

Chapter 6

*W*arm water poured through Beth's hair and down her back, washing what was left of California down the drain. She stepped onto a fluffy bathmat and wrapped herself in a thick towel. She turned the blow dryer on high, taking the chill out of the drafty bathroom.

"Danny will be here in fifteen minutes," Grandma called from outside the door.

Back in the bedroom, Beth rubbed vanilla-scented lotion across her body. She rummaged through her suitcase. He said it would be some place nice, so she pulled out a slim-fitting, black dress that came modestly below her knees. For the final touch, she put on the pearl necklace her dad gave her for Christmas. She suspected it was going to be a wedding gift.

Beth rolled the pearls between her fingers and thumb, thinking of Dad checking her car before she left as Mother cautioned her not to pick up hitchhikers or leave valuables in her car. Mother planted fears in her mind. She was the one who told her about the rapists impersonating police officers. She would not be happy that Beth was going on a date. Well, it's not a date. She's just chaperoning Grandma. She'd make the best of the dinner since Grandma was so excited about it.

Beth pulled powder, lipstick, and mascara out of her toiletry bag. That was it for make-up. She was a natural girl but had bought makeup for the wedding and started wearing it lightly, practicing. After the wedding was called off, she kept wearing it, plus a little concealer under her eyes, especially at work, trying to look put-together, as if she were okay.

Looking in the mirror, Beth brushed a little powder over her cheeks and nose. She opened her mouth slightly as she applied mascara to her short eyelashes.

She heard Danny's voice coming from downstairs.

Snap. She was late. Again. She quickly applied a natural-toned lipstick and took one last look at herself in the mirror. Maybe the dress was too much. Who was she trying to be? A glamour girl? Was she trying to impress him? No. It was just a nice restaurant. She hurried downstairs into the kitchen.

Danny stood in the doorframe, wearing a T-shirt underneath his unzipped ski jacket and faded blue jeans.

"Sorry, I'm overdressed." Beth tucked the pearls under the neckline of her dress.

"You're not overdressed. Maybe I'm a little underdressed—sorry about that. You'll find all kinds at Cornucopia. The great thing about the UP is that nobody cares what you look like. By the way, you look nice, and I like the pearls."

Heat rose to her face, and she smiled and pulled the pearls out.

"Both of you ladies do."

"Thank you. Now don't forget your pasty." Grandma handed him the aluminum foil-wrapped package.

"Ah, that's right. Thank you."

Beth slipped into her boots. "Don't you want to keep it here in the refrigerator while we're gone?"

"My Jeep is a refrigerator, at least till March. You can't leave food in a car much past when the bears come out of hibernation. Had a black bear break into my Jeep last year."

"We have break-ins in LA, but not by bears."

"Yeah. Anyhow, I'll keep it in there all night until I get to work."

"Then you eat a cold pasty?" Beth put on her jacket, and the three of them stepped out of the house.

"No, I put it on the engine block a half hour before lunch. I only lost one that way. I put it on the engine, and no sooner did I get a call. When I looked later, I couldn't find the pasty. There was some happy crow somewhere along Highway 41."

It had been snowing earlier, but the sky had cleared. Under the starry night, Beth kicked through several inches of powder. "Do you think the roads are okay?"

"We'll be fine," Grandma reassured her. "Danny has four-wheel drive. Up here on the hill, it snows every day. Anyway, we Yoopers got *sisu*—we don't let a little snow slow us down."

From the backseat, Beth looked out at the white road, which was bright well past the headlights due to the moon in the clear sky. She appreciated the beauty of the road when she didn't have the stress of staying on it.

In downtown Quincy, Danny parked in a lot near an old sandstone building. He bounded out and around the SUV, opened the doors, and offered an arm to each of the ladies. "Be careful. It's icy under the snow."

Cornucopia. The name fit the place, with its earthy décor, natural woodwork, and eclectic art.

Grandma waved across the room to a gray-haired woman who was sitting alone in a booth. "I need to talk to my friend about something. You and Danny go ahead and sit down."

Danny turned to the hostess. "Hey, Jill. How've you been?" Small-town cop. He probably knew everybody.

"Right this way." The hostess clicked her heels on the tile floor as she led the way. "A booth for three. Is the third person here yet?"

"Looks like we might have lost one." Danny nodded toward Grandma, who was engrossed in conversation across the room. He winked at Beth.

"Three people," Beth said firmly. "My grandma will join us in a minute."

"Enjoy." The hostess set three menus on the table. "Aimee will be your server."

The server had a bounce in her step, and a brown ponytail swung behind her as she looked to each table with a broad smile. As she approached their booth, she asked, "What can I get you to drink?" When she looked at Danny, blood drained from her face. "Danny?"

"Hey. Good to see you." He smiled enthusiastically. "I'll have a Coke with no ice."

"I'll have water with lemon," Beth said.

The waitress didn't acknowledge Beth, staring at Danny with her jaw slack.

"Beth—Aimee. Aimee—Beth, Lou's granddaughter."

"Oh." Aimee offered a smile. A polite smile. "You're Lou's granddaughter? Didn't you just get married?"

Danny looked confused.

"No." Beth hid behind her menu.

Aimee frowned. "I thought—"

"You thought wrong." Beth instantly regretted her tone.

"Is someone joining you?"

"Yes," Beth said firmly as Danny said, "No."

Danny pointed across the restaurant. "Lou was going to join us, but she's talking to Senja." Then Danny addressed Beth, "Aimee's in your grandma's prayer group."

"I'll be back to take your order." Aimee left.

"Excuse me." Beth set her menu down, slipped out of the booth, and strode to Grandma's table. "Are you abandoning me?" she whispered.

"Beth, this is my dear friend Senja. Senja, Beth."

The woman, younger than Grandma, smiled pleasantly. "I'm going through a crisis. Louisa's helping me sort it out." She winked at Grandma.

"She needs me." Grandma patted her friend's arm.

Senja, sitting bright-eyed with her shoulders pulled back, didn't look like she was in crisis-mode.

"*I* need you," Beth pleaded. "Mother will kill me if she finds out I was on a date."

"He's *my* date." Grandma cast Danny a wave. "Thanks for entertaining him."

A waiter approached carrying a tray with cups and a tea-pot. "Here are your drinks, ladies."

"Sheesh." Beth trudged back to her booth.

Danny sat with his back against the wall and his legs stretched out on the seat. "We lost her, hey."

"She's consoling her."

"Senja?" He straightened and faced Beth. "That's weird."

Aimee returned with iceless Coke and lemon-less water. "Have you decided what you want to eat?"

"Could I get lemon, please?" Beth asked.

"You want lemon for dinner?" Aimee scrawled on her order pad.

"No. I want lemon for my water. I haven't had a chance to look at the menu yet."

"Give us a minute," Danny said, and Aimee left.

After looking over the menu, Beth stared out the window. Cars made their way through town. A couple walked arm in arm down the snowy sidewalk. It was so different from home.

"It's beautiful out there, hey," Danny interrupted her thoughts.

"I haven't been here in the winter before. We'd always visit in the summer. My grandparents would visit us in California in the winter."

"Makes sense to me. Grandpa Sam liked to escape the snow for a couple of weeks every year."

"You called him Grandpa, too?" Beth asked.

"You all lived so far away, and my grandparents died when I was young so he and Grandma Lou kind of adopted us."

"I guess that makes us cousins," she teased.

He raised an eyebrow. "I assure you I don't see you as a cousin."

This is not a date, Beth thought. She followed Dr. Benley's rules for relationships. Dating is for the purpose of courtship, for determining a suitable match for marriage. She wasn't going to be staying in the UP, so she shouldn't be dating at all. Besides, there should be no dating after a breakup for at least six months to a year, depending on the commitment level of the prior relationship, and she was about as committed to Alan as she could be. She could go on and on with all the things that were wrong about her being on a date with Danny—her head hurt thinking about it. She looked across the restaurant. Grandma was opening a menu.

Aimee returned, without lemon, and looked at Danny. "What you want?"

"Ladies first." He nodded to Beth.

"I'd like a Greek salad with dressing on the side and a bowl of beef barley soup. And lemon for my water."

"The usual?" Aimee asked Danny.

"Yeah, but make it a large order of breaded mushrooms," he added as Aimee walked away.

"You have a usual?" Beth asked.

Danny smiled. "Life in a small town. That's why people like it."

Beth had never considered the advantages of small town living. Mother didn't talk much of Quincy, but when she did, it wasn't with particular fondness. She made it sound like people who lived in small towns were stuck. "Have you lived here your whole life?"

"Most of it. I did a stint as a trooper downstate, but moved back up here when there was an opening. There are problems here too, but not as much crime as in the city. It's a good gig."

"What happened in that accident last night?"

The sparkle dimmed from Danny's eyes and his lips formed a flat line across his face. "She's pretty banged up."

"I'm sorry to hear that. Did you know her?"

"Not well, but we were in the same graduating class."

As Aimee neared the booth, Beth felt her icy glare. Aimee dropped a basket of breaded mushrooms on the table and a few rolled off the top.

Danny shook his head and seemed to snap out of his funk. It must be hard to be a cop, Beth thought.

As they ate the mushrooms, Danny took a sip of Coke between each bite, but his glass never seemed to get more than half empty as Aimee passed by frequently with a pitcher to refill it, while Beth's empty glass sat on the table.

"Excuse me." Beth held up her glass when Aimee topped off Danny's Coke. "Could I get more water? With lemon?"

"Sure, I'll get right on it." Aimee set the pitcher on the table and slid into the booth next to Danny. "They scheduled me for next weekend, so I won't be able to go out with you." She smirked at Beth, and then presented Danny a pathetic pout.

"That's too bad. But the tips are good here, hey."

"Yeah, they better be tonight." Aimee stood. "Your food should be up."

Aimee returned a short time later with Danny's usual, a turkey artichoke sandwich, and Beth's Greek salad, drenched in dressing. Beth didn't want to complain, but she did ask, "And the soup? Maybe some water?"

Aimee's cheek muscles forced the corner of her lips up into a smile.

The service was bad, but only half-bad—bad for Beth, but not for Danny. Would he notice? She usually overlooked bad service, but this seemed personal.

"They do a good job. This is one of my favorite places." Danny took a bite of his sandwich and a sip of Coke. "This is real turkey. Here, you should try it." Danny held the un-eaten side of his sandwich out to her. "Go on."

Beth leaned across the table and took a small bite. "That *is* good."

He took a sip of Coke and another bite of his sandwich. "Why aren't you eating your salad?"

"There's a bit too much dressing."

"You ordered that with the dressing on the side, didn't you?"

She nodded, pleased he noticed.

"That's odd. Aimee usually gets everything right."

Aimee came by the table with Beth's soup and a glass of water. Still no lemon.

"Aimee, can you remake Beth's salad without the dressing?"

"Oh, no." Beth pushed a few drenched leaves to the edge

of the bowl. "That's not necessary. I'll eat it." She ate some of the dryer lettuce, and then tried the beef barley. "This soup is good."

"This sandwich is exceptional." A glob of mayo stuck to his chin.

"You really like food, hey," Beth deadpanned. She reached out with her napkin and dabbed his chin. Danny smiled and met her gaze, his brown eyes, dark and penetrating. Beth pulled her hand away and looked down.

She picked at her salad.

"Do you like country music?" he asked.

"I've grown fond of it recently, enough to buy cowgirl boots on my way through Nebraska."

"Allie Nantuck will be here next week. Do you want to see her?"

"Yeah," Beth blurted and then cocked her head. "Are you asking me out?"

"I have an extra ticket, and it's yours if you want to see her. I'm going, too, and will even give you a ride if you need one." Danny pierced her defenses with humor.

What was she thinking? No rebound relationships. No dating unless you're compatible. Follow the rules if you want your relationship to work. Panic set in. "Are you the firstborn?"

"What?"

"Are you the oldest kid in your family? How many brothers and sisters do you have? What's your birth order?"

"Slow down, lady."

"Now you want me to slow down? Yesterday I wasn't going fast enough." She shouldn't be out with him, although it was Grandma's fault they ended up at a table together, alone.

"I'm the baby. I have an older brother and sister."

Beth gulped. "Dr. Benley wrote in *Before I'm Intimately Yours* that the best match for a lastborn is either a firstborn or an only child. I'm the youngest of two, so I'm also the baby. Two babies equal chaos."

"I have a feeling that anybody matched with you will be chaos—but it would be fun." Danny raised his eyebrows and smiled. He had a slight gap between his front teeth, though the imperfection made him more handsome. "Let's not get ahead of ourselves. I'm just asking you to a concert, not to marry me."

Don't date someone you wouldn't marry, Dr. Benley's words echoed in Beth's head. "I shouldn't go to the concert."

"You want to."

"No." She met his stare.

"You're a tough nut to crack. What's going on inside that beautiful head?" Danny took a bite of his sandwich.

He was confident, maybe a little cocky, but she liked being desired. The boys in her high school had never pursued her. She had guy friends who were like brothers at Apollos, the Christian college she attended. She and Alan became friends soon after she started working at the Resource Center, and their friendship somehow turned into an engagement without a pursuit. She had watched movies play out like this, but she never thought it would happen to her. Anyway, she had a list of non-negotiables. "I'm a Christian."

"So am I." He popped a mushroom in his mouth. "I go to church with your grandma."

Grandma ambled over with her jacket hung over her arm. "Are you talking about me? My ears were itching. How's your date going?"

"You said this wasn't a date, just dinner." Beth raised her eyebrows.

"Every day is a date. Today's the eighth." Grandma chuckled.

"I'm trying to get her to come to a concert with me next week, but she's as stubborn as you," Danny said.

"Well?" Grandma asked.

"I said no." Beth folded her arms and leaned back

"Don't say no yet." Danny shot her a wink. "Sleep on it for a couple days, and I'll ask you again."

That evening, Beth sat cross-legged on her bed with her journal and pen in hand. She flipped back through the pages of the past year. The engagement. The wedding plans. The breakup. She couldn't bring herself to put anything about Danny in that book. Danny might be a new chapter, a new book of her life. She closed her journal and tossed it on the floor. After two days in the UP, she felt like a new person. She'd need a new journal. She would buy one in town—perhaps at Robin's Nest.

Chapter 7

"She died." Rich sat on the bench next to Danny looking uncharacteristically empathetic.

"Kristine?"

"Yeah."

Wow. Twenty-eight years old. The third classmate to go. One had been killed in a logging accident not long after high school. Another, the class valedictorian, had died in a freak scuba diving accident in Belize. Sad. Now Kristine. Too young.

"She had a son," Rich added.

"Really? That's tough." Even though situations like this happened all the time, it hit harder because Danny knew her. He had told Beth he didn't really know Kristine. Their relationship had been years ago. They weren't in touch. He didn't know who she was today. Guilt washed over him. There was a reason he hadn't been forthcoming. He knew God had forgiven him for his indiscretions during his wild years, but he was still ashamed to share his past.

Rich put his hand on Danny's shoulder. "The funeral's Thursday morning. Are you going?"

"I'm not sure her husband would want to see an ex-boyfriend."

"I'm sure he'd welcome the support. They weren't together anyway. I heard she moved back here with her parents, but he was still in Wisconsin with their boy." Rich stood and slammed his locker. "Stay safe. And write some tickets for once."

Beth lay in bed and stared out the window through falling snow at the top of an overgrown apple tree. Years before, a tire swing hung from that tree. Grandpa pushed her high in the air and she felt like she was flying. Beth longed for those days. When life was simple and the world made sense.

She'd had fun with Danny the night before—too much fun—she liked him and she didn't know what to think about that. When she sat up, she noticed her journal on the floor. Full of lies. She sighed and headed downstairs.

Standing at the kitchen range, Grandma stirred a pot. "I heard your footsteps so I put the *puuroa* cooking. It's steel-cut oats, so it'll take fifteen minutes. In the meantime, would you like tea, dear?"

"That'd be great."

As Grandma poured tea, Beth read aloud the title of a bound book that was sitting on the other end of the table next to another teacup, "*Les Misérables.*"

"Yes. A wonderful story of how grace redeems one man and obsession with the law consumes another." Grandma joined her at the table.

"I've seen the movie. It was good."

"The book is better. The book is always better. How was your time with Danny last night?"

"You abandoned me."

"Senja needed me."

Beth and Grandma sat in silence, looking out the window. Chickadees flittered between the bird feeder and apple tree.

"Look at the birds of the air." Grandma paused dramatically. "They don't sow or reap or store away in barns, yet God feeds them."

"You're the one feeding them," Beth countered.

Grandma chuckled. "We are his hands—his body. Have you decided what to wear to the concert with Danny next week?"

"I don't think I should go."

"You should go. I have plans on Saturday." Grandma smiled. "It would be good for you to get out."

"How did you decide to marry Grandpa? How did you know he was the one?"

Grandma leaned back in her chair. "Well, honey, he was a hard worker, he had a nice smile, and he kept after me until I said yes." She paused. "He never stopped pursuing me either—until the stroke."

Grandma served two bowls of oatmeal and set them on the table along with an almost-empty bottle of maple syrup. "This is the last of the syrup. I enjoy a little in my *puuroa*."

"I'll try it too, if there's enough."

"Don't worry about using it. We can get more from the Johnsons."

"Danny's parents?"

"Yes, they tap maple trees in the spring and sell the syrup to friends. I'll call Evelyn, and perhaps later you can run over to pick up another bottle."

"I'm not sure I'm ready to meet his parents."

"Don't look so horrified. They're lovely people."

That afternoon, Beth lay on her bed reading a Jan Karon book, but her mind had trouble escaping to Mitford. Her journal lay on the floor where she had tossed it the night before. She had bought it a year and a half ago, because she liked the cover—*Love Never Fails*. Ha. It failed her.

She put down her book and grabbed the journal. She flipped through the pages from the last year—getting to know Alan, the checklist of desired qualities. Everything seemed to fall into place. The timing was right. They were perfect for each other, not even having had a single heated argument—until the end. Why hadn't it worked out?

Beth shut the journal.

The breakup with Alan was making her re-examine her

core beliefs. Following the rules hadn't worked. She ended up with a broken heart. She was angry with Alan, angry with herself for the decision she had made, and angry with God. She had done her part. Where was God's blessing on her life?

Grandma called from downstairs, "Beth, I'm going out to light the sauna. Do you want to help?"

"I'll be right down."

Beth came downstairs to find Grandma putting on her boots.

Grandma wore her winter jacket and stocking cap. "Sweetheart, I'm going out to turn on the water. Would you gather the newspapers in the living room? I'll need paper to start the fire."

After Beth gathered newspapers in a brown paper bag, she went upstairs and added her journal to the bag.

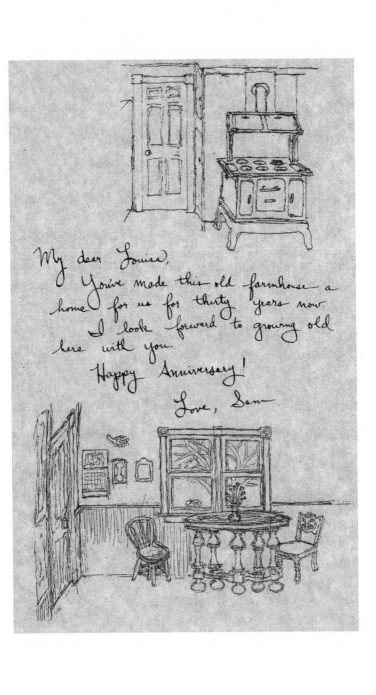

My dear Louisa,
    You've made this old farmhouse a home for us for thirty years now. I look forward to growing old here with you.
    Happy Anniversary!
        Love, Sam

Chapter 8

*B*eth slipped on her boots and jacket and then walked out to the sauna. Four inches of light powder already covered the ground that Mak had plowed the night before. Did he work weekends, too? Snow removal on the island must be a never-ending job.

In the small building with weathered, pine-board siding, Grandma scooped ashes out of the stove. "Just in time."

Beth crumpled newspaper and handed it to Grandma, who shoved it into the firebox. She stacked kindling on top of the newspaper.

Grandma reached for a chunk of firewood under the dressing room bench. "I can't quite get it. This arm again."

"I can help. I can build a fire." Beth grabbed the small log that Grandma had fumbled. "Maybe you better go to the doctor and get your arm checked out."

"I'll make an appointment with my friend Marcella. She's a massage therapist. I'll make one for you too if you'd like. She'll come to the house." Grandma sat on the cedar bench in the sauna. "Now I'll tell you what to do. Lay a few of these larger pieces of wood over the kindling. You need to open the damper or it will get smoky. There are matches in the dressing room."

Beth followed her instructions.

"Blow gently on the newspaper until the kindling starts burning," Grandma said.

As flames flickered up from the kindling, Beth pulled her journal out of the paper bag.

"What's that, Beth?" Grandma asked.

"It's the last year. It's full of lies. I'm letting go, moving forward." She tossed the journal into the stove.

"Oh, my child."

Tears welled up in Beth's eyes. "I just want to forget it. A year and a half of my life wasted."

"Sweetheart, our experiences make us who we are, the painful ones as well as the joyous ones."

"This experience has made me mad. All I wanted was real love. Why even try to do right when things don't work out anyhow?" Beth wiped her tears.

Smoke began to billow from around the journal.

Grandma held out an iron rod with both hands. "Pull it out with this poker. Don't burn it. Move on, but one day, it won't hurt so much. You may want to look back and see how you've grown. Give it to me, and I'll hold on to it so you don't have to look at it. I won't read it—I promise, and I always keep my promises. If you still feel this way when you leave, we'll have a special burning ceremony."

Beth hesitated, but then took the poker, hooked its claw on the journal, and flipped it out of the stove. It landed on the concrete floor, and Grandma patted the back of the smoldering cover with a wet washcloth. Beth bit her lip. She liked the idea of watching her memories of Alan go up in smoke. He had hurt her. He had said he loved her. A lie, because love is a choice and he had chosen to break her heart. "Why are relationships so complicated? I grew up thinking it was so straightforward. I mean, look at my parents. They have like, the perfect marriage."

"Everyone has difficulties." Grandma squeezed Beth's arm. "You'll get through this."

With the fire roaring, Grandma instructed Beth to pack the stove with firewood. "It should be up to temp in an hour."

"I think you should see a doctor about your arm," Beth said as they walked back to the house, the snow falling lightly.

"I'll try the massage. If that doesn't help, I'll think about it."

"You promise?" Beth asked.

Grandma only smiled.

An hour later, Grandma peeked into the sauna room. "I usually sauna at 165 degrees, but I'll take it easy on you since you're half Finn," she teased. "It's at 145 degrees. The temperature's still going up, but we can open the window for you."

"I can handle a little heat. I *am* a California girl." Beth breathed in the cedar scent.

"It's a bit of work to have an outdoor sauna up here in the winter. You have to haul the wood, turn on the water, and drain it when you're done so the pipes won't freeze." Grandma sat on the dressing room bench and removed her shoes.

Beth waited for Grandma's lead as to what kind of sauna this would be—naked or clothed. Mother had told her stories about sauna-ing as a young woman at church gatherings. In the Finnish-American culture, same-sex saunas were often in the nude.

"When your grandpa decided to build a sauna, I wanted it in the basement with an electric stove, but he had pictured a sauna here in this spot by the pond, where he could step out and jump in the water to cool off. The kids would skinny dip."

Beth laughed. "Mother told me about that. She said Uncle Scott and his friends would sauna and tell her, 'Stay in the house and don't look out the windows.'"

Grandma chuckled. Beth continued to stand fully dressed. "Jeremy and I loved to swim in the pond and then warm up in the sauna when we were kids."

"At a certain point you get too old for that. After your mom and uncle left home, it became a pain to come out here and light the sauna. Your grandpa was finally going to give me my wish and build a sauna in the basement, but then he had the stroke..." Grandma's voice trailed off as she furrowed her brow and looked to the floor. She popped her head up. "...but you're right. It's nice to be outside when you take a breather, even in the winter. I still like a quick roll in the snow. I'll teach you the traditional way to sauna."

Beth fidgeted nervously.

"Well," Grandma continued, "I thought you might not be quite accustomed to the culture, so I did wear a bathing suit."

"Phew." Beth breathed a sigh of relief. She pulled off her shirt to reveal her suit underneath. "So did I."

In the steam room, Grandma sat on the top bench. On the wall to the right of the bench, a thermometer was almost up to 150 degrees. A galvanized pail was set on the lower bench at Grandma's feet, and Grandma filled it with a hose attached to a spigot on the wall.

"Are you going to roll in the snow tonight, Beth?"

"I- I don't know. That sounds cold."

"Once you get your core body temperature up, a quick roll is easy. It's refreshing to cool off. One can comfortably stand outside for five minutes. Now climb up here and we'll get a steam going."

Grandma ladled water onto the stove, and it sizzled and disappeared. Steam rose to the ceiling.

Intense heat fell from Beth's head down the rest of her body and radiated to her bones.

"This will get a sweat going." Grandma took a washcloth, wrung it out, and placed it on her face. "They call this an *apteekki*, an apothecary. All the impurities come out of your skin. You can't get clean like you can in a sauna."

After fifteen minutes, Beth was red and wet from sweat. "That's about all I can handle." She stepped off the bench.

"Don't quit. We're just getting going. Let's run out into the snow. Quickly." Grandma led the way out of the sauna. "Come on. You have to do it while you're still hot." Through the dressing room and out into the cold, snowy night, Grandma ran to a snowbank, turned around, and plopped down into it.

Beth plopped down next to her. She laughed. It was invigorating.

Grandma threw snow into the air and it came falling down on them. "That's a long enough breather. Now let's warm up."

They both ran into the sauna about as fast as they had come out, but with their arms clutched close to their chests and shivering.

In the sauna, Grandma poured a ladle of water on the stove. Beth leaned back against the wall and closed her eyes as the water sizzled on the rocks. Once again the steam warmed her core. Grandma's medicine was working on Beth. As impurities came out of her skin, grief left her soul.

"The sauna builds *sisu*. It takes us to our limits, the extreme hot and cold." Grandma poured another ladle of water.

Beth pulled her knees up to her chest and wrapped her arms around her legs. As she looked down at her feet, her confidence grew. "Grandma, I'm going to the concert with Danny."

Chapter 9

"*B*eth, I checked with Evelyn Johnson and she does have more maple syrup. Would you mind running over there?"

Beth hesitated.

"What's wrong?"

"Well…" Meeting Danny's mother was the last thing Beth wanted to do. There was a long silence.

Grandma looked at Beth, confused.

"I'll look like an idiot knocking on her door to buy maple syrup."

"Evelyn's a delightful woman. She's expecting you. I'd ask Danny to pick up the syrup, but he refuses to take my money. So irritating."

"But there's also the snow."

"It's a short drive. You'll be fine. I'll give you money for the syrup and you can take them a loaf of cardamom bread as a thank you. They could sell all their syrup before summer ends, but they always seem to have a bottle for me even late in the winter. I'll dry my hair, and we'll have a light supper when you get back."

Beth took a deep breath. *Sisu.* "Okay. I'll do it."

"They're down the road two houses on the right, past the

crosscut." Grandma handed Beth a ten-dollar bill.

Before heading out of the house, Beth changed into dress pants and a nice top. She put on lipstick.

As she drove down the snowy road past the little house with darkened windows, the snow stopped. She pulled into the driveway and her headlights lit up the Johnsons' sauna. Smoke curled out of its chimney, and a bright window lit the white bark of a birch tree next to it.

She got out of her car. The stars were bright, dimmed only by an even brighter moon. There was no need for porch lights on a night like this. Beth jumped, startled to see two men standing behind a truck. She knew one of them.

"Hi, Danny."

A smile stretched across his face. "This is my friend Russ. Russ, this is Beth."

"Hi, Russ." Beth moved around the truck to shake hands with the bearded man. As she moved, the guys circled to the other side. Steam rose off their bare chests.

"It's nice to meet you." Russ held his arms stiffly in front of his skinny body. "I've heard a lot about you."

"Good things, I hope." Beth laughed. "I'm picking up syrup for Grandma." As she moved toward them, they sidled away. She wanted to tell Danny she'd go to the concert, but not with an audience. "Grandma and I took a sauna earlier. I suppose you're having a breather." Beth felt proud of herself for using the correct terminology. Snap. She realized... "Oh, my. I'm so sorry."

"I was hoping you'd want to see more of me, but you caught me at a bad time." Danny's words swirled like fog in front of his mouth, but the steam wasn't rising as fast off his body.

She held a flat hand to her temple like a blinder and scurried to the house.

Her heart hammered as she knocked on the front door. With the darkened foyer and the moon lighting the yard, the door's window reflected the scene behind her like a mirror. The backsides of the two men running to the sauna. *Oh, my.* Beth closed her eyes tightly until the sauna door shut.

The foyer light turned on, and the door opened. "Hello, you must be Beth. I'm Evelyn." The tall, slender woman with brown shoulder-length hair spoke eloquently, enunciating each word. She held out her hand. "If you had come a half hour ago, you could have visited with Danny. Now he's in the sauna. Come on in. You must be cold. You're beet red."

Beth stepped into the house with hardwood floors, a vaulted ceiling, exposed wooden beams, and a curved staircase. Her throat tightened and she looked down at her feet.

"Danny told us so much about you. I'm so glad to meet you."

Beth looked up, surprised by Evelyn's enthusiasm—surprised Danny had already told his mom *so much* about her.

"Dale, come meet Beth," Evelyn called toward the back of the house. She put a hand on Beth's arm. "Come in and visit with us. Let me take your jacket."

"I can't stay. My grandma's getting dinner ready. She told me to give this to you."

Evelyn inhaled deeply. "Cardamom bread, how delightful."

Dale appeared in the threshold of a door, which led to a formal dining room. "It's nice to meet you." The balding man smiled broadly as he gripped Beth's hand.

"Dale, go get a bottle of maple syrup. It's for Lou."

Dale disappeared into the back of the house. Beth looked at the pictures displayed on the wall. Three graduation photos. A family photo with a much younger Evelyn and Dale, a preschool age boy, a toddler girl, and a baby boy. In another family picture, Danny smiled broadly showing the gap between his front teeth. He looked about ten.

"That's our son, Jack, and our daughter Susan." Evelyn motioned to the graduation photos. "And Danny, of course. He's our baby. Do you have siblings?"

"I have an older brother."

"And that's it?"

Beth nodded.

"So you're the baby, too?" Evelyn clasped Beth's hand in

hers. "Well, I never put too much credence in that birth order stuff. Danny said you're a missionary."

"Yes, ma'am. Well, I was, ma'am. I used to coordinate a tutoring program for inner-city youth."

"Call me Evelyn. Please, relax. There's no need to be nervous."

"Yes, ma'am."

"Here you go, Evie." Dale reappeared holding the syrup.

Evelyn took the bottle from Dale and handed it to Beth.

"Here's your ten dollars." Beth held out the bill.

"We're not going to take your money. You're the first woman Danny's talked about in three years. I was starting to get worried." Evelyn laughed, throwing her head back and glancing at Dale. "I probably shouldn't have said that."

"You really should take the money." She extended the bill. "My grandma will be disappointed if I return with it."

Dale flapped his hand dismissively. "Then you should keep it and spend it on another date with Danny."

Beth felt flushed. She hadn't even been on an official date with him, and he's already talking to his parents about her. Dr. Benley would definitely not approve. Way too fast, but no harm done. She hadn't accepted the invitation to the concert. Best to end it before it starts. "I better get going." Beth opened the door. "I don't want to keep Grandma waiting. She probably has supper on the table."

Back at Grandma's, Beth sat at the kitchen table to eat reheated pasties.

"Thank you for picking up the syrup." Grandma put the bottle in the pantry cabinet. "It stopped snowing, anyhow. See, you had nothing to worry about. Did you see the full moon tonight?"

"Oh Grandma, I saw two." Beth felt her face grow warm.

"Huh?"

"Never mind. You're right. The Johnsons are very nice people. Probably a little too nice. It seems Danny told them all about me. It's a little much for only one non-date. And here's the ten dollars. They wouldn't take it." Beth put the bill on the table.

"Figures." Grandma shook her head.

"And I'm *not* going to the concert with him."

Grandma shrugged. "You can tell him tomorrow. We'll probably see him at church."

Chapter 10

"We must be going so we're not late for the service," Grandma called. "I'll pull my car out of the garage. Meet you out front."

After Beth put the final touches on her face, she hurried downstairs. Good thing she wasn't driving. It had been snowing nonstop since the prior day. She slipped on her boots, and then put on her jacket as she walked.

Outside Grandma was hitting the ground with the flat bottom of a grain shovel. Half a foot of snow covered the driveway, as Mak hadn't plowed since Friday.

"What are you doing, Grandma?"

"I'm *panking* the snow." She lifted the scoop with both hands and then allowed it to fall to the ground with a thud.

"You're doing what?"

"I'm panking a path to the garage."

"Why don't you shovel?" Beth zipped her jacket.

"Too heavy." Grandma rested on the shovel like a cane. "With my weak arm, it's easier to pank than shovel."

"Good grief. Let me help." Beth took the shovel and cleared a path. The snow wasn't that heavy, but she was breathing heavily by the time she finished. "There are reasons retirees move to warm climates."

Grandma followed behind her, and they entered the man door. She hit the overhead door opener, and light streamed into the bay revealing a maroon Subaru Outback.

"You don't have to shovel sunshine." Beth buckled her seat belt.

"I don't want to hear it." Grandma fiddled with her seatbelt for a bit before she finally snapped it together.

Grandma drove them down the highway, through Quincy, across the bridge, up the hill, and into Pinehurst's parking lot. The church sat in a glade surrounded by red pines.

In the small sanctuary, Beth glanced around but didn't see Danny. She was hoping to give him a definitive no. She followed Grandma up the right aisle to the third row from the front where Grandma sat next to Senja.

"Senja, you remember my granddaughter Beth."

Beth looked into warm smiling eyes. "Did you enjoy your date the other night?" Senja winked.

Beth giggled in spite of herself. "Yes, I did." She took a seat next to Grandma. "You said I'd see him today," she whispered into Grandma's ear.

"He attends the second service. We should see him between services. Pastor Chip always runs over."

Senja leaned forward. "Louisa and I have shared a pew for many years."

"Like cows returning to their stalls," Grandma quipped.

"Same pew every week." Senja squeezed Grandma's arm.

"I started coming here after Sam died, and I sat right here next to Senja. I've been here ever since. A creature of habit."

"I was glad you joined me." Senja smiled at her friend. "I felt like such an old maid, sitting by myself."

The pianist began to play softly, and the worship leader invited everyone to stand. Grandma raised her hands and closed her eyes while she sang.

After the gathering song, the congregation took their seats. An older, dark-haired man peered over his glasses as he announced upcoming events.

"That's Mike Rogers," Grandma whispered. "He's one of the deacons."

"Ladies, be sure to sign up for the Women's Tea. It will be held at The Tea House downtown. Ladies from ages 16 to 116 are invited." Mike laughed at his joke. "Bella Atkinson will be speaking. Sign up by next Sunday so they can have an accurate count."

"Have you ladies signed up yet?" Senja whispered. "You love The Tea House."

"Yes I do." Grandma's eyes lit up.

"So you'll come?"

Grandma looked at Beth and raised her eyebrows.

"When is it?"

Grandma opened her bulletin. "In two weeks, the Saturday after next."

Beth grimaced. "Mother wants me home by then."

Mike invited the congregation to join in a presentation of their tithes and offerings. A young girl played "Amazing Grace" on a tiny violin.

The fifty-something pastor moved to the podium. "Thank you, Reina. That was beautiful." Chip Atkinson's voice was soft. "To learn to play the violin takes discipline. Cynthia carts Reina off to Suzuki lessons every week and makes sure she practices half an hour every day. Reina doesn't always want to practice. In fact, on most days, she would rather be playing dolls. We often think of discipline as punishment, but it's not. Discipline is the hard work that makes us grow, helps us learn." Pastor Chip spoke with quiet confidence.

"Reina's his granddaughter," Grandma whispered in Beth's ear.

"She's incredible. How old is she?"

"Maybe seven—I'm not sure."

"At the beginning of Hebrews 12, we are told to endure hardship as discipline." Pastor Chip looked over the congregation. "Are you going through a tough time now? Don't make light of the Lord's discipline."

Beth's jaw tightened, and anger swelled up within her. Was

she supposed to view her broken engagement as God's discipline? An all-knowing, all-loving God should protect his children, especially when they are trying their best to follow him.

She had trouble concentrating on the rest of the sermon while she replayed the last year over in her mind. God could have stopped her from getting engaged to Alan. He should have helped her make a better decision. It didn't make sense.

On their way out of the sanctuary, Grandma introduced Beth to Pastor Chip.

"Becky's daughter." Pastor Chip shook Beth's hand, studying her face. "It's nice to meet you," he said warmly.

"Yes, it's nice to meet you." With a line forming behind her, Beth moved into the narthex. As people exited the sanctuary, an equal number of people moved in the opposite direction for the next service.

When Danny entered the church, her heart skipped a beat, and she scolded herself. Now's the time to hit the brakes. *Thanks for the invite, but no thanks.* Then Aimee, Quincy's worst server, burst through the door and quickened her step to catch up with Danny. Beth's chest tightened. She felt betrayed. Like the time someone stole her Corolla's hubcaps right out of the Resource Center's parking lot. Was she jealous of Aimee?

"Hey, Beth." Danny smiled broadly and stepped ahead of Aimee, who stiffened and frowned.

Beth felt victorious, yet unsettled.

"Good to see you again. I'm sorry we didn't have much time to chat last night." He winked.

"Danny." Beth's jaw dropped. He wouldn't say anything about that, would he?

Aimee joined Danny again by his side.

"Hi, Aimee," Beth said tentatively.

"It's good to see you again." Aimee responded, but Beth didn't think she meant it, not with that phony smile. Aimee draped her hand on Danny's shoulder. "Come on, Danny, the service will start soon." She sauntered into the sanctuary while Danny lagged behind.

"See you after church, Beth?" Danny asked.

"Perhaps. We're going to attend Sunday school."

"Join us at The Tea House for lunch after church, Danny," Grandma offered.

"Maybe. I'll have to see what Aimee's doing." Danny walked into the sanctuary.

Beth shrugged it off. Perhaps she misread things and Danny wasn't even interested in her. He probably only asked her to the concert because Aimee wasn't available. Beth looked back through a window into the sanctuary where Danny sat with a group of people about her age, probably graduate students from the college. Aimee sat next to him, shoulder to shoulder, with plenty of pew to her other side.

After church, Beth and Grandma sat at an oak table at The Tea House, which occupied the second floor of an old, Jacobsville Sandstone building in Douglass. Windows overlooked the Portage Canal, which cut off the Keweenaw Peninsula from the mainland and formed what the old Finns called *Kuparisaari*, Copper Island. Antique artifacts and prints hung from the walls. Oriental rugs covered distressed hardwood floors.

A waitress handed Beth and Grandma each a menu, a simple, single page printed on office paper with the date centered at the top. "Today, we have tomato basil soup served with a chicken salad sandwich or spinach mushroom quiche."

"Yum. They both sound good." Beth's mouth watered.

"Do yous know what you'd like to drink?" the waitress asked.

"Should we try the Raspberry Lemon Herbal tea?" Grandma asked.

"That sounds good to me."

"I'll bring yous your tea and be back for your food order." The waitress left.

"Yous? I've heard that before," Beth whispered.

"It's like the southern y'all. It's Yooper. Mary's a native."

"Which entrée are you going to order?" Beth couldn't make up her mind.

"We could order one of each and split them."

"Good idea."

Mary returned with a ceramic pot like Grandma's. Steam rose out of its spout, and Beth could smell the lemon.

"What can I get yous to eat?"

"We'll have the specials, one of each, and two extra plates, please," Grandma requested.

Beth sipped her tea. "This tea has fresh lemon in it. It's fantastic."

Grandma took a sip. "That's what makes this place so special."

Beth looked out over the frozen canal where Quincy Hill stood barely visible through a veil of falling snow. She had spent some time with Grandma as a child, but had since only known her from a distance. They hadn't ever talked heart-to-heart. She grasped Grandma's wrinkled hand. "I'm so happy we have this time together."

"Me too, dear." Grandma squeezed her hand. "It didn't look like you had a chance to tell him no today." Grandma looked amused.

Beth groaned. "I wasn't expecting him to be so nonchalant."

"So if he had asked you about the concert again, then you would've said no?"

"Right."

"Or was it because he had company? That Aimee is a nice girl. So sweet."

"Grandma." Beth set her teacup down. Sweet was not the adjective that came to her mind when she thought of Aimee. She changed the subject. "You said Grandpa never stopped pursuing you."

"Not until the stroke. Then I was his 24-hour nurse. No time off. No breaks. But he died at home, and that was the best gift I could've ever given him."

As they sat in silence, Beth's mind wandered to the future. "What should I do now, Grandma? Should I go to grad school? Look for another ministry job? Find an office job?"

"What do you want to do?"

"I don't know. I'm waiting for direction from God."

"We plan our way and the Lord directs our steps." Grandma looked like she was going to say more, but then Beth's cell phone vibrated with a text message.

Sorry couldn't do lunch. Get back 2 me re concert. Now u have my #. Danny

"It's Danny. How did he get my number?"

"He's a law enforcement officer. He has ways of interrogating people." Grandma smiled.

"What's the deal with Danny and Aimee?"

"They have been friends for a long time. Beyond that, it's not my place to say. But I'll ask you this—Would Danny ask you to the concert if he were dating Aimee?"

Beth turned her focus to her phone, took a deep breath, and typed a reply. *Yes, I'll go.*

A few moments later, her phone vibrated. *Pick u up at 6:30 Sat. Concert at 7.*

Later that evening, Beth called California. "Hey, Jules."

"Hi, Beth. How's my old friend?"

"Old?" Beth chortled. "I'm not the one who's married with two kids. How's the weather?"

"The same. Seventy degrees and sunny, the same as yesterday, and the day before." Jules laughed. "How is it there?"

"It snows all the time. Seriously, like every day. It's insane, but beautiful."

"Beth, I have to tell you something. Alan's been seeing the receptionist at the gym."

"I have to tell you something—" Beth paused for dramatic effect. "I don't care."

"I thought you would be devastated."

Beth smiled. "Jules, I have a date. He's a cop."

"You have a date? Are you serious? You've been there for three days, how could you possibly have had time to even meet anybody?"

"He's the first person I met when I got into town. I already had dinner with him. He's taking me to see Allie Nantuck on Saturday."

"Beth, it's way too soon. You just broke up with the man you were going to marry. Dr. Benley says—"

"No, Jules." Beth cut her off. "Alan broke up with me, and it sounds like he's not wasting any time, either. Besides, I don't care what Dr. Benley says. Danny is nice, and a gentleman. He seems perfect."

"I'm happy for you, but be careful. Before anything comes of this, you make sure he's willing to move to Southern California. I don't want to lose my best friend."

"You can't lose me, Jules. Love you."

Chapter 11

$\mathcal{F}$or nearly an hour, Beth hadn't heard anything but muffled voices and occasional laughter from the other room where Marcella gave Grandma a massage. Green tea steeped in the ceramic teakettle on the table. A fire burned hot in the old antique stove while Beth lost herself in the fictional town of Mitford where Father Tim deliberated over his choice for breakfast. Would he stick with his diet? Beth topped off her tea.

The volume in the other room increased. "I'm fine." Grandma sounded agitated.

"But Louisa!" Marcella's voice carried through the wall.

Beth didn't want to eavesdrop, so she reached across the table and turned on the small, one-speaker radio.

"The Michigan Department of Natural Resources has issued a number of limited nuisance permits to take wolves. There have been reports of family dogs having been killed by the predators. Ralph Anders, DNR spokesperson, said the wolf population is thriving and these permits will have no impact on the long-term health of the pack."

Beth shivered. Wolves?

"Speaking of dogs, Linda Grover called to report she's missing her Chihuahua-Maltese mix named Bridget since this morning. She lives in Quincy, so I don't think the wolves got her. With the cold temps and snow, a small dog like that will not last long. If you've seen Bridget, please take her in and call the station. We'll put you in touch with Linda.

"Officers responded to two neighbors upset over each other's snow removal procedures on Suomi Drive in Quincy last evening. This is going to be a long winter."

Beth shook her head with an internal laugh. Missing dogs. Snow removal techniques. Small town news had a certain charm.

"Adele Hintsala called to say she's missing the diamond from her engagement ring. She's offering a reward of one hundred dollars to whoever finds it. She lost it yesterday and had only gone to Shop-Mart and the library."

Beth studied the purity ring she had moved back to her left ring finger. A simple silver band engraved with the words *True Love Waits*. She missed her diamond engagement ring. But now in Grandma's kitchen, separated from California by many miles, it didn't hurt so much. She had moved on geographically and, with that, emotionally.

"Hello, you must be Beth." A young, blonde woman with soft features and sassy, layered hair stepped into the kitchen.

"Hi, Marcella."

"I'm all done with your grandma. She'll be out in a minute. I'll wash up and then get set up for you." Marcella ducked into the bathroom.

"Good morning." Grandma walked with a spring in her step to the kitchen sink.

"How was your massage?"

"It was good. She massages harder when she's worked up." Grandma filled the glass with water from the tap. "She told me to drink this to flush out toxins."

"How does your arm feel?"

"It feels good. No trouble at all." She held her glass in her left hand and tipped it to Beth.

"Your left arm wasn't the problem."

"The right one is fine, too. Still a little weak, but it has much more movement."

"That's good, Grandma."

"Finlanders." Marcella shook her head as she came back into the kitchen. "Lou, I'm quite serious about you needing to see a doctor for that arm. The muscles don't feel right. Maybe you need physical therapy. Beth, I'll be ready for you after I change the sheets."

"Grandma, you said your arm feels better."

"It does. That might have done the trick." Grandma wagged her right arm back and forth.

Beth sighed. "Grandma."

"What can I say? I'm a stubborn Finlander. You know what they say, 'You can always tell a Finn, but you can't tell her much.'"

A few minutes later, Marcella reappeared. "The table's ready, Beth. You get situated under the sheet, and I'll be in in a few minutes."

In the living room, Beth slipped out of her pajamas and snuggled under the sheet.

Marcella came in. "What should I start with first? Maybe your neck after all that driving?"

"Sure."

Marcella dug into her tight muscles and Beth exhaled. She closed her eyes.

After the massage, Beth groggily dressed and returned to the kitchen where Grandma and Marcella continued their argument.

"You should get that arm looked at by a doctor," Marcella asserted.

"The massage helped."

"It's moving a lot better, but I want you to get it checked. I'm concerned. I often have a sense about these things. Don't put it off, okay?"

Grandma mumbled something.

As soon as Marcella left, Beth pressed her. "Marcella's right. The sooner you get it looked at the better. Grandma, are you going to see your doctor?"

"There's an old Finnish proverb that says, '*Jos sauna, viina ja terva ei auta niin tauti on kuolemaksi.*'"

Beth laughed. "I have no idea what you just said. The only Finnish words I know are *makkara, nisu,* and *sauna.*"

"'If sauna, liquor and pine tar will not be of help, the disease is fatal.' And I don't drink, so I might be in trouble." Grandma jokily grimaced.

Chapter 12

"Can I help you, miss?" Behind the front counter at Robin's Nest, a slim, older man in a button-down shirt and dress pants peered at Beth through thick, round glasses. "Becky?"

Beth smiled politely and shook her head. "Where are your journals?"

He stepped out from behind the counter and limped toward her. "Walk this way."

She followed him to the back of the store, past displays of copper bracelets, copper-roofed bird feeders, copper ashtrays, and copper license plate holders. One license plate had an outline of the Upper Peninsula and the words *Say Ya to Da UP, Eh!*

"Right here." The man motioned to a number of blank books at eye level. He opened a journal. "Feel that."

Beth took the book and rubbed a page between her thumb and index finger. "It's thick."

"That's right."

She closed the book and studied the scene on the cover—budding birch trees near a stream. Below the image was the word *Hope* in gold embossed letters. She found the price on the back of the journal—$25.00.

It wasn't like her to spend so much money on something frivolous. She was a bargain hunter, a thrift-store shopper who worked at a nonprofit. Well, now she was unemployed. She set the journal back on the shelf.

"When you spend a lot of money on a journal, you'll only write the important words. Try writing on the sample paper." The clerk directed her to an open book on a small wooden stand near the metal rack. He put a metal pen in her hand. "The pen makes a big difference, too. We have those up by the counter."

Beth drew loops across the sheet.

"See how that glides?"

Solidly connected to the paper, the pen uniformly released ink. "Yes. It is smooth."

"That's right."

"But it's a lot of money." She still had some cash from selling the ring, but that was it.

"We stock cheaper books on the bottom shelf so we can compete with Shop-Mart. I'll let you think about it." He limped away.

Beth knelt to inspect the books at the bottom of the rack. She picked up an affordable journal and opened it. The paper was thin, like what she usually wrote on. Cheap. It didn't match the excitement she felt about Danny. She set the inexpensive journal back on the rack. She stood and grabbed the *Hope* book. Was it really worth $25?

"*Hyvää päivää.*"

Beth turned to see Mak's smiling face. "Hello, Mak. Hey, thanks for plowing for me and Grandma this morning."

"Yous welcome." Mak browsed the expensive journals and selected one titled Imagine. "You found your way to Robin's Nest."

"Yes, I did. How's the book writing going, Mak?"

"Fine, fine. Filled up da last journal writin' 'bout two young loves courtin'. She's a young schoolteacher who took a single room schoolhouse on da prairie. He's a cowhand. I've gots to do research. Don't know much about da West. They say write what you know, but there ain't no market for books 'bout plowin' and makin' wood."

"I look forward to reading it."

"It needs lots of work before it's ready to be read. I like my character. He reminds me of myself—a smooth talker, and handsome, too." He snorted. "Lorna might dispute that, but somebody's got to appreciate my qualities, and it might as well be me."

"Women like reading about perfect men." Beth smiled encouragingly.

"Now I'm thinking of da conflict. Every good book has conflict. Yous got your protagonist who wants something and your antagonist who stands in her way."

Beth held the journal to her chest.

"You found da good journals. It's a lot of money, but you'll only write da important words." Mak laughed. "That's what Sam told me to get me to buy my first one, and now I'm hooked. I suppose it's true, too."

Beth followed him to the front of the store, where Mak pointed to a display case of pens. "That silver one's like da one I showed you at Lou's."

"That costs a face cord of hardwood?" A tag in front of the pens read $70. "Wow."

The clerk chimed in, "When you spend a lot of money on a pen—"

"...you'll only write the important words." Mak and Beth finished in unison.

"That's right."

"I shouldn't. I'm already spending way too much on a journal."

"This one here's on clearance." The clerk pointed to a brass pen. "Not as popular as the silver, but it'll cost only half a face cord of hardwood."

"Sam, this is Beth."

Beth extended her hand. "Nice to meet you. My grandfather was a Sam, too."

"He had a good name." Sam chuckled. "My full name's

Samuel Clinton, like the president, no relation."

"I'm Beth Dawson."

"She's up here visiting her grandma," Mak added. "That's Lou Herrala."

"Aha." Sam snapped his fingers. "You must be Becky's daughter. You look like her."

"Yes." Beth sighed. How many times had she heard that?

"I had Becky in eleventh grade. I taught math." He peered at her intently. "Where's she now?"

"She lives in Los Angeles." Beth handed him the journal.

"Los Angeles? I knew she'd go far. She was a strong-willed child. I would explain something, and she'd keep asking me to explain it again and again until she got it." He rang up the sale. "I was a young teacher then, a few years out of college, and she made me work for my paycheck. That'll be $26.50."

"I'd like a pen, too. That one." Beth pointed at the brass pen sitting in a velvet-lined box. Still expensive, but at half price it was a deal she couldn't pass up.

"There you go." Mak thumped the counter. "You need a quality pen and quality paper to get the full effect."

"That's right." Sam took the pen out of the glass case and closed the velvet box. "You're visiting the UP from California in the middle of the winter? You have that backward. Your grandma should be visiting you." He punched a few keys on his register. "That'll be $63.60."

Beth handed him cash.

"How long are you staying?"

"A couple of weeks. I don't know how much of this winter I can take." Beth nodded toward the front window and the snow falling outside.

Sam gave Beth her change. He dropped the pen and the book into a bag. "Like your journal says, *Hope*. Winter in the UP reminds us that we have hope, that spring will come, trees will bud, and we will have new life. Hope that is seen is not hope—that's why Yoopers have real hope. But spring always comes."

"Except for that winter of '79." Mak's voice boomed. "Snow

fell even into June, maybe July. Then it started snowing again in October."

"That's right. I remember that. That was my second winter in the Keweenaw," Sam reminisced. "We got over 350 inches."

"Thank you, Sam. Have a good day, Mak." Beth headed to the door.

With the men's voices fading into the background, Beth could hear Mak. "Three-hundred-ninety inches north of Calumet. That whole decade of da seventies was cold. They was talkin' global cooling."

Mother graduated from high school in 1980. No wonder she left thinking the Keweenaw has endless winters. Beth stepped out of the store. She looked up, stretched her arms to her sides, and closed her eyes. Snowflakes gently settled on her eyelashes.

A few doors down from Robin's Nest, she stepped into Shear Delight. A middle-aged woman got up from a styling chair.

"You must be Beth." The woman approached the desk.

"Yes, I have an appointment."

"I'm ready for you. You can come right back."

The woman led Beth to the first of four stations. "I'm Nancy. You can sit right here." She motioned with her arm.

Another stylist cut a toddler's hair while the mother looked on.

Nancy stood behind Beth and combed her long blonde hair with her fingers. "What would you like done?"

"I'd like to look older, wiser—sassy."

"We could take some length off, and layer it. Would you like that?"

"Sure. Do you know Marcella? She said she does massages here."

"Of course, I style her hair."

"I'd like my hair to look like that."

"Okay, we can do that, but I wouldn't go too short. If Danny asked you out with your hair long, it must be working for you."

Beth's jaw dropped as she caught Nancy's eye in the mirror. "How did you know?"

"I heard from my daughter that Danny Johnson had a date with Becky Herrala's daughter. When you came in, I knew instantly." Nancy pulled Beth's hair away from her face. "You look just like your mom. Brings me back to high school. Now where is she? She hasn't kept in touch."

✳

Back at the farmhouse, Beth sat cross-legged on her bed with her *Hope* journal and new pen. Over sixty dollars. What was she thinking? She shook her head. Maybe she had lost her mind. She didn't know who she was anymore.

Beth wrote her name and cell phone number on the first page. The ink flowed on the thick, smooth paper. She added a phrase she wrote in every journal. *In the event you find this journal, please call to return. I will pay postage.*

Last fall, a kind, elderly lady had called. "I found your book in the library parking lot. The writing is beautiful and you have such a great love story. And you're getting married."

Embarrassing. But Beth was just thankful to have her journal back.

"Good night, Beth." Grandma poked her head in the door.

"Good night, Grandma."

"Are you sure you don't want to go to the funeral with me tomorrow?"

"I'll stay home. I wouldn't know anyone there."

"Sleep well, dear."

As Grandma's footsteps faded, Beth moistened her thumb and turned the page. She readied her pen. *I met him last Thursday on my way into town.*

Chapter 13

$\mathcal{D}$anny slipped into the sanctuary of the old-world church and took a seat in the back pew. Intricately carved beams spanned high ceilings, and stained glass windows lined the sidewalls. A handful of people peppered the rows. Attendance was sparse at the funeral of Kristine Smith, and, for that reason, he was glad he came. He recognized a few folks. Mak and Lorna. Louisa.

Kristine's parents sat near the front of the church next to a redheaded man and a boy. She probably married the frat boy. Either that or she had a thing for redheads.

Easels held two large, framed pictures in front of a closed casket. The blue-eyed, blonde Kristine he had known smiled at him from her high school graduation picture. They used to hang out at Grandma Lou's and steal away moments together in the barn.

Somebody's head partially blocked the other photo. He scooted over in the pew to get a better look, and as he did so, the floor squeaked. The boy in the front row turned to look, and the red-haired man next to him made eye contact with Danny. It was him—the frat boy.

They turned back around, and Danny studied the family photo. The baby in the picture had grown into the brown-haired boy in the front row. A lump rose in his throat. He saw a lot as a cop and didn't have much sympathy for those who died driving drunk, but in this case, a kid's involved. Sorrow socked him in the gut.

The service concluded, and the family stood at the front as attendees approached them to offer comfort.

Danny stayed seated. He shouldn't intrude on a personal moment of grief. Why had he come at all? He had closed this chapter of his life ten years ago. It wasn't right to attend a funeral out of curiosity.

"Danny," Mrs. Hiltunen called out.

He approached the family.

"You have my sympathy." Danny stood in front of Kristine's husband.

The man's blue eyes were bloodshot, his mop of curled locks a mess. "Thanks for coming." He clasped Danny's hand with both of his. "I'm Drew."

"Drew," Mrs. Hiltunen spoke in a stage whisper, "Danny was Kristine's high school boyfriend. You loved the same woman."

Awkward. Danny shrugged. "I was a kid then. What did I know about love?"

Drew put his arm over the boy's shoulders. "This is my son, AJ."

Danny looked down into big, brown eyes. "Hey. I'm sorry about your mom."

Stone-faced, AJ nodded, and then he shrugged off his father's affection, turned on his heels, and stepped away.

Tough kid, but underneath that impassive exterior is a boy who will likely grieve for years. How does a kid make sense of tragedy that adults can't comprehend?

"Mrs. H, Mr. H, you have my sympathy." He reached for Kristine's father's hand.

Mr. H pulled him into a one-armed squeeze. "You're a grown man now, Danny. You can call us by our first names."

"I don't think I ever knew them."

"Danny—" Mrs. H burst into laughter, which opened up a new round of sobs. She hugged him. "Patricia and Ronald. Call us Patty and Ron."

"You have my sympathy." Danny clumsily patted her shoulder.

"You were such a good friend to Kristine." Patty squeezed him tighter and lowered her voice. "You were Kristine's first love. I always thought you'd end up together. My grandson could have been yours."

Awkward. "I'm sorry for your loss, Mrs. H. I mean, Patty." As Danny slipped free from her grasp, he glanced at the boy, who slouched in the front pew.

With a heavy heart, Danny headed for the door.

In the lobby he greeted Grandma Lou, who was struggling with her coat. He helped her button it.

"Thank you, Danny." She frowned and then shrugged. "This arm."

He waved to Mak and Lorna across the room.

Mak lifted his hand and clomped over. "Sad day." Mak studied him with eagle eyes. "That boy reminds me of someone."

"What do you mean?"

Mak rubbed his brow as he shook his head. "Not da time or da place." He walked toward the door. "I left my journal in da truck. I gotta go write something down."

In his Jeep, Danny rested his head on the steering wheel. Funerals make people say crazy things. And now he was thinking them. The kid was not his. Did Patty think he was? He straightened and studied his brown eyes in the rear view mirror. He thumped the steering wheel with his palm. Full-Finn Kristine married a blue-eyed, Irish-looking man. There could have been some genes between them that produced a doe-eyed boy with brown hair. There must have been.

Chapter 14

*D*anny rinsed the razor and then scraped it one more time over his already-clean-shaven cheeks. He liked Beth, so he'd have to step it up. The city girl had class.

Earlier in the day, after his Saturday sauna, he had recounted to his folks the fiasco of being underdressed on the first date.

"Oh, Danny, I raised you better than that," his mother had said.

"I was just being myself."

"You gotta be better than yourself, son. Don't let this one get away." His dad had given him the keys to his Audi and a couple of items from his closet.

The threads were a bit much for his taste, but he didn't want to make the same mistake twice. Except for the day they first met, she was dressed to the nines every time he saw her. He thought she was cute the night he pulled her over, but he didn't realize then she was out of his league. He wondered if he had a chance with her. All he could do was try. He hoped she'd wear that sexy, black dress and pearls again.

Danny splashed aftershave on his cheeks. He slipped into his dad's pants and button-up shirt. He had refused the tie.

He had his limits. He donned the sport jacket and looked at himself in the mirror. A little less country. A little more class. He put on his Dad's wool overcoat.

Beth stripped down to her underwear. She rifled through her suitcase and pulled out a flouncy, blue, daisy-patterned skirt she had found at an upscale consignment store. The matching tank top wouldn't work, given the weather, and she hadn't packed her navy blue sweater. That would've been cute. She tossed the items aside.

"Danny's here," Grandma called from downstairs.

"Okay, I'll be right there." Snap. Where did the time go?

The khaki pants and top—no. Too business. The only other concert wear she had was the black dress. She had worn it before, so she'd have to accessorize with a scarf, which she didn't pack. Beth shivered, feeling the draft through the window. Snow was coming down hard. She hoped the roads were okay, but they'd be fine in Danny's Jeep. Just pick something. Make a decision. It was a country music concert, so she'd wear her western boots, and what better to go with boots than denim. Beth pulled out jeans and a long-sleeved, fitted, white T. It would work. She smiled, remembering Danny's words. *The great thing about the UP is that nobody cares what you look like.*

She slipped into her jeans and T-shirt and looked at herself in the full-length mirror on the back of the closet door. Perfect. She looked like a Yooper. She quickly applied a darker shade of lipstick she had picked up at Shop-Mart.

"It's quarter to. You should be going," Grandma called.

"Coming." Beth slid her lipstick into her jeans pocket and hurried down the stairs to the kitchen. "Sorry, I'm running late."

"Beth, you look great." His smooth cheeks matched his boyish grin. Gone was the five o'clock shadow, but he looked every bit as handsome—and dapper in a wool coat and dress pants.

"I should change. I have something a little nicer I can put

on." The black dress, for sure.

"Nah, Beth, this is a country music concert. Maybe I'm a little overdressed. Anyway, we need to go." Danny held her jacket open.

"You got a haircut," he said as she turned and slipped her arms into the jacket.

"You're observant." She tossed her hair over her shoulder as she bent to put on her boots. "See you later, Grandma."

Danny stepped out of the house ahead of her and offered his hand.

She took it as she descended the porch steps. "It stopped snowing."

"Another perfect evening with you." He skipped ahead of her and opened the car door.

An Audi? The luxury car Alan had coveted. Beth frowned. "Is something wrong with your Jeep?" She slid into the leather passenger seat.

"Uh, no. I'm borrowing my dad's car." He closed her door, bounded around the car, and climbed in.

Beth fastened her seatbelt. "Isn't your Jeep better in the snow?"

"This has all-wheel drive. We'll be fine." After pressing the keyless start button, Danny switched the satellite-radio station to classical music.

Although it sat lower than the Jeep, the car seemed to handle the snow-covered country road just fine.

When he turned onto the main highway, he glanced at her. "How's your vacation going?"

"Vacation?" His question snapped her back into reality. She wanted to pretend she wasn't on vacation and their relationship was going somewhere. "Good. Relaxing. I had a massage. Poked around in a few shops. That was great. I like spending time with my grandma, getting to know her as an adult." Beth frowned. "Grandma's right hand and arm don't seem to work right. The massage therapist thinks she should get it checked out."

"Yeah, I've seen her struggle with it on occasion." Danny

lowered the stereo volume. "I picked her up to take her to my parent's house for Christmas dinner, and she had trouble buttoning her coat, so she switched to a jacket with a key ring on the zipper—I assume—so she can zip it easier. She wore the coat again to the funeral and really had a hard time with it."

"You were at the funeral?" Beth wondered.

"Yeah. Have you noticed that Grandma Lou pours tea with her left hand?"

Beth shook her head. "I'm not that observant."

"Well, she's right-handed."

"I did notice she had trouble lighting the sauna stove last weekend."

"Is she going to see a doctor?"

Beth shrugged. "She agreed that it would be a good idea, but she also admitted to being a stubborn Finn."

"Yeah, Russ's grandma had a heart attack once, and she knew it, but finished canning vegetables before she called an ambulance." Danny shook his head.

They fell silent. Out the side window, stars glittered in a clear, black sky. High snowbanks flanked the road. "Do you ever think about moving to a warmer climate, Danny?"

"Every winter, around March." He laughed. "But I can't imagine Christmas without snow. I embrace winter. Play a little hockey. Ski. Snowshoe. But I like cultural stuff, too." He glanced at her. "I prefer the UP to, say, downstate where winter is cold enough to be miserable, but there's not enough snow to play in it. That's how I felt living in Ann Arbor."

"Is that what brought you back?"

"To be honest, Beth, I wasn't making good choices. I wanted a fresh start, but I knew it would be hard if I stayed where I was, so I applied to transfer when there was an opening up here. I came home and started going to Pinehurst Church. I built a house." Danny slowed and stopped at an intersection. He caught her gaze before turning his focus back to the road and accelerating. "I mean, Russ helped me with the shell, and now I'm working on the interior."

"I'd love to see it sometime." Excitement bubbled within

her.

"Can you paint?" He sounded hopeful, yet tentative. "I have next weekend off, and I already asked some friends if they could come over for a painting party—knock it out in a few hours and I'll provide the pizza and pop."

"Sure. That sounds like fun." Beth sucked in her breath, trying to catch the words as they left her mouth. What was she doing, diving right in? Meeting his parents, his friends. Not things people do when they are just on vacation.

They pulled into the campus theater parking lot and kicked through snow to the glass-façade building. While Danny checked her jacket and his coat, Beth looked around at the crowd in the lobby. She certainly was not underdressed. She had called it right. She could get used to being a Yooper. She never did like the pretentiousness of the theater scene in the city.

Danny returned wearing a white button-up shirt and a corduroy sport coat with leather elbow patches. He looked professorial, but he could pull it off.

"Danny, is that you?" A college-aged guy held out his hand for Danny to shake. "Did you borrow your dad's jacket?" He snickered.

"Uhh, I…" Danny's freshly shaven cheeks reddened.

"I have your dad for one of my engineering classes. I've seen him wear that. Who's your lady friend?"

"This is Beth. Beth, this is nobody. He used to be my friend." Danny slapped him on the shoulder.

The guy laughed, taking the ribbing well. "Have fun, hey."

The lights dimmed as they got to their seats. Beth was glad she had been running late so they didn't need to make small talk. As much as she liked talking to Danny, it was best they didn't get to know each other any better. She would be leaving for California in a week. In the meantime, she'd enjoy the concert. A date was good for her bruised ego.

"I'm so glad I could be with y'all tonight." Allie wore a simple white shirt, thick brown belt, jeans, and boots. No frills. "I wasn't sure we'd make it in with the blizzard and all, but I was told it's just lake effect. I didn't dress for the weather, but, I've got my boots."

The band played the first few chords of "The Boot Song," and Allie's rich, earthy voice filled the auditorium.

Beth settled back in her chair to the sounds of fiddles and a banjo, tapping her foot in time to the music. That was the song she heard that inspired her to buy her cowgirl boots.

After a few upbeat songs, Allie shifted gears. "I'm a sucker for a good love story." Allie's guitarist softly strummed, and Allie sat on a high stool. "One question I always ask new friends when Max and I get the chance to double date is, 'How did you meet?'"

Beth sneaked a sideways peek at Danny. He grinned. He had a great smile, and the gap between his front teeth endeared her to him.

He caught her eye. She straightened, turning her attention back to Allie.

"People's stories are so varied." Allie motioned toward her guitarist. "Max and I met at a little coffee shop in—"

"Achoo!" Danny covered his mouth, and heads turned to look at him.

"Bless you," Allie said.

"I'm all right," Danny called out, and the audience murmured with soft chuckles.

Beth passed him a tissue from her purse. He might be confident and good-looking, but he wasn't sophisticated, and that was okay with her. Less pressure.

"Anyhow, I was saying that Max and I met in Louisville. Max was playing guitar at a coffee shop that night, and he's been playing guitar with me ever since. Folks, my husband Max, my favorite guitarist." Max waved and the crowd applauded.

As the band began to play, Danny put his hand on Beth's arm. He leaned over and whispered, "This is one of my favorites." His touch lingered for a moment while she savored the sensation.

Allie sang, "We met at the cross and found grace for each

other. We met at the cross and found hope to carry on. We met at the cross and found healing to repair all the broken pieces in our lives."

Beth closed her eyes and listened carefully to the lyrics.

"We met at the cross and found love for one another because we're filled with love from up above."

"I love that song." Beth whispered, delighting in the easy connection they shared.

Wading through the crowd after the concert, Danny asked, "Did you like it?"

"Yeah, that was fun. I haven't been to a concert since—wow, my birthday, almost a year ago." A date with Alan. She willed the memory to fade.

"When's your birthday?"

"February 5th."

"Hey, Mr. Johnson." A teen boy waved to Danny. "You're looking like your dad." He laughed.

"Yeah, yeah. These kids are from my parents' church." Danny motioned to a group of students who congregated near a wall. "That fight you started last week, Jim. That was low."

"Well Henderson slashed Lahti," Jim shot back. "He didn't get called on it."

"For a while it was looking like the AHL." Danny shook his head in feigned indignation.

"Go Douglass," a boy shouted at their backs as they walked on.

"I give them a hard time because I used to play for Quincy," he explained to Beth. "Go Miners," he called back to the teens.

"Danny," a voice cried out from behind them.

He spun on his heels. "Hi."

The middle-aged woman hugged him and then rubbed his cheek with the back of her fingers. "That's the face I remember."

Danny squirmed. "Quite the concert, hey."

"Yes, it was. I cried through most of it. Kristine got me the ticket for Christmas. We were going to go together." Tears filled the woman's eyes.

"I'm sure she's glad you still went. Beth, do you want to grab our coats?" Danny nodded toward the coatroom.

"Sure, do you have the check tags?"

"What? No." He laughed. "The coatroom's unmanned. This is the UP."

When Beth returned, the woman had Danny wrapped in another hug, while his arms hung to his side and he looked to the ceiling.

"Who was that?" Beth asked as they walked to the car.

"Patty Hiltunen. Allie Nantuck has an amazing voice, hey."

Beth started to slip, and he steadied her.

"I don't think your boots have enough traction." He kept hold of her arm. "If you stick around, you'll have to get swampers, like these."

Beth looked down and laughed. She hadn't noticed the clunky boots he was wearing below his black dress pants.

Steam puffed out of the back of the Audi as Danny led her to the passenger door.

"Did you leave the car running?"

"Remote start from the lobby." Danny opened Beth's door.

A perfect gentleman, she thought. She climbed into the warm car filled with classical music. A perfect gentleman, but almost a different gentleman, except for the boots. When he sat in the driver's seat, Beth asked, "Okay, what gives?"

"Huh?"

"Your dad's car, your dad's jacket. And what's that smell? Are you wearing cologne?"

"No. It's aftershave. That's my dad's, too." He said the words sheepishly and looked away. "He has extra bottles from Christmas gifts we gave him when we were kids."

"Where's the Yooper I had dinner with last week?"

"I guess I just wanted to... You're kind of..." He glanced at her.

"I'm kind of what?"

"You're gonna make me say it?" He dropped his chin. "After seeing you last Friday in that black dress—And you looked gorgeous Saturday and Sunday, too—I just wanted to make a good impression. You're kind of a big fish."

She giggled. "If you think I'm a big fish, then you've been fishing in some pretty small ponds." Flattered, she reached over and touched his shoulder. "Everybody in LA is concerned about appearances. I prefer your Jeep." The UP was more her style. Earthy. Real. Authentic. She could just be, rather than try to become someone she was not.

"Really? Then can I turn off the classical music?" A smile spread across his face.

"How about some country?" She grinned.

They laughed.

Danny flipped through stations as they started back to Grandma's.

Parked near the front steps, Beth faced him. "Thank you for taking me to the concert."

"I'm glad you're in town and I had somebody to go with. I would've hated to see the ticket go to waste." The words tumbled out of his mouth. "Aimee and I were going to go, but then she got the job at the Cornucopia and had to work."

Beth had a sinking feeling in her stomach. "Are you and Aimee dating?"

"What? Aimee?" Danny looked confused. "I've known her since we were little kids. Aimee and I are just friends."

"Does she know that?"

He met her gaze. "I think so."

Chapter 15

*W*hen Beth stepped out of the bathroom Sunday morning, Grandma was already in her jacket and boots. A fire burned in the old kitchen stove, and the ceramic teakettle sat on top. Grandma grabbed the teakettle—with her left hand, Beth noticed—and set it on the cool modern stove. "The first service starts in fifteen minutes. Grab some *nisu* and you can eat on the way. I'll drive." The door shut with a thud as Grandma left the house.

Out the window, snow fell heavily. Beth buttered two slices of cardamom bread and ate one piece as she caught up to Grandma in the garage. Beth got into the Subaru Outback and fastened her seatbelt.

"Would you be a dear and turn the key for me?" Grandma looked straight ahead, her shoulders square.

"You can't turn the key?"

"No, and I don't understand it, because I was able to light the stove this morning, make myself breakfast and tea, but now my hand is tired out."

"Is it safe for you to drive?" Beth kept her tone low-key, trying to conceal her growing concern.

"I think so. I still have one good arm. It's just that the ignition is on the right side."

"I should drive." Beth spoke more boldly. She didn't want something to happen to Grandma—not on her watch.

"You don't like driving in the winter," Grandma protested.

"I'm getting better." Beth shoved the second piece of bread in her mouth and got out of the car. She wasn't giving Grandma a choice.

When Beth opened the driver's door, a tear rolled down Grandma's cheek. It broke Beth's heart to see her sorrow, but, at the same time, she felt a sense of purpose. She was here, in this snowy wilderness, for a reason. Grandma needed her. She placed a hand on Grandma's shoulder. "We'll figure out what's wrong, and you'll be back to driving in no time."

Beth stepped aside, and Grandma got out. With her head hung, she walked around the car as Beth slipped into the driver's seat.

A few of miles down the road, Beth broke the awkward silence. "The concert was fun."

"Oh, Beth." Grandma said with renewed enthusiasm. "Tell me all about it."

"She sang 'The Boot Song' and 'We Met at the Cross.'"

"Yeah, yeah. It was a concert. They sang songs. Tell me about the company."

"Yes, the company." She glanced at Grandma and then fixed her eyes back on the road. "He's nice." She said the words calmly.

"Just nice?" Grandma chuckled.

"And here's the church." Beth pulled into the parking lot as the snow tapered off.

"Maybe you should take an early class and attend the second service with Danny," Grandma teased.

"I want to sit with you." She was still concerned about the incident this morning. "Besides, I don't want to appear too interested." She removed the keys from the ignition.

"Are you thinking about staying longer?"

Beth shrugged. "At least through the Women's Tea, because I offered to help Danny paint on Saturday."

"So you're giving him a chance?"

Beth laughed. "No. In a moment of weakness, I agreed to help him paint. That's it. I'm putting the brakes on right now."

In her pew, Grandma put her arm around Senja and squeezed her in tight. "I'm ready to worship this morning." The music started and Grandma quickly rose to her feet, lifting her arms in praise.

As Beth stood, she felt a gentle bump on her shoulder.

Danny smiled broadly. "Hey, Beth," he whispered, "I just got off work and thought I'd catch the early service."

Beth met his gaze. Blasted brown eyes. They sat, shoulders touching.

Mike Rogers came to the podium. "I do hope you ladies plan to attend the Women's Tea on Saturday. Bella will share a message for all women, young and old, married and single."

Senja leaned over Grandma and addressed Beth. "Will you stay long enough to attend?"

Beth glanced at Danny, who winked.

"I'll sign us up." Grandma's face crinkled into a smile.

Danny slipped his boots off and rested a colorful wool stocking foot on his knee.

Beth thought nothing of Californians kicking off their sandals, but she found this amusing. Their eyes locked, and he matched her smile.

Pastor Chip took the lectern, and Beth willed herself to pay attention to the sermon.

"I lived in Los Angeles, California, for a short time after graduating from Quincy High School in 1980."

That got her attention. Beth sat straighter. Pastor Chip had graduated the same year as Mother.

"Behind my apartment building there was an orange tree. The oranges started forming on the tree in the spring. By June, that tree produced beautiful, round oranges. Since a dozen tenants shared this apartment building, I assumed that tree would be empty as soon as they ripened, but it wasn't. I picked a handful of oranges off the tree and brought them up to my apartment. I eagerly peeled the rind off one of the fruit, broke a section off, and took a bite. It was horrible. I figured out why nobody had picked the fruit.

"In Hebrews 12:15, the author warns messianic Jews not to let a bitter root grow up to cause trouble. They would have understood the reference to the bitter root comes from Deuteronomy. Moses warned the Israelites not to go their own way."

Beth jotted notes in her *Hope* journal.

"The bitter orange I had tasted thirty-six years ago was likely crossed with lemons. It wasn't an orange tree after all—it was a hybrid between an orange and a lemon tree. The problem with that orange-lemon tree was at the root. Though I did not know it at the time, that tree was a symbol of my life. I was a bitter root that Moses warned of and I persisted in going my own way."

Danny nudged Beth. "Me, too," he whispered. "I was a bitter root."

As the service ended, Grandma turned to Senja, Beth, and Danny. "Let's all have an early lunch at The Tea House."

"That would be delightful," Senja agreed.

Danny smiled. "Sounds good to me."

As they left the sanctuary, Beth and Danny queued to greet Pastor Chip.

"Good sermon, Pastor." Beth shook his hand. "You graduated with my mother, and went to California, too."

"Yes, I did. I'm so glad you could join us again this week." He extended his hand to Danny. "You made it to the early service." Pastor Chip winked.

Danny caught Beth's eye, a smug expression on his face. "Yes, I did."

As Beth turned to exit the sanctuary, Aimee stood in the doorway. "Hello, Beth." She frowned. "Danny?" Aimee pursed her lips and walked into the sanctuary.

Half an hour later, Grandma and Senja sat across from Beth and Danny in The Tea House.

Mary served Mint Melody, placing the ceramic teakettle on a stand above a candle in the middle of the table. "Danny, I'll be back with your Coke—no ice."

Grandma poured tea into her cup with her left hand, spilling a little on the tablecloth.

"Grandma, did you hear that Pastor Chip lived in LA after graduating from Quincy in 1980? That would make him Mother's age. They would've gone to Los Angeles at the same time." Beth filled her cup and passed the kettle to Senja.

"Yes, California was the place to be after the intense winters we had." Grandma said without making eye contact.

"Here's your Coke." Mary interrupted. She placed the glass in front of Danny. "What can I get yous to eat?"

After Mary took their orders, Senja unfolded her napkin in her lap. "That was a good sermon. Pastor Chip is so honest. I appreciate how he opens up about his personal struggles so we can see the testimony of Christ in his life. I'm glad he came to Pinehurst."

"When was that?" Beth asked.

"A few years ago," Grandma said.

"The sermon reminds me of some of the girls I worked with." Beth sipped her tea. "They'd be doing so well, coming to our tutoring program, keeping up their grades, making good choices. Then a guy would come along and they'd go their own way, get pregnant, and drop out of high school."

"It's a strong temptation." Senja shook her head.

"I know, but it really bothered me when I saw the guys just using them for their own selfish pleasure." Beth traced the woodgrain of the table with her finger. "It broke my heart when I saw them ruin their lives."

"Children are a gift," Danny snapped, glaring at her.

Beth's defenses rose. She didn't even know what she had said to offend him. "I know, but kids aren't ready for the responsibility of parenthood. The guys don't stick around, and the girls are left dreaming about the things they never got to do."

"Sometimes guys miss out." Danny faced the window.

"I've never married, but I've come close." Senja plunked her teacup down. "It's hard to make those right decisions."

Grandma looked to Danny with concern, but addressed Senja, "I still haven't given up on you, Senja. I even arranged Scrabble games with a couple of the eligible bachelors."

Senja laughed. "If he's still a bachelor in his sixties, he's too set in his ways for a bachelorette in her sixties who's set in her ways."

"How about Mike Rogers?" Grandma asked with a gleam in her eye. "It's been more than five years since Marianne died. I see how his face lights up when he mentions your name."

Senja lifted her cup to her mouth and blew across the top of the tea.

"I love Scrabble." Beth rescued Senja.

"Danny plays, too," Grandma said. "He and Jack used to play with Sam and me."

"We used to win." Danny turned back to the conversation.

"You thought you won, but we'd take it easy on you and make sure you had places to go, and we even opened up triple words. I wouldn't be so easy on you anymore," Grandma told him.

"How 'bout a rematch?" Danny asked. "Thursday work for you ladies? That's a day shift for me, so I'd be available in the evening."

"Not me," Senja said. "I'm tied up all week."

"You're always tied up, Senja." Grandma chuckled. "I'm available."

"It works for me." Beth leaned back in her chair. The brooding Danny was gone. It must be hard to work nights. That was likely the reason for his sharp tone earlier.

"Then it's a date," Danny said enthusiastically.

"Lou, how's that carpal tunnel?" Senja asked.

"It's strange. My arm seems to be doing fine one minute, but the next minute everything seems heavy."

"You were having trouble with it at Christmas," Danny said. "Remember when you couldn't button your coat and had to switch to a zippered jacket."

"That may be the first thing I remember. Since then I've been having trouble chopping vegetables. I had trouble putting wood in the sauna stove." Grandma frowned. "I've been able to light the kitchen stove, but those pieces of wood are quite small."

"You've been pouring the tea with your left hand," Beth said.

"I haven't noticed that."

"Are you going to see a doctor, Lou?" Senja asked.

"I don't know. It feels a lot better after the massage." Grandma lifted her hand and set it back on the table.

"Grandma, you said you would."

"I said I should."

"Will you?" Beth wasn't sure how hard she should push, but she was increasingly concerned.

"What will the doctor tell me? He'll say my arm's weak and I'm getting old. He'll tell me to join a gym, lift weights."

"Maybe Mother's right. You should move to LA." *Mother would be a lot better at talking sense into you than I,* she nearly added. Beth wasn't accustomed to bossing adults around.

"Here's our food." Grandma smiled as Mary approached the table with a large tray.

Chapter 16

*A*s Beth washed the dishes from a late morning breakfast, the phone rang.

Grandma stood and retrieved the handset. "Hello?" The black spiral cord was twisted, keeping the phone tethered within a foot of the wall. She glanced at Beth. "Okay, anytime."

"Who was that?" Beth scrubbed sticky steel-cut oats from the bottom of a pot.

"It wasn't for me. They were trying to reach someone else." With a satisfied smile, Grandma reached around Beth and filled the teakettle with water. "What do you want to do this week?"

"See that you call your doctor." Beth dried her hands and sat at the table.

Grandma placed the kettle on the wood-fired stove. "My arm has stabilized. If it gets any worse, I'll call."

"Promise?"

"Promise," Grandma agreed. She joined Beth with a newspaper and pen.

"Good. You said you always keep your promises. Let me know if you notice anything change with your arm."

Grandma turned to the daily crossword puzzle. "I'm looking forward to Scrabble on Thursday."

"I'm sure you are." Beth said with a hint of sarcasm.

"He's a nice man, that Danny."

"He might be, but it's too soon and too fast." Beth wrinkled her nose. "Dr. Benley would not approve of one of his devout followers going on three dates within a month of being jilted. And neither would Mother."

Grandma chuckled. "I suppose not."

"Then why are you encouraging it?" Beth leaned back in her chair and crossed her arms.

"What are you talking about, dear?"

"You were supposed to go out to dinner with us, but you ditched me. You knew he and Aimee are just friends, but you let me believe it was more so my competitive spirit would accept another date with him. Now you set up this Scrabble game."

Grandma looked up from the crossword. "Danny suggested Scrabble."

"Maybe, but you brought it up, knowing he loves to play. You knew Senja was too busy, and I don't know what you have planned, but I have a sneaking suspicion you'll find some excuse to leave us alone."

Grandma furrowed her forehead. "I need to find a thicker pen." She stood and sorted through a pen box attached to a bulletin board next to the phone.

Beth frowned. There was definitely something wrong with Grandma's right hand. "That's it. It's time to call the doctor."

"Oh, Beth. This isn't the first time I've used a thick pen."

The front door squeaked open. "Delivery."

Grandma bobbed her head toward the door. "Beth, would you get that?"

Beth went to the front door. "Flowers!"

"Bring them here. Maybe they're for me," Grandma teased.

Beth brought the arrangement of wildflowers with two yellow roses to the kitchen table where she opened the note and read aloud, "We met at the gas station. Danny." She laughed. He was thoughtful, fun. Was she falling for him?

"What does that mean?" Grandma broke into her thoughts.

"It's kind of an inside joke. Allie Nantuck talked about how she likes to find out how couples met."

"I thought you met in my kitchen."

"You know, Grandma, after following all the rules with Alan and seeing our engagement go down in flames, I'm thinking to heck with the rules."

On Thursday evening, they sat at the table with the flowers pushed up against the window. It was cold and quiet outside, but warmth and laughter filled the house. The teakettle sat warming on the stove, and on the table in front of each player was a teacup. The Scrabble board, with half the tiles placed on it, sat on the table, turned to Beth.

"All vowels." Beth sighed. "This is not my night."

"You can trade them in again." Danny shook the cloth bag of letters and held it out to her.

"No thanks. I'd probably draw different vowels."

Grandma chuckled.

Beth placed an *O* and a *U*. "*YOU*, for, what's that? Four, five, six, and the double word makes twelve points." She drew. "Finally, two consonants."

Grandma arranged her letters on her tile holder.

"I stopped in to see Maribel after work. She's in rare form," Danny said.

Grandma, looking at the board, placed a *B* well above the *U* Beth had put down. "We should go visit her next week. I'd like you to meet her, Beth—while she still has some of her memory. I think she'd enjoy seeing you. She knew your mother quite well." As Grandma finished her sentence, she laid the last of her seven tiles on the board, spelling out the word *B-E-S-C-O-U-R-S*. "Now let me see. One, three, twelve, thirteen, plus fifty is sixty-three."

"Bes-curs?" Danny questioned.

"Be-scow'-ers." Grandma corrected his pronunciation. "Do you want to challenge it?"

"You want me to lose another turn?" Danny shook his

head with a smile.

"I don't mind if you do," Grandma said smugly.

"She has years of crosswords on us," Beth said. "I'm not going to challenge it. What does it mean?"

"It means to scour, clean thoroughly. It's one of those handy little verbs you can add *BE* on to. Thank you for the *U*, Beth. That one fell in my lap."

"There you go setting up a triple word, like old times," Danny said.

"It's worth it for a bingo."

"*B-I-D*," Danny placed two letters on the board off the *B* in bescours. "Three, four, six. That's eighteen."

"Good job, Danny," Grandma said. "What did Maribel lose this time?"

"Her ammunition."

"I better block the other triple word." Beth placed her letters. "*S-E-A*. Nine points for me."

Grandma rearranged her tiles.

"More consonants," Beth said after picking tiles. "Maybe I can mount a comeback and at least come in second. Did you find the ammunition?"

"Yes."

"She can't blame it on Vance this time." Grandma chuckled.

"Vance still has them, because when I found them, I kept them right where they were in the back of the drawer of that old dresser. I don't mind her shooting squirrels, but I don't want her shooting a law enforcement officer whom she's mistaken for Vance. Beth, what's the score?"

"Grandma has 179, you have 83—"

Grandma's hand fell on the board, upsetting the tiles. Grandma stared in disbelief at the ruined board.

"It's okay, Grandma. We can put it back together." Beth flipped the tiles right side up and tried to re-create the board.

Danny gathered the pieces that had fallen to the table.

"It's no use." Grandma's eyes welled with tears.

"It's all right, Grandma Lou. We'll start over. Thanks for

giving Beth and me a chance," Danny joked.

Grandma pressed her lips together tightly, the corners turning upward slightly as though attempting a smile. "I'm going to call it a night and head to bed. You two can play. You need the practice," she teased, but her voice didn't hold its usual ring. "Excuse me."

After she left the kitchen, Beth looked down at the mess of the board. "She needs to see a doctor. I'm going to insist she call tomorrow morning."

Danny put the tiles back in the bag and pushed the board aside. He reached across the table and grabbed Beth's hand. "It'll be okay."

"Thank you." Beth pulled her hand away. "Do you want more tea?"

"I'll have a glass of water."

Beth filled two glasses of water and handed one to Danny. "Let's sit by the woodstove for a bit. I'd like to warm my feet."

They sat on chairs in front of the old stove.

"Good night, kids," Grandma called from the bottom of the stairs.

"Good night," Beth and Danny said in unison.

Beth pushed her toes under the stove. "I'm beginning to see a greater purpose in my coming here—to help Grandma." She glanced at Danny and then lowered her head. "I don't know if you know—if you've heard. It's not exactly a secret. I came to Michigan to figure out my next steps because…" How to say it? She took a deep breath. "My fiancé called off our wedding. We were going to get married on Christmas Eve."

Familiar feelings of hurt and rejection washed over her, yet she had a sense of relief. She felt her shoulders relax as she sipped her water.

"I'm sorry, Beth. That's tough."

She stared at the stove, seeing flickers of flame through a small viewing window. "Yeah, my life turned upside down, so I'm trying to figure out a new plan."

There was a long silence.

"I understand," he said finally. "I have a past, too."

Chapter 17

*D*anny leaned back in his chair with his feet under the stove next to Beth's. "A few years ago, before I moved back, I had a girlfriend." Danny had sensed deep pain in Beth's voice when she talked of her broken engagement. He remembered his own pain all too well. "We weren't engaged, but it was heading in that direction."

Beth met his gaze, her eyes filled with compassion.

"We had been living together for six months," he continued. "One day, I came home from work and she was gone."

"Wow." Beth stiffened, looked away, and stared at the fire.

"Beth." He said her name tentatively, but she wouldn't look at him. He had just wanted to empathize with her, but he obviously struck a nerve. How much should he tell her about his past? It seemed awkward to have the conversation now, but deceptive to have it later.

"I ran wild for a few years," he continued.

"Have you slept with many women?" Beth twisted a silver ring around her left ring finger.

He stared at the fire with sorrow. He'd tell her the truth and let the chips fall where they may. "I woke up in bed with women I didn't even know, sometimes more than one. I justified it because, in my heart, I had lust and I knew that was as much of a sin as actually doing it. So I just did it." Danny took a sip of water.

Beth pulled her feet from under the stove and sat up straight. "Did you just say you woke up with more—"

"That was in the past. I was a different man."

"I hope so." There was a sharp edge to her voice.

"Look, Beth, I wasn't trying to make this about me. I was just trying to say I understand how you feel. With your fiancé breaking up with you. We both have a past." He offered his hand. "Truce?"

"I don't have a sexual past." She waved his hand away.

Danny put his hand back in his lap. "But you were engaged, so I thought…"

"You thought wrong." She crossed her arms. "You always remember your first and I wanted my first to be my husband. And me to be his. No comparisons. You know—you love your future spouse so much, you wait to share the gift of sex with that one person." She held her hand out and he read the engraving on the silver band. *True Love Waits.*

He'd only dated one virgin in his life—Kristine—and she wasn't eager to stay one. Beth talked about purity with the teen girls, but she even extended those rules to her own engagement. He bit his lip. He couldn't undo his past.

In the stillness, the floor creaked above them as Grandma Lou retired for the night, and then it was quiet.

"I gave up on love." He immediately regretted saying it. It seemed too cynical, too melodramatic, even for a hopeless romantic, which he'd admit to being, but he wanted her to understand. "There were so many rules in the church I grew up in. I couldn't live up to their expectations, so why try?"

Beth was quiet.

"I knew the way I was living was wrong. I finally left Ann Arbor and moved back home, made a fresh start. Aimee was a big part of that. She helped me plug into her group of friends. I got back in touch with Russ. He had moved back after being away for a while, too. He's good for me. A bit goofy, but a good guy."

She finally smiled.

He exhaled. Whew. "You were telling me your story. I'm here for you. You can tell me anything or nothing."

"Thanks." Beth leaned back in her chair and slipped her feet back under the stove. "Tell me more about Aimee and Russ."

Danny laughed. "Russ is a character. He's got a cabin deep in the woods, about a quarter mile off the road. He parks his truck by the road. In the winter, he drives a snowmobile in. An ATV in the summer. He lives off the grid."

"That's hard core."

"Yeah, hey. And Aimee, she's a good kid. I was friends with her older brother, Rob, growing up. Before she got a job at the Cornucopia, she was a waitress at another restaurant in town, the Heikki Lunta. When I moved back into town, I kind of became a regular there, so we'd chat, and she invited me to Pinehurst. She doesn't have a car, so I pick her up on my way to church, when my work schedule allows it."

"So you never slept with her?"

"No. Of course not."

"Are there things you're not telling me?"

"Well, yeah—"

"No," Beth interrupted. "I don't want to know details. I just... I'm just disappointed."

A lump rose in Danny's throat and his eyes stung.

"Are you crying?" Her voice softened.

He blinked tears away. "It's dry in here with the wood heat." He didn't deserve her. Not just for what he'd done, but for who he was. A wave of shame rolled over him. "I'll go now." He stood.

"Don't go." She held his forearm and pulled him back down to the chair. "I'm sorry I was judgmental. I don't want to be like that."

"You're okay with my past?"

"We're not even dating, so your past doesn't matter."

"And if we were?" he asked.

She stared at the stove, hot coals reflecting in her eyes.

"I should be going. It's nearly eleven o'clock." Danny stood again. "Are you still going to help me paint on Saturday?"

She stood, grabbed his hand, and squeezed. "I'll be there." Holding hands, their eyes locked.

He was tempted to kiss her, but in light of their conversation, he decided it was best to back off and take his cues from her.

"Good night, Danny."

"Good night."

Beth watched from the doorway as he pulled out of the driveway and turned right. Snowflakes began to fall. Taillights traveled down the road until they disappeared when he turned into his driveway. Minutes later lights brightened the windows of the small house a quarter mile across the field.

That night she curled up on her bed with her *Hope* journal and pen. She turned to a blank page. *I'm not sure what to think,* she wrote. *When I'm with him, I feel alive, but I'm disappointed, saddened to learn Danny has a sexual past.* Sorrow filled Beth's heart. *It's crazy, because I'm leaving anyhow, but I thought my plans might change if it worked out with us. I was hoping he'd be the one, but I guess that's out of the question. But the time hasn't been a waste,* she added. *I'm here for Grandma. Her arm is getting weaker.*

Chapter 18

$\mathcal{T}$he next morning, Beth looked out at the banditry of chickadees feeding at the bird feeder in a choreographed dance. Each took a turn to bury its beak into the freshly fallen snow, retrieve a seed, and flutter off to the apple tree to eat it. The ceramic teakettle sat on the trivet, steeping with the already-familiar aroma of green tea. Beth poured herself a cup.

"Here you go, dear." Grandma set a bowl of oatmeal in front of her.

"Thank you." Beth drizzled Johnsons' maple syrup over it. "Grandma, you need to call your doctor today."

"Oh my child—"

"You promised."

"I did."

Toast popped. "I'll get that," Beth said. "You call."

Grandma searched hand-scribbled notes on the bulletin board next to the wall phone. She picked up the receiver, cradled it between her ear and neck, and dialed using her left hand.

"Hello, this is Louisa Herrala. I need to schedule an appointment with Dr. Seid."

Beth spread thimbleberry jam on her toast.

"Beth," Grandma asked as she held her hand over the mouthpiece, "would you be available next week to take me?"

"Of course."

"Okay, I'll see him then. Bye." Grandma hung up the phone.

"I'll call Mother tonight to let her know I'll be staying another week."

"Brave move." Grandma chuckled.

That evening, Beth called home.

"Hello, Beth." Excitement filled her dad's voice.

"Hi, Dad." She was glad he answered. He could always cheer her up.

"It's good to hear your voice. How are you? Tell me all about winter in the UP."

"It's beautiful up here."

"It is. Have you been getting out in the snow?"

"I even rolled in it, when Grandma and I took a sauna."

Dad laughed. "That's wonderful."

"I went to a concert, too. A singer named Allie Nantuck."

"I've heard her on the radio. They play her song 'We Met at the Cross.' It's a good song."

"Yeah. I like that one, too."

"I'm surprised your grandma's into that style of music. I thought she pretty much stuck with hymns."

"Grandma's pretty open-minded, Dad, but I didn't go to the concert with her. I went with this guy who lives next door to her."

"Oooh. Rebecca," he called out, "Beth's on the phone. You're going to want to hear this."

"Wait." Beth massaged her temple.

"I'm going to want to hear what?" Beth could hear Mother's voice faintly.

"I have you on speakerphone," Dad said. "Tell your mother about the concert and your date."

"You had a date?" Mother's voice was shrill.

"I just went to hear Allie Nantuck. Grandma's neighbor had an extra ticket. He's nobody special."

"Elizabeth, you should not be going on a date, not yet. You need time to heal. You should wait at least six months after a major breakup. Don't you remember what Dr. Benley said? At least six months."

"Mother, it was just dinner and a concert."

"You had dinner with him, too?" Mother scolded.

"With Grandma." It wasn't a lie, because that's what it was supposed to be, and she was at the same restaurant.

"Rebecca, it was an innocent date while she's on vacation. It's not a big deal." Dad tried to make peace.

"Oliver, I'm her mother. It's a big deal to me that she's making right choices."

Beth and Dad were both quiet.

"It's been two weeks since you called." Mother said finally. "Have you talked Grandma into moving out here?"

"I tried. She's not interested."

"Humph. Well, then it's time for you to come home. Leave tomorrow and drive to Minneapolis. Shop at the Mall of America for a couple of days. I'll pay for your hotel. You shouldn't be traveling too far on the weekend, so set out from Minneapolis on Monday."

"That's what I'm calling about. I'm staying for a while yet."

"Elizabeth, two weeks is long enough for you to have pondered your situation."

"I'm going to go to the Women's Tea tomorrow night, and I want to make sure Grandma gets in to see the doctor next week."

"What's wrong with her?" Mother asked.

"Something with her right arm—weakness, maybe carpal tunnel. Anyhow, she'd been too stubborn to make an appointment, but she finally did, and now I want to make sure she doesn't back out."

Beth heard a click, and then Mother's voice became clearer. "You're off speakerphone. Your father said he loves you. I'm glad you're there to push your grandma to go to the doctor. That's why I wish she would move out here. Why she insists on staying in that old house by herself, I don't understand. Let me know what the doctor says."

"I will, Mother." Beth sighed. "The Women's Tea is going to be at The Tea House in Douglass. Have you been there?" She said the words brightly, attempting to redirect Mother's attention.

"No, that must have opened recently. It wasn't there the last I visited the UP."

"We've been there a few times. It's beautiful. Lots of antiques and it overlooks the water. They have these neat ceramic teakettles they put on a stand above a candle. The pastor's wife, Bella, is going to speak at the Women's Tea."

"Bella?" Mother sounded confused. "I thought Pastor Higgin's wife was Lisa. Did they get a new pastor?"

"Yes, a few years ago."

"Your grandma didn't tell me. She doesn't always remember to tell me things and sometimes she forgets she has already told me something. Is she thinking clearly?"

"Grandma's sharp as a tack. It's just her arm that's giving her trouble."

"Have you made any decisions about your future plans, Elizabeth, your next steps?"

"No, but the first Sunday I was here Pastor Chip talked about going through hard times, and I—"

"Pastor Chip? What's his last name?"

"Atkinson. He had insight I had never thought about before—"

"Elizabeth," Mother interrupted. "I need to go."

Beth heard a click and the line went dead.

Chapter 19

*D*anny took a stool next to Mak at the counter of the Heikki Lunta. The red, wood-clad diner sat on a steep side street in Douglass and overlooked the canal that cut through the middle of the Keweenaw Peninsula.

"*Hyvää päivää*," Mak bellowed. "Good morning."

"Morning, Mak. Tammy, I'll get coffee, too," Danny said when the waitress stopped to fill Mak's cup. "When you have a minute, put in an order of pancakes and bacon."

"Sure thing." Tammy plunked a cup down in front of him and filled it.

Danny sipped his coffee.

"What's new?" Mak forked a piece of *pannukakku* into his mouth.

"I'm in town picking up painting supplies for this afternoon. Some friends are going to help me knock out the rest of the house. What's new with you?"

Mak set his fork down and picked up his pen. "I've got an idea for da romantic Western I'm writin'. I'm trying to flesh out da emotions for a scene." Mak gazed at him intently.

"Why are you looking at me like that?"

Mak lowered his voice. "How'd you think a man would

feel if an old love married someone else, but popped out a kid who looked just like him?" He put his hand on Danny's shoulder. "You want to talk about anything?"

Danny's stomach tightened. "What are you talking about?"

"I got to thinkin." Mak gulped his coffee.

"That was your first mistake."

"That boy at da funeral looks a lot like you when you was a kid. You and Kristine were high school sweethearts. I know how that is when you're young and in love. Lorna and I... Never mind. Just thought it would be a good plotline for my novel."

"He's not my kid." Danny's heart pounded. "Come on, Mak, stop making stuff up. This is real life, not fiction."

"I'm just running with an idea. How would a guy feel? Hypothetically, if it was true."

Was it possible? No way he had a kid. Danny stared into his coffee. "Mad that the girl didn't tell him. Conflicted if he should say anything."

"That's it." Mak scribbled in his journal. "Talk it out."

"The first thing to do would be to find out the kid's birthday. See if the timing works. How would he do that?"

"You're the cop? Don't they teach you that in cop school?"

Tammy plopped Danny's breakfast down in front of him.

He pulled his smart phone out of his pocket. "People always post pictures of their kids' birthdays on Facebook."

"That's good, that's good." Mak jotted a note in his journal. "Wouldn't work in a Western, but let's just run with it for now."

"I friended Kristine's husband on Facebook." Danny pushed the untouched pancakes back and set his phone on the counter. He scrolled through Drew's timeline. "Bingo. Here's a birthday picture—last February."

Tammy made the rounds with a coffee pot. "Cute kid," she commented as she passed by.

Danny put the phone in his lap. "See that cake."

Mak pulled reading glasses out of his pocket and leaned in.

"Seven candles on it." Tension released from Danny's shoulders. "The timing doesn't work at all. It's been almost ten years since I was with her."

"Eight," Mak said.

"What?"

"Eight candles. I count eight. That one's not lit." Mak sat up and made another note in his journal.

"Hi, guys." Russ sat on the stool next to Danny. "Pancakes, hash browns, and bacon, extra crispy," he said to Tammy as she passed by. "And coffee."

"Sure thing." Tammy went to put in his order.

"Russ, how many candles are on this cake?" Danny directed Russ's eyes to the phone in his lap. Mak leaned in, too.

"Seven."

"See." Danny elbowed Mak.

"Eight," Russ corrected himself. "That one's not lit."

Danny groaned.

"Why are you guys staring at his crotch?" Tammy stood at the counter with a coffee pot, filling Russ's cup.

"They're not," Danny snapped. "They're looking at my phone." Danny turned the phone off and set it on the counter. "The math still doesn't work for him to be my kid."

"What math?" Russ loved math.

"Hypothetically, a man was with a woman almost ten years ago and she has a kid who turned eight—the math doesn't work."

"When did he turn eight, and what was the gestation period?" Russ took a drink of coffee.

"Truth is better than fiction." Mak's pen flew across the page.

Danny stuffed his phone in his pocket. "Tammy, can I get my bill?" he called out.

"Sure, hon. Not hungry?" Tammy ripped the ticket stub off her pad, set it on the counter, and walked away.

"It doesn't mean the kid's mine." Danny pulled cash out of his wallet.

"I haven't seen any blue-eyed couples produce a brown-eyed child." Mak jotted a note.

"She cheated on me. She might have cheated on him."

Danny spun on his stool and stood. "I've got to go buy paint and pop. Russ, can you pick up Aimee for the painting party?"

"Sure, man. Can I have your pancakes and bacon?"

Chapter 20

A foot of snow covered Beth's car. It had snowed all Saturday morning, and it was still snowing when Beth went out to the garage and got in the driver's seat of Grandma's Outback. She arrived at Danny's before the vehicle even had time to warm up. His Jeep was in front of his house, blocked by three other vehicles and banks of snow. She parked next to a truck lettered with *Saarinen Contracting*—the truck she had seen the night Danny and Russ were outside the sauna.

The sky brightened, and the sun peeked through the thinning clouds as the snow tapered off. She glanced at the dashboard clock. Twenty minutes late. Would she be the last to arrive? At least in California, people assumed there was traffic when she ran late.

Beth knocked on the door, but nobody answered. She could hear laughter inside, but couldn't see through the fogged-up window. She opened the door and yelled, "Hello." Just like a Yooper, she thought.

"Hey, Beth." Danny came to the door, smiling broadly, a splotch of paint on his T-shirt.

"Hi." She kicked her boots off on a rubber mat with thick, raised edges. She slipped off her jacket and looked for a place to hang it.

"I'll take that." Danny folded the jacket over his arm.

Russ approached with a paint roller in hand. "It's good to see you again."

"Hey, everyone, Beth is here," Danny called out.

"Hey, Beth," said a brown-haired man on a ladder who was cutting in paint on the wall next to the ceiling.

"That's my brother, Jack." Danny nodded toward the man. Beth could see the resemblance.

"That's Sydney over there." Danny pointed to a woman who was rolling paint on a wall.

"Hi, Beth." Sydney looked young, perhaps still in college.

"Welcome," Aimee said as if she owned the home. "We're glad you could make it."

"Hi, Aimee."

"This is it. The living room's here, the kitchen's over there, and the dining room's over there. The tour's over," Danny joked.

"Nice." Beth smiled.

"Come on. I'll show you." Danny walked through the living room and down a short hall. "The bathroom's right there. It still needs paint." Even if the door were closed, one could see the toilet through the gap between the frame and the wall. "Not quite done."

Danny motioned to his right to an empty room with unpainted walls. "That'll be my office when it's finished, or I guess the guest room."

Beth followed Danny into a slightly larger bedroom opposite the other.

He added Beth's jacket to four already on the bed. "This is the master bedroom." Dark burgundy walls. Taupe carpet. White trim. "I finished off one room so I'd have a place to relax." He motioned to heavy blankets covering the windows. "Those are my darkening shades. I work rotational shifts, and sometimes I have to work nights. When that happens, I need to sleep during the day."

"It's a nice house," Beth said. "I like it."

"It's simple. Only 1100 square feet on the main floor, but there's a walkout basement, so when I get around to finishing it, I'll have a 2200-square-foot home. I could put two bedrooms down there, and maybe even a sauna." He winked.

Beth's cheeks grew hot. Two moons. Unable to shake the image, she turned away. A computer sat on a desk in one corner of the room. Facebook was open showing a birthday picture of little Danny. Adorable. "Is that a throwback Thursday picture? I saw the family pictures on the wall at your parents' house. I like that little gap between your front teeth. You were a cute kid."

Danny stared at the screen as though he had seen a ghost. "We should get to painting."

"Are you okay?"

"Yeah." Danny walked out of the room. "That's not me," he mumbled.

Back in the living room, Aimee played hostess, cleaning up after the workers and asking the crew if they needed water or wet paper towel. Beth frowned. She wasn't even sure she liked Danny, even if she decided to stay longer, so why did Aimee annoy her? Worse than being a hostile waitress, she pranced around like Danny's girlfriend, saying things like, "We so appreciate your help."

"Could you get the bathroom ready to paint?" Danny asked Beth. "Put the plastic drop cloths over the counter, toilet, bathtub, and floor. Put painter's tape around the cabinets."

"I can try."

The work in the bathroom was tedious, at least for Beth, because she lacked the patience to do things that require precision. She did appreciate that no one was looking over her shoulder, telling her what to do. Danny seemed to trust that she would do it right.

After completing her project, she returned to the living room. The crew, having finished painting, gathered supplies on a tarp. Aimee removed the drop cloths from the clustered furniture in the middle of the living room.

"I'm going to make a pizza run." Danny looked at Beth.

"Who wants to go with me?"

"I'll go." Aimee bounded to his side, triumph in her eyes.

He smiled meekly. "The problem is that my Jeep's blocked. I was thinking maybe Beth could take me."

"You can take Russ's truck," Aimee suggested. "I'm sure he wouldn't mind."

"I don't mind," Russ said, oblivious to the competition for Danny's company.

"Thanks, Russ. You guys take a break. We'll pound out the kitchen, bathroom, and office after lunch. While we get the pizza, you can go downstairs. The pop's outside." Danny left with Aimee.

Beth wiped moisture from the living room window and watched them drive off with Aimee sitting in the center seat next to Danny. Let it go, she told herself. She didn't need more drama in her life. She did not need a boyfriend, but she had to admit, the sight of the two of them leaving together unsettled her. Did she really like Danny, or was it just her competitive nature coming out?

"C'mon, Beth." Russ waved from the basement door.

Beth descended the stairs into unfinished space. "Ahh, a man cave."

A pool table stood at one end of the basement, and a foosball table at the other. The basement was damp and cold, with a concrete floor and block walls. A furnace separated the space, with sheet metal ductwork coming up and branching out.

Jack opened a vent. "It'll heat up soon enough with all of us down here. Are you up for pool, Sydney?"

She nodded, and they grabbed cues.

"Do you play foosball?" Russ asked Beth.

"A little."

"Get you a pop?"

"Something without caffeine, not diet, if he's got it."

Russ opened the basement door to the outside. Snow was piled over two feet deep and imprinted with the bottom third of the door. The soda pop sat on top of the snow. Russ returned with a Coke and a Sprite. He took his position on the other side of the table.

Beth dropped the ball, and they whacked it back and forth a couple of times. She flicked the ball into the goal that Russ was defending.

"You play a little, hey."

"A little each week. I ran an afterschool tutoring program. Foosball and other activities are what get the kids to show up—and they stay for the tutoring." She dropped another ball, and Russ sent it flying to her end.

"Did you go to school with Danny?" Beth engaged Russ in conversation as they played.

Russ struggled to answer as he concentrated on defending his goal from Beth's quick hands. "Not exactly—I was homeschooled. We became friends through hockey."

"Danny said you're a contractor."

"When I can get work." Russ paused between sentences, focusing on the game. "It's pretty slow in the winter. It's a great time to hire a contractor, because guys like me are desperate for work. Nobody thinks of doing projects until the snow melts, but then in the summer, there's too much competition. The market is saturated."

Saturated? Alan's mother, a professional businessperson, used language like that, but this Yooper guy? "So why are you a contractor if there's not enough work in the winter and too much competition in the summer?"

"Because I…" Russ focused on the foosball table, flashing his eyes back and forth, as Beth kept slamming the ball toward his goal.

"Yeah!" Beth slid another bead over. The score was 2-0.

"Nice. I'm a contractor because I can't imagine working for somebody else. I did it once, and I'm never going to do that again."

Beth dropped the ball into play and whacked it toward his goal. "Danny said you live in a cabin off the grid."

Russ looked up from the table with a broad smile. "Yeah, it's a little cabin, but it works. I'm independent."

Beth scored again and slid another bead over. She popped

the tab on her Sprite and took a swig. Because she wanted to hear more about his living off the grid, she eased up on her play and the game became less competitive. "So, how do you live without electricity?"

"I have a propane fridge and I use LED lights run off batteries. I charge them when I come into town. I have one charging upstairs, along with my laptop. Danny doesn't mind sharing his electricity."

Beth blocked a couple shots on goal, then managed to push the ball to Russ's end.

"The coolest thing about the cabin is my composting toilet. I have an outhouse, but who wants to go outside to use it in the winter?" Russ spoke with passion. "It's a Swedish toilet, called the Diverter. The key to a good composting toilet is diverting the solids from the liquids. The better the solids dry, the less it stinks."

Beth looked up in disbelief. Wow. Intense. What's up with the preoccupation with toileting in the UP?

"Score! Finally, I put a point on the board." Russ slid a bead over.

"Pizza." Danny descended the stairs with two boxes in hand.

Aimee followed behind holding another two boxes.

"Russ, could you give me a hand with this?" Jack grabbed a 4' x 8' sheet of plywood, and he and Russ placed it over the pool table.

Sydney pulled a couple of stools and a few chairs to the makeshift table, while Danny and Aimee set the pizza on the plywood.

Danny folded the tops back on the pizza boxes. "Dig in." He sat and waited for his volunteers to serve themselves first.

Aimee, showing no interest in the food, took a stool at the opposite end of the table from Danny. She looked solemn.

Beth sensed tension. Maybe Danny and Aimee had a DTR—a define-the-relationship talk. If so, it hadn't gone well for Aimee. Beth took no pleasure in her pain. Rejection was hard.

"Beth and I played foosball." Russ stacked a paper plate with pizza slices.

"You play foosball?" Danny asked Beth.

"A little." She took a bite of cheese and vegetable pizza.

"After we eat, let's have a game of doubles." Russ flashed a smile at Beth. "Me and Beth against you and Aimee."

"No, I want to be on Aimee's team." Beth would try to make peace.

"Boys against girls? Come on." Danny rolled his eyes.

"Okay." Aimee shrugged.

At the end of a spirited game, Beth raised her hands in the air, victorious. "Goal. 10-8."

Aimee high-fived her, and they laughed.

"Good job defending, Russ. You blocked a lot of shots." Danny slapped him on the back. "Okay, let's see if we can pound out the rest of the house. Let's put Russ and Sydney in the office, me and Jack in the kitchen, and Beth and Aimee in the bathroom."

Aimee grimaced. "I don't think—"

"Let's get 'er done." Danny led the way upstairs.

Beth and Aimee gathered supplies in the bathroom. The space was large enough for both of them, but small enough that it forced them to work side-by-side.

"Are you going to the Women's Tea tonight?" Beth asked.

"No. I work Saturday nights. Remember?"

"Oh, yeah." Beth decided to keep her mouth shut and not make any more conversation.

Aimee opened a can of paint. "Beth?"

"Yes?"

"I'm sorry I've been so cold to you."

"That's o—"

"No, it's not okay." Aimee stirred the paint. "We both know I like Danny. I guess I had the wrong impression. I thought it was mutual, not that he's ever really—"

"You don't have to explain."

"Look…" Aimee took a paintbrush out of a plastic tub. "We've never dated. I got a little competitive when I saw you with him. I hadn't ever seen him date anybody since he moved back, and it's not like he was dating me, but I kind of hoped we'd grow closer."

"We aren't dating. I'm not even sure how long I'll be here."

Aimee gasped, as if she could no longer maintain the façade of capitulation. "It's just not fair. I've been after that man for years, ever since I was in middle school, and then you suddenly show up and he's head over heels for you." She dipped the brush in the salmon-colored paint and pointed it at Beth.

What an ugly color. If it were to go any further with Danny, she'd need to have a difficult conversation with him on his decor. She laughed.

"What's so funny?" Aimee narrowed her eyebrows.

"Nothing... I was just thinking how awful the color is."

Aimee looked at her brush and snickered. "It's hideous, hey."

"I know how you feel, Aimee." Beth took a deep breath, expecting to have to fight back tears. They didn't come, and she lifted her chin. "My fiancé just left me." She said the words matter-of-factly.

"I *thought* that was you who was getting married. I thought Grandma Lou only had one granddaughter. But you said it wasn't."

"No, you asked if I just got married. Clearly I didn't."

"You're very honest," Aimee said with a hint of sarcasm.

"I wasn't looking for this, with Danny, and the more I learn about him, the more I'm thinking we're not a good match anyhow."

"As much as it pains me to say it, you should date him. He likes you, and he's a good guy." Aimee forced a smile, but her eyes still held sadness. "I thought I wasn't going to like you, but I think we could be friends."

Chapter 21

"*A*imee apologized," Beth said to Grandma as she drove through Douglass on their way to the Women's Tea.

"Oh?"

"I know what you mean now about her being sweet."

"And was Danny sweet?" Grandma's eyes sparkled.

"He is, was, and that's what drives me nuts. I shouldn't be dating now, much less actually liking a guy. But every time I'm around him I'm just..."

"You're just what?"

"Alive." Beth felt heat rise to her face. "You know, he's not the little choirboy you think he is."

"I never thought he was. I've heard him sing." Grandma snickered.

Beth turned and descended a side street. "I'm serious. Did you know he has a past?"

"Everyone has a past."

"No, I mean..." Beth didn't want to gossip. She pulled into the parking lot behind The Tea House, turned off the car, and met Grandma's gaze.

"Beth, do you think people can change?" Grandma searched her face.

She looked out the side window. Of course she believed people could change, but he was a Christian when he was sleeping around. He should have known better. A song from her high school youth group days popped into her head. *To leave and cleave and become one. Just the two of us in this union. True love waits.* Beth set her chin and faced Grandma. "I just don't want to begin a relationship on a poor foundation. That's why the rules are so important."

"You mean the law?"

"What?"

"You heard me, Becky. I mean Beth—you look so much alike." Grandma got out of the car.

In the restaurant, Senja stepped out from behind the hostess stand.

"Hello, my good friend." Grandma hugged her.

"Hang your jackets here." Senja motioned toward a wheeled coat rack. She examined a list, running her finger down a page of names. "You're at the daffodil table. You'll find your names on place cards there. Have fun."

About thirty women had already gathered in The Tea House. Each table had a unique arrangement of silk flowers— roses at one, lilies at another. On one side of the room, a microphone was set up between two large speakers.

Grandma and Beth found the daffodil table where another woman was seated. "Hi, Louisa. I was delighted to see your name at my table."

"Beth, this is Karen. She's in my prayer group."

"I've heard so much about you." The middle-aged woman stood and smiled enthusiastically. "Congratulations. Did Alan come out with you?" She hugged Beth, so she missed seeing her pained look.

"No, I came alone." It would be like Grandma to share the good news of the engagement but not the bad news of the breakup.

While Karen and Grandma chatted, Beth sat and picked up the list of teas. Cups sat upside down on saucers. A ceramic kettle of hot water rested on a stand above a candle.

Mary came and took the orders—oolong for Grandma, chamomile for Karen, and herbal spearmint for Beth. A few minutes later, she delivered individual tea sachets.

A college-aged woman stood in front of a microphone and strummed her guitar. "Ladies, you'll find printed lyrics on your tables."

Grandma lifted her arms in praise as a chorus of voices filled the room.

After a few songs, the guitarist said, "I was at the concert last Saturday and had the privilege of hearing a song that's been playing on the radio. Join me in singing 'We Met at the Cross,' by Allie Nantuck."

As Beth sang along, her thoughts drifted to Danny. His gentle touch. The easy comradery they shared.

When the guitarist finished, Senja stepped to the microphone. "Thank you, Missy. Thank you for joining us, ladies. Mary will be coming around with wonderful *hors d'oeuvres*. There are hundreds in the back, so help yourself to as many as you'd like. They're all included in the price."

"There was an admission price?" Beth whispered.

"I took care of it," Grandma whispered back.

"So without further ado," Senja said, "I present you Bella Atkinson."

Bella stepped to the mike with a broad smile. "I am thankful to be here with you today to discuss a topic near and dear to all of us, no matter what our season of life. In one of my favorite childhood books," Bella held up a worn, hardcover book, "Anne of Green Gables asks Marilla, 'Do you think that I shall ever have a bosom friend in Avonlea?' We long for bosom friends. Kindred spirits, Anne calls them. People to whom we can confide our inmost souls."

Beth was still a fan of Anne. As Bella spoke about friendship, Beth jotted notes in her *Hope* journal.

After the talk, a middle-aged woman approached their table. The hugger Danny had talked to at the concert.

"How are you doing?" Karen asked with an empathetic tone.

"One day at a time." The corners of the woman's lips drew down.

Grandma stood and hugged her.

"Thank you." She pulled away, and then dropped her chin with an expectant look to Beth.

"Patty, this is my granddaughter, Beth."

Patty took Grandma's seat. "You're the girl Danny's dating."

Beth grimaced. "We're not really dating."

"My daughter Kristine and Danny dated in high school." Patty grabbed Beth's hand and held it between hers. "I guess you're his type. Petite, blonde, and beautiful." Her eyes filled with tears. "I just wish we could go back in time and rewrite the past. If she'd stayed with Danny, he would've kept her on the right track. Life would've been different." She pulled a wadded napkin from her pocket and dabbed the corners of her eyes.

Karen put a hand on Patty's shoulder. "But then you wouldn't have AJ."

Patty shook her head. "I'd still have AJ."

"Patty." Grandma handed her a fresh napkin. "Are you still working at Health and Human Services?"

"Yes, I am," Patty said.

Beth stepped away to have a conversation with somebody—anybody—else.

"What was that about?" Beth asked Grandma when they were out on the sidewalk.

"It was a feel-good talk over tea and *hors d'oeuvres.*"

"I know that. I'm talking about that awkward conversation with Patty."

"She's grieving. Her daughter just died in a car accident."

Chapter 22

"When we get to Maribel's, honk the horn. We don't want to surprise her." Grandma held a glass jar of warm chicken soup as Beth drove her through the falling snow down the road past Danny's house and his parents' house. "I would've called to let her know we're coming, but she doesn't answer her phone anymore—not since Vance came out to sell her satellite TV."

Past a stop sign and a mile down a gravel road, Beth turned left into a driveway. Old farm equipment cluttered the yard, where the snow lay undisturbed between the house and a rickety old barn. In what was once a field, alder brush and trees encroached on the house and barn. She honked and parked next to a plow truck.

Grandma and Beth got out of the car and walked to the wood-sided house with a few patches of paint here and there that had not yet peeled. As they approached, an elderly woman came out onto the stoop in a calico nightgown with a rifle in hand. Her dark, sullen eyes looked in their direction.

"Hello, Maribel," Grandma called out.

"Louisa!" Maribel's face broke out in a smile and she patted down her short, straight, salt-and-pepper hair.

"Are you up for visitors?" Grandma asked.

"I sure am. I sure am. I milked the cows and I don't have any chores to do until afternoon."

Beth glanced back at the undisturbed snow.

"Maribel, I brought somebody for you to meet. My granddaughter, Beth."

"Who's that?" Maribel asked loudly as if the women were still across the yard.

Grandma and Beth climbed the steps of the front stoop.

"Ahh, Becky!" Maribel's eyes lit up, and she patted Beth on the shoulder. "You're here. I'm so glad." She wrapped Beth in a hug. "Today, we'll sort through things."

Beth looked at Grandma, who shrugged.

"Come in. Come in." Maribel led the way into the kitchen and set the rifle next to the hutch. "I've got so much stuff I can hardly move around. I'm so glad you've come to help. Where's Chip? We'll need him to move the dresser. He's such a nice boy and so strong. So strong. When are you two gonna get married, Becky?"

Beth looked to Grandma, unsure how to respond.

"We don't have time to sort today, but we'll visit for a few minutes." Grandma held out the Mason jar. "We brought chicken soup. I'll heat it up and dish you up a bowl."

"I love soup, but I'll heat it up later, after we visit." Maribel took the jar and walked across the squeaky linoleum floor to the refrigerator. "Have a seat. Have a seat."

Grandma and Beth sat at the kitchen table, which stood in front of a window much like at Grandma's, except the screen had half a dozen pieces of duct tape stuck to it and the bird feeder outside was empty and falling apart.

"I have coffee. Would you like coffee?" Maribel asked.

"Water would be fine for me," Grandma said.

"Water for me, too," Beth said.

Maribel pulled Mason jars from the cupboard and filled them with water at the tap. She took a seat in front of a mug of coffee. Holding it in both hands, she leaned back in her chair and crossed her legs. She faced Beth. "How's California?"

"Fine, thank you." Beth took a sip of water.

"Maribel, how have you been doing?" Grandma asked.

"I'm okay. I'm okay. Except for the crime. Never thought I'd live to see the day when there was so much crime in the UP. Crime in the UP." She leaned forward and banged the mug on the table, sloshing coffee.

"What crime is that?" Grandma asked.

"Burglaries. Ever since that TV guy came, things have gone missing. That Vance—he got one of my house keys. He lets himself in and takes stuff."

"What's missing this time?" Grandma asked.

"My ammunition. My ammunition." Maribel scowled. "What am I going to do? I can't shoot the squirrels, and they're making such a mess in my attic. I can't defend myself if Vance comes back again. I even reported it to law enforcement, and Officer Johnson searched the house and couldn't find a trace of it. Vance took it." She sighed. "At least the mere brandishing a weapon, even if it's unloaded, is enough to scare off intruders. That is, if I'm awake. Vance comes at night. He comes at night."

"Maribel, are you okay in this house by yourself?" Grandma asked.

Maribel scoffed. "I do fine."

Beth nudged Grandma's leg with hers under the table. Grandma turned to her and whispered, "Shush, child. Don't make this about me."

"I just need a little help sorting. Becky, when can you come back to help me? That reminds me." Maribel stood." I want to show you the dresser. Come, let me show you it. Let me show you it."

Maribel led the way down the hallway to a cluttered, dusty bedroom. An embroidered blanket, mostly hidden by piles of papers, hung from the edges of a twin bed. Boxes were stacked in the middle of the floor. A wide, antique dresser with a vanity mirror stood along the back wall.

"My parents bought this dresser for our wedding gift. It's meant for two people. With Henry gone, I have no need for it. It's too big. It's too big. If I could get rid of it, I'd have a little more room to move around in here. I want you to have it."

Beth hesitated for a moment and then said gently, "Thank you, but I don't have room to bring it back with me."

"Yes, that's what you said." Maribel furrowed her brow. "But I told you Chip should come and get it and store it at his folks' house. I'm telling you, when you get married, you're going to want this. When you get married, you're going to want this. You and Chip need a big dresser that can hold both your clothes."

"Chip?" Beth looked to Grandma.

"Maribel," Grandma said, "Rebecca did *not* marry Chip. She married a man named Oliver. This is Rebecca's daughter, Beth."

Maribel looked confused, flustered.

"Daughter? Rebecca's daughter? What's your name?"

"I'm Beth."

"You look like Becky."

"Yes, I do."

"*Oofta.*" Maribel walked out of the bedroom. "I need a nap."

Back in the car, Beth buckled her seatbelt and asked again, "Chip?"

Grandma smiled. "Yes, your mother and Chip dated."

"Chip Atkinson?"

"The very same."

Beth drove out of the driveway. "They were going to get married?"

"That's what Maribel said. They never got engaged, but it was pretty serious."

"Why didn't you tell me?"

"It wasn't my story to tell."

"You didn't tell Mother that Chip Atkinson is your pastor?"

"She didn't ask."

"She knows now, because I told her about The Tea House women's talk and Bella Atkinson speaking. She hung up on me."

Grandma sighed. "Sometimes wounds don't heal when they're not properly treated."

Beth stopped at the stop sign, looked both ways—more so out of habit and duty than necessity—before proceeding onto the paved road. "How did Maribel's husband die?"

"Henry." Grandma's voice was pensive. "That was tragic. He died maybe fifty years ago, when he was young—twenty-eight, twenty-nine. He couldn't have been thirty. He died of Lou Gehrig's disease. It was heartbreaking."

"What's that?"

"It's dreadful. At first, they thought he had a stroke, because his speech was slurred. Then he had trouble swallowing, and even choked once, but Maribel patted him on the back until it came out—that was before the Heimlich maneuver. He went downhill fast after that. He became bedridden and died within a year."

"It sounds horrible." Beth pulled into the driveway.

"Maribel wasn't the same after it. She couldn't keep up on the farm. She let the strawberry fields go. Maribel did custodial work at Douglass State for years."

"Did they have any kids?"

"No. They hadn't been married long, a few years. She had a miscarriage, and then Henry got sick."

Beth pulled into the garage and shut off the engine. Tears moistened her eyes. "That's such a sad story. I'm glad Danny is looking after her. He's a good guy."

"Yes, he is, dear."

Chapter 23

$\mathcal{B}$eth drove Grandma over the old, double-decker Lift Bridge as snowmobile traffic passed underneath on what was once a railroad track carrying ore off Copper Island.

"Turn right after the bridge. It's over there." Grandma nodded to a repurposed sandstone train depot with an awning over an elevated cement platform.

"We can take you right away, Mrs. Herrala," the receptionist called as they entered the clinic. Grandma went through a door held open by a nurse, and Beth took a seat in the waiting room.

She checked Facebook on her phone. Cat pictures. Recipes. Rants. Nothing of interest, except for pictures of people she loved. Julie's kids. Selfies of girls from the Center. She entered *Danny Johnson* in the search function. Too common of a name. She narrowed the search. *Danny Johnson Quincy Michigan.*

There he was, with his dark brown eyes and an easy, gaptoothed smile. Should she send him a friend request? That would be a bit too declarative of her interest. Probably better to wait and see if he friends her.

She checked her e-mail. Mostly spam. Junk mail. A note

from Julie, asking for an update on Danny. A note from her mother, apologizing for hanging up so abruptly. Mother wanted her to come home. More junk mail. Beth scrolled down to the messages from the week before. A note from Alan. *Alan?* Her stomach turned with the feeling one has when looking over the edge of a canyon. *Big News* was the subject. Her heart hammered. Should she delete it? Ugh. Curiosity got the best of her. She opened the message.

Beth, I hope you're well and having fun, wherever you are. I'm leaving the Resource Center at the end of the month. I found a job out East about an hour from D.C. I'll live with my mom until I can find my own place. I'm excited about the opportunity. The kids ask about you. Carmen's doing a good job with the tutoring program, but she can't work full time while she's still in school. Things were awkward between us when we both worked here. I hoped we could still be friends, but I realize now that would've been difficult. So sorry for everything. All the best, Alan

Why couldn't he have left before she quit the job she loved? Jerk. Tears welled up in her eyes, and she blinked them away. Why was she still so weepy over him?

She looked out the window at snowmobilers passing on the trail alongside the frozen canal. In Los Angeles, the weather was in the seventies. She missed the sun. She missed her friends.

She opened the messaging app and texted Julie. *Jules, what's up?*

An ellipsis popped up on the screen... Julie was typing. *Laundry. Never ends.*

Miss you, Beth replied.

U coming home soon? Even after Julie got an iPhone, she retained texting patterns from the flip phone days.

Not sure. Alan's leaving the Resource Center.

No way. Now, after you left? RU going to go back there?

Beth leaned back. The tutoring program was in full swing. She missed the kids—but if she hadn't left, then she wouldn't have met Danny. Like that was going anywhere anyway.

Don't know. Still in shock. She pressed send. Maybe she

should call her boss, Gary, to ask if he'd hire her back. But for now, she had another pressing matter.

She typed another message. *Going to stay for a bit. Grandma's having trouble with her arm. Can't start car. I'll play chauffeur until we figure it out.*

How's your boyfriend?

Haha. Not my boyfriend. He's okay. I'm not sure about him. He has baggage.

LOL. Don't we all?

Yes, but don't know if I'd want to deal with it.

Another text message popped up from Julie. *Baby still sleeping, but Lydia woke from nap, crying. G2G.*

"Got to Go." Beth laughed, translating the *textese*. Julie was married with two children, but she texted like she was a teenager.

Bells above the door clanged and a very pregnant, young mother entered, pushing a stroller with a toddler boy. Two girls—perhaps three and five years old—bounded in with jackets unzipped, no hats, and no gloves. The mother brushed snow off the kids' blonde heads and Beth thought with amusement how Yooper kids develop *sisu* at such a young age. The little boy waved as he rolled by.

Beth sighed. Would she ever get to experience motherhood?

"It'll be a few minutes, Mrs. Saari." The receptionist handed the young mother a clipboard.

Beth picked a newspaper off the end table and scanned the headlines, mostly news from downstate. She flipped it over and saw the weather forecast. The outlook for the next seven days—snow every day, mid-twenties. A snow tally reported three inches in October, eighteen inches in November, sixteen inches in December, and, so far, fifty-three inches in January. Fifty-three inches in twenty-seven days? Incredible.

It was hard to believe spring would ever come. She remembered the words of Samuel Clinton at Robin's Nest. *Hope that is seen is not hope.* The UP snow certainly did not allow its residents to see hope for spring.

Grandma entered the lobby, rubbing her neck.

Beth set down the newspaper. "How did it go? What did the doctor find?"

"It went fine. Dr. Seid thinks it's something with a nerve."

They left the clinic and walked to the Subaru Outback.

"He wants me to see a neurologist as soon as possible," Grandma said.

"Really?" Beth followed Grandma around to the passenger door.

Grandma pulled the handle, but it sprang back, and the door remained closed. "He said I should be open to neck surgery."

"That sounds serious." Beth searched her face. "Why did he say that?"

"The doctor saw atrophy in my right arm, muscle loss." A hint of concern washed over Grandma's face before she stepped to the side and successfully opened the door with her left hand. She plopped into the seat, and then leaned back and swung her legs in.

"So when are you going to call to make an appointment to see the neurologist?"

"He had his assistant call to make it right away. It's in two weeks."

Beth closed Grandma's door, and then walked to the driver's side and climbed in. "It looks like I'm staying for another two weeks," Beth decided.

"The neurologist is in Marquette."

"Okay, where's Marquette?"

"It's ninety miles east. It's a bit far to drive in the winter, especially for somebody who doesn't like winter driving."

"I'm getting better," Beth said in her most chipper voice, attempting to conceal her anxiety. "This is fluff, and the roads are dry."

"We'll have to see. The weather starts to warm in February, and we get hit with nasty, wet blizzards. It might be better to go in the spring."

Back at home in the kitchen, Grandma opened the pantry

cabinet and took out a bag of rice and a box of raisins. "Let's make *riisipuuroa.*"

"What's that?"

"Your mother didn't make it? It's my comfort food." Grandma set a pot on the counter. "It's soupy rice—boiled in milk with sugar, cinnamon, and, sometimes, raisins."

"*Arroz con leche.* The Mexican families I worked with made that dish."

"*Riisipuuroa* is Finnish more by the name than the ingredients. Could you start a fire in the stove?" Grandma took a measuring cup from a drawer.

Beth grabbed a canvas sling and retrieved firewood from the porch. She knelt in front of the stove, loaded it with newspaper and kindling, and added several pieces of wood. After lighting the newspaper, she gently blew on the fire until the kindling burned on its own. Then she closed the door. No assistance. No coaching. She felt rather proud of herself.

Grandma set the rice to boil, and Beth filled the teakettle. She put it on the old stove, and they sat at the table. Beth looked out the window at the falling snow. Again. Three weeks since she had arrived and it had snowed every day. "Grandma, where are the chickadees?"

"They're off looking for food."

"Is your bird feeder empty?"

"I believe it is. Would you be a dear and fill it up? There's a bag of seed by the back door."

With the bag half full of sunflower seeds, Beth waded out onto the back deck, grimacing as snow fell into the tops of her boots and cold stung her ankles. She opened the hinged roof and, with the bag propped against her hip, scooped seeds out to fill the feeder. The bag wasn't heavy, so why hadn't Grandma kept it filled? For such a creature of habit, these changes in Grandma's routine raised concern.

The rice simmered until *al dente.* Grandma added the milk, sugar, and cinnamon. When the rice softened, she turned off the burner and added raisins.

Beth sliced *makkara.* She sampled a piece and placed the

rest of the sausage on a plate.

Grandma packed a tea ball and dropped it in the kettle. "I suppose we should update your mother."

Beth nodded. "She'd want to know."

"Would you call her?"

Beth hesitated. "I can call her, but that'll have to wait until after eight o'clock. Mother doesn't like to be interrupted at work." Beth was glad to put the call off until later. She tired of Mother lecturing her.

The porch door slammed shut.

"That's Danny," Grandma said. "He's filling the wood hopper."

Beth felt flustered, suddenly concerned about what she looked like. She polished the knife with a dish towel and then held it up to see her reflection, checking for food in her teeth. She set the plate of summer sausage on the table, where she joined Grandma and waited.

She had briefly seen Danny at church on Sunday, the day after the Women's Tea. He had sat with her and Grandma, but then she didn't see him after the women's Sunday school group. It felt strange, as if their budding relationship had ended without closure. She had told him she was going to stay through Grandma's appointment. Maybe he would come in to say good-bye, thinking she would be leaving soon.

The front door creaked open and Beth jumped up.

"Calm down, girl." Grandma chuckled as she got up from her chair and called out, "Come in, Danny."

Beth could keep her cool as long as she didn't look into those eyes. She sedately followed Grandma to the front door.

"Hi, Grandma Lou. Hey, Beth." Danny stood in his uniform, looking past Grandma, who quietly disappeared back into the kitchen.

Danny was glad he caught her before she headed back to California.

"Hi, Danny." Beth looked down at her feet.

"You're still here."

"I'm still here."

"Grandpa Sam used to ask how you can tell the difference between a Finnish introvert and extrovert."

"How's that?"

"An introvert looks at her feet. An extrovert looks at yours." Danny laughed.

Beth looked up and smiled.

"Will you be leaving? Your car's buried under two feet of snow. Should I clear it for you?"

She met his gaze. "No. I'm staying for a while yet."

Danny sat on the hall bench and unlaced his boots. He had woken up that morning not caring the relationship was over, figuring the pain was not worth the reward, but he felt compelled to see her, even if it was to say goodbye. Now that she was staying, maybe there was still hope.

They joined Grandma Lou in the kitchen where she stood at the stove, stirring a pot using her left hand. "Would you like tea and *riisipuuroa*?"

He nodded. "I'd love that. I'm glad to see your stove's burning. You haven't been going through as much wood lately, and it's the dead of winter."

"Beth started the fire today."

"She did, hey." Danny draped his arm around Beth's shoulder. "We'll make a Yooper out of you yet."

"And I'll teach you to up-speak." Beth nudged him playfully.

"How did it go at the doctor's?" Danny over-emphasized his up-speak.

"It could be a nerve in my neck." Grandma Lou dished the porridge into bowls. "I'm going to see a neurologist in Marquette."

"When's that?"

"February 10th. Come sit down." Grandma Lou carried her own bowl while Beth grabbed the other two.

"You got a ride?" He'd check his schedule. Maybe he wasn't working that day.

"I'm going to drive." Beth put a bowl in front of him.

"All the way to Marquette in February?"

"I can do it." Beth squared her shoulders.

He took a bite. "This is delicious." He faced Beth. "So you'll be here for your birthday?"

She beamed. "You remembered."

"You bet." Of course he remembered. He couldn't stop thinking about her. "I tell you what. I'd like to take you on a special birthday outing. It'll be a surprise, but dress warm. Set aside the whole day." He winked at Grandma. "Grandma Lou, is it okay if I take your granddaughter out?"

"Please do." Grandma's smile stretched across her face.

"How about it?" Danny asked Beth.

Beth stared, blinked.

They seemed to have a connection, so what was her problem? Danny rubbed his neck.

"Okay," she finally said, and for a brief moment, her blue eyes sparkled.

"This is Rebecca Dawson."

"Hi. It's me."

"Hi, Elizabeth. You caught me in the car."

"I thought I would."

"I'm sorry I had to cut it short the last time we talked. I was just a little surprised that you weren't coming home yet."

Yeah, right, Beth thought. You were surprised to hear the name Chip Atkinson.

"Did Grandma see the doctor today? Did they figure out what's wrong with her arm?"

"She might have a pinched nerve in her neck. She has a referral to see a neurologist. I'm going to stay, at least until after the appointment."

"Oh good, I'm glad you're there to help her. When's the appointment?"

"In two weeks."

"You're going to be away for your birthday?" Disappointment twinged Mother's voice.

"It looks like it."

"Very well. Let me know what they find. You're not dating that boy anymore, are you, Elizabeth?"

"He's hardly a boy. He's twenty-eight years old. His name is Danny." Beth felt a burst of confidence. Where did that come from? She didn't often stand up to Mother.

"Elizabeth, Dr. Benley said you should not be dating for at least six months after a major breakup."

"Mother—"

"Don't get too comfortable there. It's not a place you want to end up. Everybody's into everyone else's business."

Beth fought back a giggle. Best not to mention Maribel's comments about Chip and the dresser.

"It seems charming at first, but then—"

"Mother, I have to go."

"Don't lose your head," Mother said.

"Good-bye." Beth hung up the phone.

Chapter 24

*B*eth carried a pan of freshly baked *nisu* as she walked with Grandma down the sidewalk in Douglass, after having circled the block twice before finding a place to parallel park. The issue was not so many cars, but too many snowbanks.

"Senja's apartment is up there." Grandma motioned to a tall brick building. Rows of windows towered above a ground level business that read *Chen's Wok*. "My next favorite restaurant after The Tea House."

Beth followed Grandma through the lobby of the historic Sheldon House. In the confined space of the elevator, the smell of cardamom through the foil made her mouth water.

"Now the party can start," Senja announced, when they entered her fourth-floor apartment.

"Party?" Beth laughed. "I thought this was a prayer meeting."

"It's a prayer meeting and a party." Senja chuckled.

"Hello, my dear friend." Grandma hugged Senja and then motioned toward the pan Beth carried. "We made *nisu*."

"Thank you. I'll take that into the kitchen." Senja reached out and took the *nisu*. "Beth, make yourself comfortable. You should see familiar faces."

Beth and Grandma left their boots by the door and hung their jackets on empty wall hooks next to other jackets. Beth made her way into the living room with her *Hope* journal in hand. At the far end of the living room, two windows looked out over the canal to a lit ski hill.

Beth indeed saw faces she recognized among the half dozen women.

Karen sat primly on a wooden dining room chair. She rose and greeted Beth with a hug. "This is my friend Shu-wa." Seated in an upholstered chair and holding a teacup with both hands, the slender woman bowed her head toward Beth. "Shu-wa's from Taiwan. She's working on her doctorate at Douglass State."

"Nice to meet you."

Aimee lounged on a sofa. She scooted over and waved for Beth to sit next to her. "This is Robin Clinton." Aimee motioned to the woman opposite her on the couch.

Beth extended her hand. "Samuel's wife?"

"You know Sam?" The older woman's face brightened with delight as she squeezed Beth's hand.

"Yes, I've been in Robin's Nest."

"Wonderful."

Senja, followed by Grandma, carried two plates of sliced *nisu.* She set them on a coffee table. "Ladies, as always, help yourselves to tea and coffee in the kitchen. Louisa and Beth brought *nisu.*"

"Beth, it's good to see you." Bella crossed the room with a warm smile and offered her hand.

"I enjoyed your talk at the tea." Beth looked into sincere, smiling eyes. She wondered if Bella had any idea her husband used to date Mother.

"I missed the tea." Aimee wrinkled her nose. "I have to work every Saturday night."

Bella patted her shoulder. "It won't be long before you graduate and you're working at your dream job."

Aimee frowned. "I hope so."

"Let's get started," Senja said as she sat. "We'll begin with praise."

Each woman closed her eyes and bowed her head.

"We praise you, God, for the blessings in our lives." Senja's voice rang out, melodious.

"We thank you for our families," Grandma said. "I thank you for time I have with my granddaughter." She opened her eyes and peeked at Beth.

"We thank you for providing for our needs," Shu-wa said.

"Thank you for Louisa's *nisu*," Senja said.

The women laughed and then continued to jump in with sentences of thanksgiving.

"Thank you for new friends," Aimee said, squeezing Beth's arm.

After several seconds of silence, Beth felt compelled to say something. "Thank you for giving us rest."

"And now, sisters," Senja concluded, "we'll share prayer requests for this coming week."

The women took notepads, journals, or scraps of paper out of purses and bags and waited expectantly. Beth opened her *Hope* journal and flipped to a blank page.

"You'll only write the important words in that one." Robin laughed.

Beth's laughter was met with more laughter as the other women saw what she held in her hand.

Bella held up her journal with familiar embossed letters, but the word *Faith* paired with a scene of a sunset. "That's what Sam told me."

"And me." Karen held up her journal embossed with the word *Believe* and a scene of a starry night sky.

As the women shared prayer requests and took notes on each other's concerns, Beth remained silent. She would have appreciated prayer for her budding relationship with Danny, but she didn't want to get into that with strangers, especially not with Aimee there. Besides, it felt weird to be in a town where everyone seemed connected in some way. They all knew Danny. Mostly, Beth's mind was on Grandma, but she was right there in the room, and it should be up to her to ask for prayer for her own health.

"Is there anything from anybody else?" Senja asked.

Beth looked across the room at Grandma, who met her gaze. Beth raised her eyebrows.

"Anything?" Senja asked again. She turned to Grandma. "How's your arm?"

"It's okay."

Exasperating. Beth shook her head. Was it Grandma's generation or her personality? In any case, she wasn't forthcoming about anything.

Chapter 25

*F*rom the living room window, Beth watched Mak plow in his silver, four-door pickup truck with a red plow shaped like a V. He pushed snow far beyond the house and, as he approached the bank, straightened the blade and pushed the snow up. Back-and-forth in an intriguing dance. After he had cleared the rest of the drive, he plowed around Beth's car, but it was still hopelessly buried. She missed driving it.

"I'll take your car to go pick up food," she told Grandma.

The Co-op sat on a side street in Quincy among old houses built at the turn of the twentieth century. On the front of the building, a mural depicted the history of the Copper Country—Native Americans forging tools from float copper, loggers clear-cutting virgin timber, immigrant miners working deep underground.

Beth parked on the side of the building and entered under a hand-painted sign—The Copper Country Co-op, Public Welcome.

"Hello, how are you?" A middle-aged cashier, who seemed to genuinely care, caught Beth off guard. The woman continued to look at her as if waiting for a response.

"I'm fine." Beth pushed a shallow-basket cart through the

store past bulk dry goods, a large vat of honey, natural cleaning products, and shelves of packaged products labeled with terms like organic, non-GMO, and gluten-free. In the natural beauty product aisle, she noticed a familiar face. "Hello, Marcella."

"Hi, Beth." Marcella smiled warmly. "I love your hair."

"Thank you."

"How's Louisa's arm?" Marcella asked with concern.

"It's not getting better. She has an appointment with a neurologist in Marquette."

"That's good. I'm worried about her. But all the way in Marquette? Who's going to drive?"

"I am."

"Oh." Marcella's face showed surprise and disbelief.

Beth had seen the look before, like when she was a kid and her dad caught her and Jeremy leaving the house with a large plastic tub on their way to slide down concrete steps in the neighborhood park. She had seen the look when she told her mother she planned to drive across the country to visit Grandma.

"Well, I hope the weather's okay then. Pass on my love and positive thoughts to your grandma." Marcella waved and disappeared into the next aisle.

Next to the deli was a soup table with steaming beef barley kale and curry squash in a coconut milk base. Laminated signs listed the ingredients. Cups and covers were stacked on a ledge above. Small sample cups sat on the table. Beth carefully ladled a sample of the beef barley kale into a cup and tasted a spoonful. Delicious.

"*Hyvää päivää*," Beth heard from behind her, and she turned to see Mak, who was dressed in his flannel jacket and orange hat.

"*Hyvää päivää*," Beth returned the greeting, mimicking Mak's accent.

"There you go." Mak laughed.

He was a unique Finn. Someone once told Beth, perhaps incorrectly, Finns were humorless. She wasn't sure if that was a joke, because she did know Finnish humor was dry. When

Grandpa Sam told a joke that fell flat, he would say, "Yous got to be smart to get that one," followed by a wry smile. In any case, Mak had an easy laugh, even when he wasn't telling a joke.

"Thank you for plowing for me and Grandma this morning."

"Yous welcome. I's glad to be in da truck to warm up. Fell off a roof this mornin'."

"Are you okay?"

"Oh, yeah. I's shovelin' a roof for another client and I slipped, ended up knee-deep in da snow bank below. I had to lay back and laugh." Mak guffawed, his head thrown back. "When I pulled my legs out, my swampers got stuck in da snow. I had to fish for 'em, but then they was full of snow, and my feet was wet, so I got in my truck and turned da heat up and did some plowin' till my feet dried. My last stop was Lou's. Now I'm pickin' up my lunch. They have good soup here."

"Yes, I tasted the beef barley kale soup." Beth licked her lips. "How are Lorna's cupcakes?"

"Delicious. But she's got another idea—makin' use of da birch bark I saved. I don't like cuttin' down birch trees, but a few years ago Asplundh cleared da shoulders along US-41. Trees was growin' up in power lines. They would have let those trees lie there and rot, but that's premium firewood right there, birch. I stripped all da bark off da wood before splittin' it up, and I flattened it all usin' my cider press."

"What's Lorna going to do with it?" Beth ladled soup into a one-quart container.

"She's got this idea to make birch bark decorations—ornaments, baskets, mini-canoes. Maybe she could sell 'em at Robin's Nest, or better yet, open her own shop. Maybe if she opened her own store, I could get my journals at wholesale. Sam and Robin wouldn't appreciate da competition, I suppose."

"Probably not." Beth snapped a cover on the soup container. "How's the book coming along, Iris?"

"Good, good. Conflict's brewin'. Da guy Iris created

hasn't been completely forthcomin' with his lady. Lots to work through from his past. Every couple has issues to work through, and—believe me—they'll work through them, 'cause I'm writin' a small-town Romance where you can't keep a past hidden."

"I look forward to reading it, Mak. When will it be finished?"

"It's hard tellin'." Mak shrugged. "Once I finish da story, then comes all da editin'. I'll get feedback from my beta readers. That's da humblin' part. Writin' makes ya feel like an idiot."

"Take care, Mak." Beth moved to the vegetable aisle and picked from a selection of roots—carrots, beets, potatoes, and rutabaga. It would be fun to make more pasties.

"Did you find everything you need?" the cashier asked when she placed her produce on the counter.

"Yes, thank you." Beth unloaded her soup. "I'm not a member."

"That's okay; I'll ring it up under Louisa Herrala. Then she'll get the credit."

"Yes, how did you know I was—?"

"You look like Becky, and I heard that Becky's daughter was up visiting Louisa. I knew instantly it was you, when you walked in the store." The cashier weighed the produce and the soup. "That will be $18.49."

Beth handed her a twenty-dollar bill.

The cashier took change from the drawer and counted it out in her hand. "How did you like the flowers Danny got you?"

Her face warmed. Mother wasn't kidding that everybody's into everyone else's business.

Chapter 26

"Danny's here," Grandma called from downstairs.

Beth rolled over and grabbed her phone—9:23 a.m. Late again. What a way to begin her twenty-sixth year. Every New Year she would make a resolution to be punctual. It hadn't mattered at the Resource Center. She worked second shift, didn't have a specific time she needed to be in, and always put in more than the required forty hours. Beth sighed. She hated that she was always running late. The prior night, she had intended to go to bed early so to get enough sleep, but she got lost in a book and didn't finish it until after midnight. She must have shut her alarm off and gone back to sleep, or slept through it entirely. Either way, she was late.

She got out of bed, grabbed jeans and a T-shirt, snuck downstairs, and slipped into the bathroom. She readied herself as quickly as she could.

"Are you sure you won't have any tea, Danny?" Grandma asked as Beth came into the chilly kitchen. "Beth needs to eat breakfast."

"Sheesh, Beth, you haven't had breakfast yet? The day's a wastin.'" Danny stood in the doorframe in his boots and jacket. He wasn't smiling.

"Sorry, I overslept." She had never seen him so crabby. "Good morning to you, too."

"Oh, yeah, good morning, and happy birthday." His smile seemed forced.

"It'll only take a few minutes to make eggs and toast," Grandma offered.

"That would be great." Beth went to the fridge and grabbed the eggs.

"I'll take that." Grandma took the carton from her hands. "You sit down, birthday girl."

Danny sighed, took off his jacket and boots, and joined Beth.

She poured two cups of tea and slid one across to Danny. "Grandma, do I smell *nisu*?" Her mouth watered.

"Yes, you do. I made it for Danny."

"Oh." Disappointed, Beth looked out the window.

"Hey, Beth," Danny said, "I'm sorry I'm a crank today. I've been working nights all week. It was a long night last night, including another visit to Maribel's after my shift this morning, and I'm excited about our date and eager to go. Will you forgive me?"

"Sure," Beth said, not quite ready to mean it.

Grandma cracked eggs into a cast-iron skillet and scrambled them right in the pan using her left arm.

"Grandma Lou, do you want me to start a fire for you?" Danny asked.

"I would so appreciate that."

"Danny," Beth asked, "what are we doing today?"

His eyes lit up. "Snowmobiling."

"I'm not dressed warm enough for that."

"I borrowed a snowsuit from Russ's sister." Danny smiled broadly and went out to the front porch with the canvas sling.

Grandma put bread in the toaster. "And you can grab a sweater out of the front closet."

Danny returned to the kitchen with wood in the sling and knelt in front of the stove. Grandma served Beth the eggs and toast and joined her at the table.

"Have you ever been snowmobiling?" Beth asked Grandma.

"Never," Grandma said. "Sam had a—"

"Wait! Wait!" Danny held his right index finger up and his left hand over his mouth. Beth and Grandma stopped the conversation and looked at Danny who, with his eyebrows raised and his mouth gaped open, sneezed, and then said, "I'm okay." He turned back to the stove, lit a match, and with it lit the paper. He shoved a few pieces of kindling into the stove.

Grandma started again. "Grandpa Sam had a snowmobile when your mom and Scott were kids. But I wouldn't get on it."

"Are they dangerous?" Beth frowned.

"They're not dangerous," Danny interjected, "if you drive them safely."

"Beth, don't let me worry you," Grandma said. "I regret I didn't go. I worried too much when I was young, when I had nothing to worry about. What's a life not lived?"

"A long life?" Beth suggested tentatively.

Grandma chuckled.

With the stove lit and packed with wood, Danny retrieved the teakettle from the table and placed it on the antique stove. "Grandma Lou, your tea will taste better heated on this." He smiled at Beth, "Okay then, you take your time. We'll go when you're ready."

"I'm ready."

Snow fell heavily, and through it Beth saw Russ's truck and a windowless trailer behind it. Danny skipped ahead and went around the truck to the driver's door. Beth took note that she had to open the passenger door herself—she was capable, but out of the habit when she was with Danny. A gift was sitting on the passenger seat, the size of a CD case. She hadn't purchased a CD in years, but it was more personal to pick out a CD than give an iTunes gift card.

"For me?" She smiled.

"Yes, for you. I wanted to see your reaction when you saw it."

She climbed into the truck and held the gift on her lap.

He looked at her with a cheeky grin. "Open it."

Beth ripped the paper, pulled the CD out, turned it over, and read, *Torn for You.*

"They're Christian," Danny offered.

She wasn't so sure. On the cover of the CD was a picture of the band—long hair, leather, tattoos, and scowling faces.

"Let's put it in." Danny put the truck in drive, made a broad sweeping turn with the trailer tailing behind, and pulled out of the driveway.

Beth took the plastic security seal off the jewel case, removed the CD, and slid it in the player.

An electric guitar hammered a steady beat, and then singing, or rather, yelling began. It was unintelligible, and Beth stared blankly out the windshield. It was snowing heavily and Danny was driving too fast for her comfort. She glanced over at him. He was bobbing his head back and forth to the incessant beat.

"This is awesome." Danny looked over at Beth. He turned the volume down. "What do you think?"

"I've never heard anything like it before." It was the most honest thing she could say while still being polite. "How long's the drive?"

"A half hour."

"Let's keep the volume down so we can talk." She hoped the road noise and conversation would drown out the racket that came out of the speakers. "Where are we going?"

"Eagle River, and from there we'll drive the snowmobile farther into the Keweenaw and up Brockway Mountain.

"You have a mountain?"

"We call it a mountain. I suppose by your standards it would be a hill, but it's beautiful nonetheless."

Beth tried to think of anything other than the music. Rows of trees stood along the highway. Needles competed for light at the top of tall, straight, barky trunks. "Are those tree farms?"

"Kind of. Those were planted in the fifties. The state helped landowners reforest after it was clear-cut. Grandpa Sam said he planted the red pines by the farmhouse when he first bought the property."

Even with the volume down, the thumping bass and drums pierced her skull. And Danny was still driving too fast. "Do you snowmobile often?" Beth continued the line of questions as she tried to ignore the music.

"Haven't been for a long time. Russ's family's into snowmobiling, and they used to take me along with them when I was in high school. I'd ride one of his sisters' sleds."

"How many sisters does he have?"

"Let me count… five."

"Five? That's a big family."

"That's not half of it. He has seven brothers."

"Twelve kids?"

"Thirteen kids, counting Russ."

"That's amazing."

"Anyhow, I used to go snowmobiling with them, so I do have some experience. I'm telling you this so you won't be afraid to ride with me, but I'd rather snowshoe. Take a walk in the bush."

"Then why aren't we doing that?"

Danny glanced at Beth. "If you're still here, I'll take you to see the Hungarian Falls in the spring when the snow starts melting."

"That'll be…" Beth caught herself. She didn't need another absent-minded agreement.

"Stunning," Danny supplied a word.

"I'd like to try it, but I'm not that coordinated," she said.

"You'll do fine. It's like walking."

She had heard that before.

"But, today," Danny continued, "we're on another adventure." He turned up the volume on the stereo. It was a ballad. "Ahh, listen to the lyrics of this song."

Nice melody. Gospel message. Not half-bad, but it was still not her type of music.

"Could we turn this off and talk?" she asked.

"You don't like it?" He shut off the stereo.

"I thought you liked country music, like Allie Nantuck."

"I do. I like a variety of music."

"I thought we shared—"

"Wait! Wait!" Danny held up his right index finger and, with his mouth gaped open, he gasped for air. He sneezed into his left sleeve, inhaled, and shook his head. "I'm okay."

"Why do you do that?"

"Sneeze? Doesn't everybody?"

"No, make a big production of it."

He glanced at her.

"Could you keep your eyes on the road? And slow down."

"What's wrong with you? Why are you so critical today?"

"I don't know." Beth blinked back tears. "I guess it's good that I'm learning all your imperfections now. You're handsome and charming. And so open and honest. But you're not perfect."

"You're critical and sad because I'm not perfect?"

"I guess it's better to know sooner than later."

"That I'm not perfect?" he asked.

Beth laughed through her tears. It was the time of the month when she had the ability to be simultaneously mad, sad, annoyed, and amused. "Yes." She looked at Danny with a smile and wiped tears from her cheeks. "It's not healthy to have unrealistic expectations for a relationship."

"I'm not sure what to say. The academy taught us to deal with one emotion at a time."

The snow tapered off. They passed a snow thermometer, a billboard of sorts, thirty feet tall with a red arrow pointing to last year's snowfall of twenty-five feet.

The winding road descended before them and rose up in the distance. Clumps of snow stuck to evergreen trees. Rocky bluffs guarded the valley to the north of the road. Calm came over Beth.

They drove through Phoenix, a small town with two road-side bars and parking lots full of trucks with empty snowmobile trailers.

"Danny, do you have unrealistic expectations for me?"

"What?" Danny turned left onto a smaller road.

"Do you think I'm too perfect?"

"Ha." Danny laughed.

Beth huffed. "You don't have to put it like that."

"I'm sorry. I don't expect you to be perfect. I'm not interested in you because you're perfect."

"Then why *are* you interested in me?"

"At first, I thought you were hot."

"Hot?" She cocked her head.

"Beautiful," Danny corrected himself. "And then God started knitting our hearts together."

"I don't know if God is knitting our hearts together."

"He will if we allow it."

"I've only known you for a month."

"Isaac married Rebekah right when he met her."

She raised her eyebrows. "You can't take Old Testament stories and make them prescriptive for today."

"Huh?"

"Never mind."

They rose out of the valley and crested a hill where, in the distance, Lake Superior stretched out like the Arctic Ocean. White extended from the shore for miles, and beyond that there was open water to the horizon where blue met blue.

"What's not perfect about me?" The words escaped her mouth.

"To start with, you're always late."

To start with? Maybe she *didn't* want to know.

"And you— "

"Wait! Wait!" Beth held up her index finger and then pretended to sneeze.

He laughed.

"I hate that I'm always late." Beth felt more centered as they entered Eagle River, a sleepy town built next to tiered falls. "What else were you going to say?"

"You're kind of judgmental."

Her heart sank. That's what bothered her most about her mother. She looked out the passenger side window.

"Beth, are you okay?"

"I don't want to be judgmental. I just don't want to mess up my life because you messed up yours."

"So my sins are bigger than yours?" Danny asked.

Tears rolled down her cheeks. "I didn't say that."

"Look Beth. I don't want to be judgmental about your judgmental-ism. That would make me something worse—a hypocrite." He reached out and squeezed her hand.

Chapter 27

"Look." Danny motioned out the window of the truck as they pulled the snowmobile trailer through Eagle River. Scores of deer gathered in a clearing of trees near the edge of town. Danny slowed.

"Amazing." Beth found the camera app on her phone and held it up. "Is it a deer farm?"

"No, they're wild deer. They bed down near the lake in the winter where the snow isn't so deep. People feed them so more will survive the winter." Driving slowly, he turned down a street next to the clearing.

Beth unrolled the side window. "Who feeds them?"

Danny shrugged. "I don't know. The townsfolk, sportsmen, I guess."

She held the phone out the window, snapping pictures. "That's so kind."

"Yeah, and it makes for much better hunting in the fall."

"Danny." She swatted his bicep with the back of her hand. Such beautiful animals—so majestic.

"What? It's much kinder to shoot deer than it is to have them starve to death. People need to eat. That's where food comes from."

"My food comes from grocery stores. I don't like to think about people killing deer."

Danny laughed. "You'll think more kindly of hunters if you ever hit a deer with your car." He parked in a lot near the lake.

Danny pulled Russ's snowmobile out of the trailer and climbed on. "Sit behind me. Hold on."

She climbed on and wrapped her arms around him. He felt solid, safe. This was the closest she had ever been to him and she liked it, maybe too much, but with the bulk of the snowsuits and helmets, it was innocent enough.

The snowmobile screamed and lurched forward. Danny drove along the shoulders of side streets until he picked up a trail that headed away from the lake and into a hardwood forest. Tree limbs hung over the trail and suspended piles of snow.

Trail 151 followed the contour of the land—up, down, left, right, in, out. Small signs marked the groomed trail. It looked like a white gravel road. Stark white birch trees were scattered amongst evergreens and leafless branches of other hardwoods.

He turned onto Trail Number 3 and they rode northeast into the Keweenaw. The hypnotic drone of the snowmobile blocked every other thought in Beth's head except for the scenery and Danny's presence.

On occasion he tapped her hand and pointed to one side or the other—a valley, a lake, a rocky bluff. Turn after turn, he navigated the trails like a highway system. They came to an intersection marked Brockway Mountain Drive. It was a seasonal road, not plowed in the winter, but groomed like the other trails. The mountain drive rose steadily in elevation with an occasional switchback. Road signs cautioned sharp turns on the winding road.

Trees hugged both sides of the road at first, but then the road followed the edge of the mountain rising up on the left and dropping down on the right. She could see miles out over the land. She felt nervous, as if they could fly off the edge of the road, so she squeezed Danny. Her fear of falling over the

precipice disappeared, not because she was holding on tighter—she knew holding him wouldn't make a difference if they
went over the edge—but because holding Danny tighter made
her mind focus on him, feeling his body lean into the corners,
feeling his body tense as he steered the machine.

They reached the summit of the mini-mountain, where
wind swept across the top, clearing the snow from the rocky
surface overlooking Lake Superior. Danny shut off the snowmobile, and Beth continued to hold him, not wanting to let go.
He peeled her hands off his chest and set them on her knees.
He climbed off the snowmobile and took off his helmet, so
she did the same. It was cold, bitterly cold, a fact Beth hadn't
noticed when she was wearing the helmet.

"Isle Royale." Danny pointed to a sliver of land on the
horizon. "A ferry runs out of Douglass to the National Park.
Grandpa Sam took me and Jack hiking there."

"It's beautiful." Beth shivered.

"Let's find shelter from this wind and have lunch. Come
on." Danny motioned to the snowmobile.

They climbed on and Danny drove down from the top of
the mountain to a clearing where trees blocked the wind. Danny got off and opened a compartment behind Beth's seat. He
retrieved a Thermos, two plastic mugs, and a loaf of *nisu*. "I
asked Grandma Lou to bake this for us."

She tore off a chunk. "Delicious." So thoughtful of him.

He poured Beth a cup of steaming chicken soup. Danny
sat on the snowmobile backward, facing Beth. She was hungry.
Sitting on a snowmobile for an hour took a surprising amount
of energy. They ate in silence, with only the sound of wind
blowing over the trees. She liked the silence, being in Danny's presence. They passed a test of friendship, not in what was
said, but in being comfortable when nothing was said.

After they finished the soup, Danny stowed the Thermos,
mugs, and what was left of the bread. Back on the snowmobile,
he faced her, inched close, and sandwiched her hands between
his.

"We need to think this through." The words came out of

her mouth, but she wasn't sure she meant them.

"There's another one of your faults." Danny laughed. "You think too much."

"That's not a fault. Dr. Benley says…"

Danny's deep gaze distracted Beth. She couldn't look away. He leaned in and their lips met. Beth's lips parted, and she closed her eyes. Danny put his hand on the back of her head and pulled her in tight. When he finally let her go, she sat in the stillness, her eyes still closed, savoring the smell of his skin, the taste of his mouth, the familiarity between them.

"What was Dr. Benley saying?" he asked.

She turned her head away. What had she been thinking? Obviously, she had not been thinking. "I don't want to date for fun."

"You don't want to have fun on our dates?" He laughed.

"I don't even know if I'm going to stay."

"I'm trying to give you a reason. Look, I don't know where you got these ideas that you need to date somebody who's perfect and only if you intend to marry him. Let's have fun, and if God knits our hearts together, we'll make a commitment."

"We shouldn't have done that." She crossed her arms as she said more forcefully, "You shouldn't have done that."

He was silent for a moment. "You didn't like it?" A look of consternation spread across his face.

"I did, and that's the problem. Don't do it again."

"Never?"

"Maybe someday." She inched toward him. "I'm cold."

Danny pulled her into a tight embrace and held her for many seconds. "Okay, let's get your helmet back on. I need to get home and get a few hours of sleep before work."

After dropping Beth off, Danny drove down the gravel road and past Maribel's. He pulled off the road into a plowed clearing next to a maple forest where he had parked his Jeep. After unhitching Russ's snowmobile trailer, he unloaded the sled and drove it to the rustic cabin.

A cast-iron, potbelly stove roared in one corner of the cabin, and in another, Russ sat on a stool at a counter-height table working on a laptop plugged into a battery pack.

"Russ, let me ask you a question." Danny pulled up another stool after removing his boots and snowsuit. "I've been looking at a website, and I can't make sense of it. Can you tell me what you think?"

"Sure." Russ twisted the screen to where they could both see it.

Danny replicated the search criteria he had done the day before at home. *How blue eyed parents can have brown eyed children.* He recognized the link and clicked on the article he had read several times.

Russ skimmed the page. He was the most overqualified building contractor Danny had ever known. A PhD in mechanical engineering, he had worked downstate before giving it up to live an independent life in the UP. "Okay, what do you want to know?" Russ faced Danny.

"What does it mean? There are these OCA2 and HERC2 genes, and I just don't get it."

"They determine why a person has blue eyes, or not."

"Mak said he'd never seen blue-eyed people have a brown-eyed kid."

"This is about that boy who looks like you, hey."

"Right. He looks like me, and both of his parents have blue eyes." Danny's chest heaved. "I figured out what you meant about the timing. He'll be nine at the end of the month, and that'll be about fourteen weeks shy of the ten-year anniversary of when Kristine and I broke up—when she cheated on me. Is it possible the boy is Drew's?"

"All the blue-eyed people Mak knows may have both genes turned off. It's like a light circuit. The switch needs to be on and the bulb needs to work. If the bulb has burned out, there's no light no matter which position the switch is in. If the switch is off, there's no light even if the bulb is good."

"What are you talking about?" Danny asked.

"Pigmentation. Pigmentation is like the light. Blue eyes

come from the lack of pigmentation, and maybe most Finns have both genes turned off, so the kids always have blue eyes. But if one of the parents has blue eyes because only one of the genes is turned off, and the other parent has the other gene turned off, then they can have a kid with brown eyes."

"That's a relief." Danny got up from the stool, and then plopped down into a loveseat and interlocked his fingers behind his head. "Beth told me today that she appreciates my honesty, but I haven't told her about AJ. I was going to tell her, but she told me she didn't want to know any more about my past so I didn't tell her about my kid."

"He's not your kid. You don't even know him."

"That wasn't my choice." Danny fumed.

"Whoa, I know. Calm down. You would've made a great dad. I'm just saying the boy just lost his mother and he's got a father. The only father he's ever known." Russ was the voice of reason.

"Yeah, I have no right to step into his life." Danny leaned forward and put his face in his hands. He was such an idiot. "AJ's such a beautiful kid."

"Are you crying?"

"No." Danny squeezed his eyes shut. His tear ducts opened anyway and he sobbed. "I'm missing out on knowing my kid and I don't deserve Beth."

Russ sat next to him. "It's okay, man."

"It's not okay. It'll never be okay. How did I let myself become such a..." He searched for the right word. Something must be wrong with me, he thought. "Two women cheated on me, and now I'm going to lose Beth when she finds out who I really am."

"You gotta let it go." Russ draped his arm around Danny's shoulders. "Believe your sins forgiven through Christ's blood."

"It's easy for you to say." Danny leaned forward, resting his head in his hands. "You're a good person. Beth needs a man like you."

"But she loves *you*." Russ thumped his shoulder.

Danny leaned back and stared at the ceiling. "She doesn't

love me."

"She loves you. I've seen it in her eyes."

"She's in love with the fantasy of an honest man."

"You're an honest man," Russ reassured him.

"She likes to argue with me."

"It's passion. She's channeling the passion in the wrong place."

Danny wiped his cheeks with a sleeve. "We did have this connection today. It's hard to describe."

"Pursue her, man. Don't let her go."

"Thank you, my friend. That's good advice from a man who's never had a date."

Beth sat on her bed cross-legged with her journal. *February 5th—I went snowmobiling,* she wrote. *Not what I ever imagined I would be doing on my 26th birthday. Danny even let me drive it.*

She looked at her *Torn for You* CD sitting on top of the dresser. *I had fun with him, but we had a fight. We're still friends, so I think that's a good sign. We argued and now I feel closer to him. I could really like him, but realistically, how could this work? I don't know if I could live in snow country. And what would I do for a job?*

Maybe she wouldn't need a job if they got married and had kids. She wasn't opposed to the idea of Danny being the father of her children. Not opposed at all. *We have chemistry,* she wrote. *Probably too much chemistry for having only known each other a month. He kissed me.*

She stared down at her journal and scribbled out the words *He kissed me.* She twisted her ring around her finger. Could she let go of his past? He had slept with many other women. Women he didn't even know.

The thought turned her stomach. Would he be faithful in a marriage? Of course, she believed people could change. She believed in grace. But this was not the way she imagined her life. Not her dream. Not God's ideal foundation for a relationship.

She looked down at the purity ring her parents had given to her on her thirteenth birthday, a symbol of her commitment to abstinence before marriage. She was disappointed by his past, but it was in the past and at least he was forthcoming about it. True intimacy comes from honesty. She took the ring off and zipped it in the pocket of her duffel bag.

Chapter 28

Change comes in ebbs and flows until it's firmly lodged on land or dragged out to sea. Beth sat in the pew next to Grandma, who was next to Senja as usual. Danny was working, and she was glad, because Pastor Chip was preaching from 1 Corinthians 6 on fleeing from sexual sin. Danny's past still disturbed Beth. She waffled between feeling as though she might be ignoring a red flag that was telling her to run back to California and wanting to move beyond fixating on his past indiscretions.

Words from a youth conference talk she had heard years ago echoed in her head. *If you can't keep your pants up before marriage, will a ring give you self-control? There will be new temptations once you're married.* She still remembered the object lesson the speaker had the group do. She had even used the same illustration with the teen girls at the Resource Center. *If you remove your conference name tag and stick it on someone else, remove it again and stick it on yet another person, what will happen? It will lose its ability to stick. The same thing happens in marriage when intimacy has previously been breached. The bond is weakened.* She had waited for marriage, so shouldn't she expect the same of her future husband?

Pastor Chip read the familiar verse about two becoming one flesh. Beth had been taught that when two people have sex they are united in spirit, forever. It pained her to think Danny was united with many other women.

"Paul told the Christians in Corinth to honor God with their bodies, but they were giving excuses. I've heard so many things as a pastor. I've heard, 'What's the big deal?' I've heard, 'If you even look at a woman with lust, you've committed adultery in your heart, and I can't stop thinking it, so I might as well do it.' I've heard it all before, and I've even said it." Chip's voice became somber. "I told you before about my past. You know my testimony. You know that I came to the Lord as a young boy, but that I chose not to walk with him as a teenager. I lived in sin. I fornicated."

Beth sat straighter. Chip Atkinson fornicated when he was a teenager? When he dated Mother?

"I had to flee from sin. So I left California and ended up in Chicago at seminary to become a slave to Christ, and for several years after, a slave to my student loans." Pastor Chip smiled wryly.

After that, Beth had a hard time concentrating on the sermon. *Mother's not as perfect as I thought.*

Chapter 29

*F*ebruary broke January's dreary hold on the Keweenaw. The sky was bright and blue, though white still covered the ground. Beth kept the bird feeder full and the kitchen stove lit. On Wednesday, the day before Grandma's appointment in Marquette, they had their morning tea as the chickadees ate. "There's hope for spring." Beth held her cup in both hands close to her lips. "It's good to see the sun."

"Winter's far from over, dear."

"It looks like we'll have good weather tomorrow for driving."

"We can pray for good weather. February is unpredictable. January brings cold and with it lake-effect snow—a couple of inches every day. February's warmer, but we get hit with heavy, wet snowfalls. Driving can be treacherous. If the weather's bad, we will—"

Thumping boomed from the front porch.

"Danny." Beth stood, scooting her chair back. Tea spilled on the table. "Sorry, I'll clean it up."

"No, sweetheart, go ahead. I'll wipe it up." Grandma stood to do just that.

Beth hurried out of the kitchen and opened the front door

to the porch where Danny filled the wood hopper. She smiled brightly. "Hi, Danny."

"Hey." He was focused on the task, not seeming as eager to see her as she was to see him.

"Are you going to come in?" she asked.

Danny met her gaze and smirked. "Are you going to invite me?"

"You're invited. Come have tea with us." Beth led the way down the hall into the kitchen where she poured Danny's tea and set it next to her cup.

Danny took off his boots and joined Grandma and Beth at the table. "It's good you're keeping your stove lit, Grandma Lou."

"Beth's keeping the stove lit." Grandma beamed at Beth.

"You're becoming a regular Yooper, Beth," Danny said. "You should trade in your Corolla for a plow truck."

"I've watched Mak plow. I could do that." Beth straightened in her chair. There was no telling what she could do.

"Danny, you missed church on Sunday," Grandma said.

"I was sleeping. I started on evening shifts—didn't get off work until three in the morning."

"You're up early today," Beth observed.

"Not too early, it's already ten o'clock. Besides, I need to reset my internal clock—I need to be up early tomorrow."

"Why's that?" Grandma asked.

"I need to drive two ladies to Marquette. Someone special has a doctor's appointment, and her only other option for a ride is a woman who's likely to get pulled over for driving too slow."

Beth leapt out of her chair and hugged Danny.

Chapter 30

*B*eth woke early to give herself plenty of time to get ready. She was capable of not being late for things of such importance. She would not make Grandma late for her appointment.

An hour later, she stood with Grandma in the porch as Danny jumped out of his SUV and waded through nine inches of wet, heavy snow to the front steps. Using Grandma's shovel, he scraped the steps and panked a path to the Jeep. They walked cautiously down the path. Beth climbed in the back while Danny helped Grandma Lou into the front seat.

High winds had swept snow across the Keweenaw Peninsula, flattening every peak and filling every crevice. Mak hadn't plowed yet, so Danny gunned the engine and punched through the furrowed snow at the end of the driveway.

He drove down the center of the road covered in four inches of snow and marked on either side by poles—sapling trees, with the branches stripped and red ribbons tied to the tops, sticking high out of the snow banks.

"What are those for?" Beth motioned to the tall poles.

"So snowplows can find the road." Danny drove confidently, relaxed, leaning back in his seat with one hand on the steering wheel and the other holding an insulated coffee mug.

Grandma sat quietly and looked out the passenger side window.

"Is it safe to drive?" Beth asked.

"Sure," Danny assured her. "We have gutter bumpers."

"Huh?" Beth looked at the snowbanks, high on both sides of the road.

"Did you ever go bowling when you were a kid? They put up the bumpers for the kids. We've got gutter bumpers on our roads by the end of January."

"You're not making me feel any safer." Beth gripped her armrest.

Grandma Lou laughed. "We'll be fine, sweetheart."

Danny turned onto the wet blacktop of US-41. "The state salts these roads. Too much, if you ask me. Vehicles don't last long up here—they rust out within ten years."

"We could cancel," Grandma Lou teased. "The trip may be too hard on your truck."

"You're not getting out of this that easily," he said.

"No, I'd hate to cancel." Grandma lifted her chin. "I want to get the treatment started and put this behind me."

"We'll take it slow. We'll cut lunch short if we get delayed." Danny switched on the stereo and country music blasted from the speakers. He reached for the volume knob. "I'll turn it down."

"I like this song." Beth nodded her head in time to the music, remembering his head bobbing from the week before.

"Yeah, it's all right." Danny looked at Beth in the rearview mirror. "Did you bring *Torn for You?*"

Beth smiled. "It slipped my mind."

They cleared the worst of the weather an hour from home when they passed by the giant copper statue of Bishop Baraga, the Snowshoe Priest, who held snowshoes in one hand and a cross in the other. The statue rose sixty feet above a bluff on the southern tip of Keweenaw Bay.

After a leisurely lunch in the hospital cafeteria, they made their way to the neurology department, where Danny excused himself to pick up a few home-improvement items at Menards.

"Text me when you're ready," he said. "I'll pick you up outside the entrance."

Beth sat with Grandma in the lobby, filling out forms on a clipboard, reading her the questions while Grandma softly mumbled answers, "No, no, no, no, wait... I mean yes, no, no."

"Okay, can you sign?" Beth asked.

"Sure." Grandma took the clipboard and pen. "I just didn't want to tire out my arm before the appointment."

Beth shook her head. "That's like fixing your car before you take it to a mechanic."

Grandma chuckled. She awkwardly scrawled her name on the form.

"Louisa Herrala," a nurse called, holding open a door.

Grandma got up and approached the nurse. She looked back at Beth. "Coming?"

"Do you want me to?"

"Yes. You can take notes." Grandma handed the clipboard to the nurse. Beth followed them to a scale, to a blood pressure station, and finally to Exam Room 2, where Grandma sat on an exam table and Beth took a chair against the wall.

The nurse pulled up Grandma's record, entered the information from the clipboard into the computer, and asked for a few clarifications—medications, supplements—"Is there a gun in the house?"

"Gun in the house?" Grandma asked.

"We have to ask it. Government regulations."

"Do I have to answer?"

"No." The nurse finished up with the data entry, pushed the keyboard aside, and retrieved a hospital gown from a drawer under the exam table. "Put this on, and the doctor will be with you shortly."

Grandma held up the gown, her forehead furrowed. "There are three openings. How does this work?"

"Your arms go in here and here. Wrap it around again and put your right arm in here." The nurse left the room.

"I can step out, too." Beth rose from her chair.

"That's okay. I'm a Finn." Grandma stripped her clothes

off, and Beth helped her with the gown.

A few minutes later, there was a knock on the door and a thin, graying man entered the room. "I'm Dr. Adams." He shook Grandma's hand and smiled at Beth.

Beth readied her *Hope* journal and brass pen.

"I read the notes your doctor sent. When did you start having problems with your arm?" Dr. Adams asked.

"I'm not sure." Grandma frowned. "Maybe a few months ago."

"Let's take a look." The doctor pulled and pushed on her arms and legs between taking notes. "Walk on your toes."

Grandma tiptoed across the room.

"And your heels."

She complied.

Dr. Adams shined a flashlight across her arm and watched for several seconds. He did the same with her back and legs. "Can you stick out your tongue for me?" He shined the flashlight at her tongue. He tore off a corner of tissue, rolled it in his fingers to form a delicate paper feather, and tickled her toes and fingertips. "Do you feel that?" he asked.

"Yes."

He checked her reflexes, hitting a spot below her knee, and hitting the inside of her elbow on her outstretched arm. He gave no indication of his findings, not a raised eyebrow, not a *hmm* or an *a-ha*. "Let's have you change back into your clothes and sit next to your granddaughter. I'll be right back." He left the room.

"I think that went well," Grandma said, clearly uneasy.

After Grandma dressed, Dr. Adams returned and sat on a rolling chair across from Grandma. He took a deep breath and slowly exhaled as he leaned forward in his chair. "I want to refer you to a specialist to do more testing."

"What kind of specialist?" Beth asked.

"An ALS specialist."

"Oh no." Grandma gasped. She stared straight ahead, as her eyes glossed over.

"Remind me, what's ALS?" Beth asked the doctor.

"You might have heard it called Lou Gehrig's disease," Dr. Adams said.

Tears streamed down Grandma's cheeks. "Please, Lord, no."

Beth put her hand on Grandma's trembling shoulder. "That's what Maribel's husband had, isn't it?"

Grandma nodded. "It's a death sentence." She choked the words out.

"Possible ALS." The doctor attempted to soften the news. "I can't find any other cause for weakness, and your symptoms are consistent with amyotrophic lateral sclerosis."

"What symptoms?" Beth asked Dr. Adams as she patted Grandma's shoulder.

"There are signs of both upper and lower motor neuron death—muscle atrophy, weakness, hyperreflexia, spasticity, and fasciculations, which is muscle twitching. Have you noticed the twitching, Louisa?"

"Yes, for some time—months. Isn't that normal with age?"

"It can be benign at any age, but in your case, considering the prevalence and given the other symptoms, it's a sign of lower motor neuron death. Look at your forearm. Do you see how the muscles ripple?"

Grandma turned her right arm over and laid it on her lap. Sure enough, muscles flexed and fell under her skin.

"ALS is a progressive, degenerative neuro-muscular disorder," Dr. Adams said.

Beth wrote the words in her journal. "How do you treat ALS?"

"Your grandma's right, I'm afraid. There's no cure."

"It's not dying that scares me," Grandma spoke through tears. "It's the cruel process that this disease takes in getting there." Sobs shook her body.

Beth put her arm around Grandma and cried, too.

"Take as much time as you need." Dr. Adams walked to the door. "Come out when you're ready, and Shannon will make an appointment for you to see Dr. Anderson. She comes to Marquette once a month and will be here next week."

Minutes passed as the women sobbed. Grandma finally relaxed her shoulders, let out a sigh, and wiped the tears from her cheeks with the back of her left wrist.

"Grandma, what happens with ALS?" Beth looked down at her journal. "He said progressive, degenerative neuro-muscular disorder. What does that mean?"

Grandma only shook her head.

Beth texted Danny. *Ready.*

His reply came quickly. *Go well?*

She typed the three letters. *ALS*

Through tear-filled eyes, she read his reply. *Oh no. I'll be outside the lobby.*

Danny was waiting for them when they exited the clinic, leaning against the Jeep. He opened both front and rear passenger doors. They approached him, and he hugged Grandma. He helped her into the front seat.

"Thank you." Grandma's eyes had dried. He fastened her seatbelt. "Thank you, again, but the only thing that changed today was knowledge. I can still fasten my seatbelt."

Danny kissed her on the temple. When he slid behind the wheel, he met Beth's gaze in the rearview mirror. Red-eyed, he shook his head.

All were silent while Beth cried inwardly, staring out the window at the snow.

A half hour into the trip home, Grandma spoke. "I know this disease. I know what it does to people. I saw Maribel's husband waste away." Grandma trembled. Her voice seemed to get caught in her throat. "I wish Sam were here. I feel so alone."

"You're not alone, Grandma Lou," Danny said. "You've got me. You've got Beth."

"Thank you, Danny, but I told you, I know the course this disease will take. It's too much for you, too much for Beth." Grandma heaved a sigh.

"Then we'll find others," Beth said.

Grandma sniffed. "I went through this after Sam's stroke. People surrounded us in the beginning—encouragement and practical things like meals—but after a while, when days turned to weeks, weeks to months, and months to years, people moved on with their own lives. I understand it. People have their own families." Grandma turned back and caught Beth's eye. "When Sam had his stroke, you and Jeremy were teenagers, and your mom had her hands full. Scott was busy with his career." Her head drooped as she faced forward. After a long silence, she said half under her breath, "That was fear talking. Help me, Jesus. One day at a time. Besides, he said 'possible ALS.' We're not sure of the diagnosis."

Beth took her phone out of her purse and typed those dreadful three letters into the browser. *ALS*. She clicked on a site and read. *Amyotrophic lateral sclerosis destroys connections between the brain and voluntary muscles, leaving its victims paralyzed, even unable to swallow and breathe. The average life expectancy is two to five years from diagnosis. Some live longer, but with limited mobility. All this happens while cognitive functions remain intact. There's no known cause, no cure, and treatment is mainly managing symptoms.* Sobs escaped her, and Grandma looked back. Beth didn't meet her gaze. There was no sugarcoating the horrible disease.

When they arrived home, Grandma went to her bedroom, Danny left, and Beth called Mother.

"I'll be on the next available flight," Mother said immediately when Beth told her the news.

"We don't know if this is the diagnosis yet," Beth said. "Grandma has a follow-up appointment next Friday with the ALS specialist."

"Then I'll be there for the appointment," Mother said tersely.

"I'll go to the appointment with her. I—"

"I'm her daughter," Mother cut her off. "I'll go."

Beth frowned. Shouldn't Mother talk to Grandma and see what she wants?

"When your grandma wakes up from her nap, have her call me. And tell her I'll be on the next available flight."

After she hung up, Beth rested her head back on the couch. A spider crawled along the ceiling to the corner where it settled into a web.

She turned her phone back on and looked at the ALS page that was still up in the web browser. She read it again. She clicked on a link that described the diagnostic process. *An ALS diagnosis is a process of elimination. Ten percent of diagnoses turn out to be something else.* Why would Dr. Adams even mentioned ALS without having done an MRI and an EMG? It seemed premature, even irresponsible.

It's got to be something else. God wouldn't let this happen, not to Grandma.

Chapter 31

"Good. You're up." Grandma greeted her with a bright smile when Beth entered the kitchen the next morning.

"That was some nap you took yesterday." Beth sat at the table. She still felt exhausted, emotionally drained. It had been a restless night.

"When I woke, you were already in bed, so I spent quiet time with my sweet Jesus." Grandma opened the refrigerator and took out a bottle of syrup. She set it on the table. "I want to take a sauna today. Can you light it?"

"Sure." Beth studied Grandma's face. She seemed her usual chipper self. Was she in complete denial?

"First, have breakfast. I made *puuroa*."

"Do I smell peppermint? You always have green tea in the morning. You're a creature of habit."

"Peppermint today. It's mentally soothing."

"We need that." Beth poured a cup for herself. "I called Mother last night. She's coming on the next available flight."

"She knows?"

"Yes, I told her. I hope you don't mind. I probably shouldn't have."

"That's okay. I left a message for her this morning—at her

office so she'd get it when she goes in today. I said I'm having more tests next week. I didn't mention ALS, though."

"She insists on being here for the next appointment."

"That daughter of mine." Grandma shook her head. "She has always been strong-willed, and a worrier. I'm not going to concern myself with things unless the diagnosis is confirmed. There's no need to worry about things I can't control."

After Beth finished her oatmeal and tea, she went to light the sauna. She had done it before, and she could do it again. When she returned to the kitchen, she found Grandma sitting at the table awkwardly paging through a photo album using her left hand.

Beth refilled her tea, sat at the table, and held the warm cup in her hands. "Ahh, this feels good."

"Look at this picture. This is when your grandpa, your mother, Scott, and I went to Mount Rushmore." Grandma laughed. "We almost got arrested. They were doing construction and had rerouted foot traffic, but we didn't notice the signs. We made our own path through the woods and got pretty close to the base of the mountain, but then park rangers confronted us and escorted us out of the park. I did manage to get this picture though."

"How old was Mother then?"

"Thirteen. You look so much alike."

"I know. I do a double-take when I see pictures of her, thinking they could be of me."

"That was an easy vacation. She was my little helper and kept a watchful eye on Scott. She was like a second mother. She drove him nuts." Grandma chuckled.

"She drives me nuts, too. Why's Mother so pushy?"

"She's always been like that. Even when she was a toddler, she bossed her dolls. She took after me."

"But you're not controlling."

"I used to be. It wasn't until Sam had his stroke that I learned to let things go. I've mellowed in my old age. Rebecca was always the one to set the rules when she played with her friends, and if they didn't like her rules, they didn't stay friends." Grandma flipped a page and pointed to another picture. "We did it all. Wall Drug, the Badlands, the Corn Palace. That was corny." Grandma chuckled at her own joke.

Beth laughed, too. It *was* corny, and not funny, but it felt good to laugh.

While the sauna heated, they looked at more pictures of Grandma's full life.

After an hour passed, Grandma and Beth made their way to the sauna. Mak had plowed after the storm, and the driveway was clear of the fresh snow, yet soft as the snowpack melted. A thin layer of fog separated the warmer air from the cold snow in the field.

"It feels like spring." Beth extended her hand, testing the temperature.

"Don't be fooled. There's an occasional ray of sunshine, a bright day, even in the middle of a long, misanthropic winter."

"Misanthropic?"

"I got that one from Herman Melville." Grandma smiled. "It's from *Moby Dick*. Winters have never bothered me, but I'm in the mood to call it a misanthropic winter."

Beth laughed. "Now you're sounding like Mother."

In the dressing room, they kicked off their shoes and stripped off their outer garments down to their bathing suits.

Grandma opened the door to the steam room. "Here's the cure. Our tropical simulation chamber." She climbed to the top bench.

Beth grabbed the galvanized pail and set it on the lower bench. She took the hose and filled the bucket before joining Grandma on the top bench.

The thermometer read Grandma's ideal 165 degrees.

"Should we open a window for you, Beth?"

"No, I'm a Finn. I can take it."

Grandma filled the dipper from the bucket and, using her left hand, threw the water in the direction of the stove. It splattered on the floor. A shadow of disappointment fell over her face.

"I'll do it." Beth filled the dipper and tossed the water on the stove where it sizzled on the rocks. Steam rolled along the ceiling and descended the wall, stinging her face, heating her body, and warming her toes.

"Another," Grandma commanded.

Before ladling the water, Beth dipped a washcloth in the bucket and held it ready to protect her face. She threw another dipper of water at the stove. By the time the steam descended the wall, Beth leaned forward with the wet washcloth over her face. The steam stung her back.

"One more." Grandma leaned her head against the cedar wall.

"Okay, Grandma, but I'm moving off the top bench."

"I need my medicine. My *suomalainen apteekki* is the best medicine I know."

Beth ladled another scoop of water on the stove.

Grandma closed her eyes as steam rolled down the wall. "I have the full Melville quote memorized—'Ere long, the warm, warbling pervasiveness of the pleasant, holiday weather we came to, seemed gradually to charm him from his mood. For, as when the red-cheeked, dancing girls, April and May, trip home to the wintry, misanthropic woods; even the barest, ruggedest, most thunder-cloven old oak will at least send forth some few green sprouts, to welcome such gladhearted visitants; so Ahab did, in the end, a little respond to the playful allurings of that girlish air.'"

Beth pulled her knees up to her chest and wrapped her arms around her legs. A few flies came to life in the tropical simulation chamber right there in the dead of the misanthropic winter. The heat warmed Beth's core. She felt calm, relaxed... confused by Melville's quote. Finally, she said, "That was beautiful. What does it mean?"

"It means that even Ahab's mood improved when spring came, much like an old oak tree will sprout a few green leaves."

"I guess if he said that, it wouldn't have been a classic."

"That's for sure."

After they sat in silence for a spell, Grandma said, "One more steam, and then we'll take a breather."

Beth splashed the rocks, put her washcloth over her face, and waited.

After the steam settled over them, Grandma said, "Okay, are you ready? Let's go." They raced out into the cold air. "The last one back in the sauna is the true Finn."

Grandma plopped into the snow. While Grandma rolled side to side, Beth jumped up and down. When the cold began to hurt, they both hurried back to the sauna, Beth leading the way. As they approached the door, Beth stepped to the side and fell in behind Grandma, nudging her into the sauna first.

Grandma laughed. "All right, you won, Finn girl."

Chapter 32

*T*he congregation rose and sang, "Great is Thy faithfulness, Oh God, my Father, There is no shadow of turning with Thee."

Grandma stood silent, eyes closed, and arms hung heavy to her sides.

Senja, at her side, grabbed Grandma's hand and lifted it for her, and Beth lifted the other.

At the second verse, Grandma added her voice. "Summer and winter and springtime and harvest. Sun, moon, and stars in their courses above. Strength for today and bright hope for tomorrow. Blessings all mine and ten thousand beside." Tears trickled down her face.

"We sang that at Sam's funeral," Grandma whispered to Beth, after they sat.

"Happy Valentine's Day, everyone," Pastor Chip began his sermon. "It's February, and we have months to go before spring. Snow keeps falling and it seems as though winter will never end."

Beth thought with amusement how weather was a perpetual topic of conversation in the Copper Country.

"My grandson Carter asked me the other day, 'Do you think God will remember to send spring?' He's eager to get out and ride the new bike he got for Christmas. That's what he wanted, so that's what Grandma and Grandpa got him—not too practical of a Christmas gift in the Keweenaw, is it?"

Murmurs of laughter moved through the congregation, ever eager to laugh in church.

"Sometimes, life is like a Copper Country winter—spiritually, emotionally, or physically—and we feel like spring will never come. We feel like we'll never get to a place of growth and new fruit."

Beth could see growth in her own life. Her heart had come a long way in the healing process. She sensed deeper compassion for others after experiencing her own heartbreak, but she still had questions. *Where is the bright hope for tomorrow with a disease like ALS? Why do kids like Gloria need to endure such evil? Why doesn't God put an end to all the suffering?*

"We don't always see hope when we're in the midst of the situation." Pastor Chip's voice brightened. "Remember, Paul said in Romans, 'Hope that is seen is not hope.' Our job is to persevere, trust that our character is growing, and, out of that, hope will come. It's going to take a long time for two-hundred inches of snow to melt, but it will melt and saturate the soil to give life to the strawberries, thimbleberries, and blueberries."

Pastor Chip's words rang inside Beth's head. *Persevere. Trust.*

That evening, Beth met Danny at Grandma's front door.

Danny, dressed in one of his finest T-shirts and clean jeans, carried two wrapped bouquets. "Happy Valentine's Day." He held one out to Beth.

"Thank you." Taking the bouquet close in one arm, she gave him a side squeeze.

He leaned in close. "How's Grandma Lou holding up?"

"She seems like her old self after having a good cry this morning at church," Beth whispered. What a mix of emotions she felt. The excitement of her and Danny's relationship juxtaposed with grave concern for Grandma.

"How are you?" he asked.

Beth shrugged. "I'm okay. I'm waiting to see what the ALS specialist says. I missed you today. How was work?"

"Busy. Three accidents with the wet snow. Fortunately, it's still deep, so the deer aren't moving yet."

She opened her bouquet and breathed in the scent of roses. Red roses, she noted with a smile. She set the flowers on the table and pulled scissors from a drawer.

As Danny stepped into the kitchen, he held out the other bouquet. "For you, Grandma Lou."

"Thank you." Grandma eagerly took the flowers and pulled back the wrapping. "Daisies." Her face lit up. "You used to pick daisies for me when you were a little boy."

Sweet, Beth thought. Dr. Benley said you can learn a lot about a man's character by how he treats his mother—or adopted grandmother. "Here, I'll cut your stems for you."

Grandma laid her daisies on the table next to the roses.

Danny took a seat at the table. "I'm off again this Friday, so I can drive you to Marquette for your appointment."

"That's not necessary." Grandma dug under the sink. "My daughter's coming next Wednesday, and she'll drive me."

"I look forward to meeting her." Danny looked at Beth with a smile of excitement, which she met with a frown of apprehension.

"Shouldn't I?" He looked confused.

"No, it's good. It's good." Beth tried to convince herself as much as him. She snipped the flower stems.

"Let's just say it won't be as relaxing around here when Rebecca comes." Grandma set two vases on the table. "She hasn't exactly approved Beth's plan."

"Plan?" he asked.

"My plan is to stay as long as Grandma needs me... and to get to know you." Beth smiled as the room suddenly felt warmer.

"You need her approval?"

"No, of course not." She put the daisies in a vase, and then carried them to the sink and turned on the tap. "But that's not going to stop her from expressing her opinion."

Grandma chuckled, a bit forced, to ease the tension. "Danny, you're a charming young man. Rebecca will adore you."

"Let me know when she comes into town—maybe I'll pull her over. It seems like a good way to meet people."

Beth laughed, the vase slipping from her hands and clunking on the bottom of the stainless steel sink.

"Inside jokes," Grandma said. "This is getting more serious than I thought. Now let's get those roses in water, and then you kids better get going so you're not late for your dinner reservation."

Chapter 33

The week started with Danny taking Beth to the Cornucopia for Valentine's Day, and it continued with him seeing her each night thereafter—Scrabble with Grandma on Monday, dinner at the Johnsons' on Tuesday, and hanging out at Grandma's on Wednesday before Mother's flight arrived. Beth was sure Mother would like Danny, if she'd give him a chance, but they agreed it would be best if he didn't meet her right away. There would be time on Thursday for a casual encounter when Danny stopped in to fill Grandma's wood hopper.

Beth's phone rang. "It's Mother." She put the phone to her ear. "Hi, where are you?"

"I made it to Chicago, but the plane isn't going to make it in tonight—blizzard conditions. Imagine that," Mother said sarcastically.

Beth covered the phone and whispered to Danny, "The flight's delayed."

Danny whispered to Grandma, "The flight's delayed."

"Who's that?" Mother asked.

"I'm sitting here with Grandma," Beth said as truthfully as she dared.

"Anyhow, they can get me as far as Green Bay tonight. I'll

get a hotel room and drive up in a rental car tomorrow morning. Let me talk to your grandma."

Beth handed her cell phone to Grandma, who struggled to hold it up to her ear. "One second, Rebecca." Switching the phone to her left hand, she fumbled it, and it dropped on her lap.

"Here, Grandma, I'll put it on speaker." Beth put her finger to her lips and motioned for Danny to be quiet. "Mother, you're on speaker with Grandma and I."

"Grandma and me," Mother corrected.

Beth rolled her eyes, and Danny shot her a wink.

"Hi, Mom. How are you holding up?" Mother's voice sounded tense.

"I'm doing okay, dear. Taking it one day at a time."

"Good. My plane isn't coming in tonight, and I don't want to risk missing the appointment on Friday if tomorrow's flight doesn't go out." Mother sighed. "I'll fly into Green Bay tonight and drive up tomorrow if the roads are okay."

"The roads will probably be fine until you get to Baraga. From there they'll be heavily salted. Take it slow—no rush," Grandma said.

"That's the problem with that place, Mom. One can't even get there in a timely manner during a crisis."

"Dear, we're not in a crisis. We'll see what the specialist says before jumping to conclusions. We're not going to worry about anything."

"Speak for yourself. This is serious."

"Yes, sweetheart, it is serious, but worrying doesn't change anything."

"You're always positive, Mom. I love that about you. I'll call you tomorrow when I leave Green Bay. I need to board my flight. I love you."

After she hung up, Beth turned to Danny who looked at her wide-eyed.

"Mother's intense," Beth said.

"You think?" Grandma chuckled.

Mother didn't waste any time the next day, arriving midmorning after a four-hour drive.

"Hello," she called as she opened the front door.

"Rebecca," Grandma yelled from the kitchen.

"I smell *nisu*. I could smell the cardamom from outside." Mother stepped into the kitchen carrying a duffel bag.

"Mother," Beth exclaimed.

They all met in a three-generation embrace.

"I'm so glad you could come home." Grandma's smile spread across her face.

"I didn't think I'd ever see a UP winter again." Mother stepped back and studied Grandma. "Mom, you're looking well. I'm glad."

"I don't feel sick. My arms are a little weak, especially the right one, but I feel pretty good."

"How long are you staying?" Beth asked.

"Until Sunday afternoon. I wish I could stay longer, but I can't take much time off work. I have a project due at the end of the month. I wish there was somebody I could trust to manage the project in my absence, but I've got to be there."

"That's too bad," Grandma said. "It would be nice to spend more time with you."

"We'll have plenty of time to spend together in California. I talked to Oliver, and we want you to move to California and live with us. Our house is a ranch and Jeremy's bedroom is empty."

"Slow down." Grandma chuckled. "Let's take things one step at a time and see what the doctor says on Friday. Now sit down and have some tea and *nisu*. In a bit, we'll go pay Maribel a visit."

After tea, Mother drove the three of them down the country road.

"Honk," Grandma instructed as Mother parked next to Maribel's old plow truck. "She keeps Henry's old gun handy."

Mother honked the horn, and the three women waited in the car for Maribel to come out onto the stoop. She honked again. No Maribel. "Do you think she's okay?" Mother asked.

"Let's go see." Grandma opened her door.

"No. We don't want to get shot," Mother protested.

"We won't." Beth opened her door and got out of the car. "She lost her ammo."

When the three women stepped onto the small porch, Beth knocked, but there was no answer.

"See if it's open," Grandma said.

Beth tried the knob. "It's unlocked."

"We better make sure she's okay." Grandma pushed the door open. "Maribel," she called as she stepped in.

There was no answer.

Beth and Mother exchanged nervous glances and followed Grandma into the house.

Mother caught up with Grandma. "A woman her age, or even your age, Mom, shouldn't be living alone in a house this far out in the country."

"Don't start, Rebecca."

Beth crept forward. "She has to be here. Her truck's still outside." She poked her head into the living room. Maribel lay on the couch, snoring softly. "Ah, she's in here napping." Beth whispered the words, facing Grandma and Mother.

"Hands up!" An angry voice cut through the quiet.

Beth spun back around to find Maribel pointing a rifle at her. "Ahh!"

Grandma moved forward. "Maribel, it's us, Louisa, Rebecca, and Beth."

Maribel cocked her head and then lowered her weapon. "Louisa." She smiled. "You startled me. I didn't even hear you drive in. Sorry about that."

Beth tried to calm her racing heart. It's unloaded, she told herself as she realized her shoulders were shaking. Mother put her arm around Beth.

Maribel set the rifle down, and then she looked from Beth to Mother and back again. She clapped her hands in delight. "You're twins. You're twins."

Mother beamed as she gave Beth a squeeze. "What a lovely compliment."

Beth shook her head and laughed, letting go of the stress

of looking down the barrel of a gun. Being called a twin of a woman twenty-eight years her senior was hardly a compliment. But the joy on Maribel's face. At least she had fond memories of Mother.

"I'm Rebecca, and this is my daughter, Beth."

Confused, Maribel frowned at Beth. "Have we met?"

"Yes, Mrs. Myers, a couple of weeks ago."

Maribel studied Mother. "So you and Chip *did* get married. You had a baby and she grew up. I told you that you could take the dresser. Don't you want it?"

"I didn't marry Chip. I married a man named Oliver."

Maribel frowned. "But you loved Chip. I don't remember Oliver, but I am getting old. Sometimes that happens when you get old. You and this Oliver fellow can have the dresser."

"I live in California, and I can't take a dresser on the plane." Mother moved forward and patted Maribel's arm. "It's good to see you."

"It's good to see you, too. It's good to see you. The dresser is beautiful, but I want to get rid of it. It's a dresser for two people, and, now that Henry's gone, I don't need it. Come, I'll show you." Maribel led the way down the hall to the back bedroom. "Look at this. It's beautiful. Here, I'll clear it out, and you can take it now."

"We can't take it now. We don't have a way to haul it," Mother said.

Maribel ignored her objection and pulled yellowed papers, dull pencils, corroded batteries, and worthless sundry out of the drawers. She looked over her shoulder at Beth. "What did you say your name was?"

"I'm Beth."

"Do you have a husband, Beth?"

"No, I don't."

"A boyfriend?" Maribel peered at Beth.

Beth looked at her feet.

"Do you have a boyfriend?" Maribel repeated her question more forcefully.

"Um." Beth hesitated.

Mother raised her eyebrows.

"No, not really," Beth muttered.

"You will. It's good to be prepared." Maribel cleared knick-knacks from the dresser top and laid them on the bed. "You can have the dresser. You can have the dresser. It's a good dresser."

"It's a beautiful dresser. I saw it when Grandma and I came over before."

Maribel nodded in satisfaction. "It's a dresser for two people, and I need more space. I'll have Danny bring it to Louisa's house. Maybe you can marry him."

Beth blushed, Mother furrowed her brow, and Grandma chuckled.

Maribel reached deeper into the top drawer, clearing the rest of the junk. "He's a good boy. He watches out for me. He's a law enforcement officer. There's been crime lately. I never thought I'd see crime in the UP. Ever since Vance came, things have gone missing." She grinned as she held up a box. "Look, my ammo."

Back in the car, Mother set the topic of conversation as if Maribel hadn't mentioned Chip. "This Danny has his hands full, helping you and Maribel."

"Taking care of the orphans and widows," Grandma said.

"He sounds like a nice guy," Mother acknowledged.

"Mother, that's a positive statement," Beth said.

"Nice guy, wrong location."

"You can meet Danny on Sunday at church, maybe sooner if he stops in to check on Grandma."

"I won't be going to church." Mother pulled out of the driveway. "I'll need to pack for my flight out."

Grandma chuckled. "You brought a few clothes in a duffel bag."

"You'd like Pastor Chip's preaching," Beth said.

"I'm sure he's a good speaker. He's always had a way with words."

Beth leaned forward in the rear seat to assess Mother's expression. "What happened with Chip? I never even knew you had a boyfriend in high school. You were always so against teens dating."

"We started dating when we were fifteen. Tenth grade. We both wanted to move someplace warm after high school, so we applied to USC—and got accepted." Mother said the words robotically.

"Right after the 70s, right? That must have been wild."

"The 70s went into the 80s. So, yes, it was wild. We had no idea what we were getting into. We wanted the sunshine and the beach. He was only at USC for a year, though. He went home for the summer and never came back." Mother's voice quivered. "He broke my heart." After all those years, Mother said it as if it had just happened. She shook her head, glanced back to Beth, and her face softened. "It worked out for the best, though. There would be no Beth or Jeremy if he hadn't."

They fell silent as Mother approached the stop sign, stopped, looked both ways down the abandoned road, and crossed the intersection.

Beth was stunned at Mother's uncharacteristic openness.

"I'm being silly, I know," Mother continued, as they reached Grandma's driveway. "It's been over thirty years after all, but I haven't seen Chip since then. I'd feel awkward sitting in his congregation."

Grandma, seated at the kitchen table, sipped tea through a straw, while Mother and Beth stood at the kitchen counter and cut potatoes and rutabaga. The old kitchen stove radiated heat that defied the wet, blowing snow outside.

Thumping echoed from the front porch. A shiver ran down Beth's spine, and she resisted every urge to drop her knife and run to the door.

"What's that noise, Mom?" Mother asked.

"That must be the neighbor boy, Danny, filling my hopper. Beth, could you go let him in?"

"Sure." To give the illusion of self-control, Beth gently laid her knife on the cutting board, rinsed her hands, and wiped them on a dish towel hung from the door pull beneath the sink before slowly waltzing to the front door.

"Hey, Beth." Danny was dressed in uniform.

"Hey, Danny," Beth whispered. "Are you ready to meet her?"

"Heck, yeah," Danny said.

Beth smiled. "Watch your language around her, sailor."

Danny laughed. They sat on the bench while he took off his boots.

"We visited Maribel today," she whispered. "She wants us to get married and take her dresser."

"Maribel's trying to set us up?" Danny grinned.

"She cleared out the dresser," Beth said. "She wants you to pick it up and bring it back here."

"Did she find anything in the dresser?"

"Yeah. She has her ammo back."

Danny sighed, shaking his head.

"Danny, come in. What's taking you?" Grandma called.

Danny and Beth stepped into the kitchen.

"Mrs. Dawson?" He removed his hat.

"Yes, you must be Danny. I've heard so much about you." Mother extended her hand with a professional smile.

Chapter 34

*B*eth sat in the back seat while Mother drove Grandma to Marquette for the appointment with the ALS specialist.

"What a relief to have blue sky and dry roads," Mother said.

"I was hoping for bad weather so Danny could drive us." Grandma chuckled. "Beth could have kept him company while you and I visited in the back."

"Grandma."

"Don't encourage her," Mother said. "The last thing she needs is another broken heart."

"Mother."

"He's not the type to break hearts," Grandma countered.

"He's a nice guy," Mother said. "I'll give you that, but I know plenty of nice guys for Beth back in California."

"Hello? I'm right here, and I can hear everything you're saying."

Mother glanced at Beth in the rearview mirror, and Grandma laughed.

Beth was optimistic about the day's appointment. The additional testing would confirm this was something else. It would have to be something else, because Grandma seemed too healthy in every other respect. It was just a little weakness in her arms. Beth didn't want to think of the gradual, though noticeable, changes in Grandma—favoring her right arm, not being able to light the stove, not being able to feed the birds, trouble holding the phone, drinking tea through a straw. It was too disturbing to consider. It was impossible to think she would actually have ALS.

After an uneventful one-and-a-half-hour drive to Marquette, they arrived early enough to have a leisurely lunch. "Now we'll have to find a place to reheat these pasties," Mother said.

"Let's put them underneath the hood," Beth suggested.

"What?"

"That's how Yoopers do it."

Grandma laughed.

"We're not Yoopers," Mother said.

"I'm becoming one." Beth tossed her hair.

"For crying out loud," Mother said. "We'll find a microwave."

The women found a microwave in the hospital cafeteria along with salt, ketchup, and plastic utensils. After lunch, they went to the neurology department, checked in, and waited for the nurse to call them back. When the nurse called, "Louisa Herrala," all three women stood.

"Sit down," Mother instructed Beth, "and wait here for us."

Beth clenched her jaw. Didn't it make sense for her to go? She'd been with Grandma since she began having trouble. She encouraged her to see a doctor, sat with her in Exam Room 2 when she got her "possible" ALS diagnosis, and she'd stick with Grandma if the diagnosis really was ALS. She crossed her arms in front of her.

"Why are you still standing there? Sit down," Mother said.

"Okay, Mother." Beth sat stiffly on a chair.

When the women returned after three long hours, Beth knew immediately. Mother's eyes were red and puffy. It was the first time she'd seen her mother defeated. Grandma's face was wooden. Tears welled up in Beth's eyes, and she stood with arms stretched out. They met her embrace, and all three women sobbed.

Others in the lobby averted their eyes, not wanting to be witness to one family's realization that life had irrevocably changed.

Mother held out the keys to Beth as they approached Grandma's car. "You drive."

After they distanced themselves from that dystopian clinic—after silence created a vacuum into which their anxiety could escape—Beth asked, "So what happened in there?"

"You would not believe how young the doctor is," Mother said. "She's barely older than you."

"And she's a neurologist?"

"Fresh out of residency."

"I like her," Grandma said.

"Does she know her stuff?"

"I'm afraid so," Mother said. "Her residency was at an ALS clinic in Minneapolis. She has seen many cases of ALS, and she knows the symptoms."

"Your mom grilled her, and she had answers for everything. She gave me the same examination, pushing and pulling on me, tickling my toes with tissue, checking my reflexes, looking at my skin, having me walk back and forth. She agrees with Dr. Adams."

"An ALS diagnosis is a process of elimination," Beth said. She had spent hours researching on the Internet. "Has she eliminated other possibilities?"

"She did a nerve conduction test," Mother said. "Mom passed—and that was a test we hoped to fail. She doesn't have any peripheral nerve damage."

"And she poked me with needles," Grandma said.

"The EMG?"

"Yes, the electromyogram," Mother said. "Dr. Anderson said the muscles should be quiet, but there was static, like bacon frying, coming through the speakers of the machine, and she said that means the muscles are getting bad signals from the motor neurons."

"So this is definitely ALS?" Beth asked.

"Probable ALS," Grandma's voice cracked.

"Probable? We still don't know?"

"No." Grandma sighed.

"How will we know?" Beth asked.

Grandma and Mother were silent for several seconds as they looked at each other, and then Grandma took a deep breath and spit out the words, "When I become paralyzed and die."

Mother sobbed quietly in the back seat.

Beth still had too many questions. "How can she not know for sure this is ALS?"

"It's a brain disease," Mother said. "You can't look inside the brain."

"But Grandma had the MRI today, too."

Grandma explained, "That will check for other diseases—I can't remember what—but it's unlikely to find anything. She'll let me know the results by mail, unless it changes the diagnosis."

"No wonder the appointment took you three hours," Beth said.

"Yes, it was exhausting," Mother said.

"What's next?"

"She wants me to come back in three months." Grandma said. "She'll monitor the disease progression and make referrals to a physical therapist, occupational therapist, pulmonologist, and all the other 'ists' to help me manage the symptoms."

"They have ALS clinics in larger cities," Mother said. "You see the neurologist, physical therapist and all the others on the same day. I'll find a clinic for you in LA."

"It's too far to commute." Grandma lifted her chin.

"You have to move out to LA," Mother said firmly.

"Let's not make any decisions yet." Beth pulled out a George Beverly Shea CD from the center console. "I'll turn on some music, and you can both get some rest."

Mother and Grandma laid their heads back and closed their eyes.

Chapter 35

*A*t home that evening, while Grandma napped in her recliner and Mother cleaned the cupboards, Beth curled up on the couch as she wrote in her *Hope* journal. *I'm so sad. It's not fair. Hasn't Grandma suffered enough already with Grandpa's stroke? God, heal her, please.*

Mother tiptoed across the living room floor and whispered to Beth, "We're going to the Co-op to pick up dinner."

Beth nodded, reflexively compliant. She closed her journal and stood as her chest tightened. Why didn't Mother at least ask if she wanted to go? Why did she treat her as though she was still a child? Beth put on her jacket and boots. Maybe Mother wanted her to drive.

Darkness had already fallen on the Keweenaw when they walked out of the house. Mother's rental car chirped and the headlights flashed two shadows on the gray stucco farmhouse.

"I'll drive," Mother said.

Beth got in and slammed the door. Why was she even going? Mother would be the one to decide what they were having for dinner.

Mother started the car. "I need you on my side."

"What do you mean?"

"We'll give my mother a couple of weeks to get used to the idea. I need you to support my decision to have her move to California."

So that was it. Mother wanted to form an alliance to get Grandma off the island. "Grandma will do what she wants."

"Yes, she will. She's stubborn."

At least she's not controlling. Beth almost laughed at her unspoken comeback.

"What's so funny?" Mother glanced at her before turning onto US-41.

"She *is* a bit stubborn," Beth acknowledged. "It's a family trait."

"I didn't raise you to be stubborn."

They made their way down the hill and into Quincy.

"Anyhow," Mother continued, "you're not going to be able to take care of Grandma on your own. She'll have more support in Los Angeles with all of us there, and the hospitals are better. I need you on my side."

Beth looked at the passing road while her mother droned on. What could she say to make Mother understand? Grandma's entire life was here on Copper Island, where she belonged. *In fact, maybe it's where I belong.* Beth swallowed.

In the Co-op, standing at the deli counter, Mother ordered sandwiches for herself and Grandma. She courteously offered Beth the privilege of ordering her own. "You wait for the sandwiches, and I'll pick up a few other things for dinner."

After Beth ordered, she turned to the table of soups. Only one soup remained so late in the day, Tomato Basil. She ladled a bit into a sample cup, brought it to her nose, and inhaled. It smelled wonderful. She took a small sip and—

"*Hyvää päivää,*" bellowed a gruff voice.

Beth dropped the sample cup. She turned. "Mak."

"Sorry about that. Yous city guys aren't used to sudden greetings. You got tomato basil on da floor."

"I was startled, but I wasn't scared." Beth laughed. "I knew I wasn't getting mugged by an old Finn yelling *hyvää päivää.*"

Mak peered over the counter and flagged down the deli

sandwich maker. "Could we get a paper towel? A small spill here."

Beth took the offered towel and wiped the floor. "How's the book coming along, Mak?" She threw the mess in the garbage can.

"Fine. Fine. I have lots of tension brewing, and I'm 'bout to write da dark moment—when it seems all hope is lost. Every good Romance has a dark moment." Mak nodded toward the produce where Mother was engaged in conversation with another middle-aged woman. "I saw your mom over there. For a minute I thought it was you, but then I realized it was Becky. I said '*Hyvää päivää*' and she looked at me like I's crazy."

"Well…" Beth smiled.

Mak offered a short, belly laugh. "What's the occasion for her visit?"

Beth bowed her head and brought her hand to her forehead.

"What's wrong?"

Beth took a deep breath. "Grandma has ALS."

"What's that?"

"Lou Gehrig's disease."

"Oh, no." Mak's forehead puckered. "That's what Henry Myers had."

Beth nodded slowly.

"I'm so sorry." Mak put his hand on Beth's shoulder. "Lorna and I will stop in soon."

"Beth?" The deli sandwich maker put three wrapped subs on the counter.

"Thank you." She grabbed the items.

"There's not much soup left." Mak held the cover open. "You was here first."

"Thanks, Mak, but I'll have to pass. It's probably not on the approved shopping list anyway. See you later." Beth waved and then crossed the store to find Mother.

She added the sandwiches to Mother's basket. "Who were you talking to?"

"That was Judy Martin, or at least she was Martin. She's

been married a couple of times."

"How do you know her?"

"Everybody knows everybody up here. She knows Danny. Her niece used to date him. They were…"

"They were what?"

"Never mind." Mother walked to the checkout.

When they returned to the house, they found Danny and Grandma sitting at the kitchen table, laughing and wiping tears from their eyes. The old stove was getting up to temperature, and the teakettle sat atop the newer kitchen range.

"Hi, Danny." Beth set a paper grocery sack on the table.

"Hey, Beth." He stood. "Mrs. Dawson."

"Hello, Danny," Mother said stiffly. "We have our dinner, so if you would excuse us."

"What?" Danny frowned, looking to Grandma. He seemed confused by the inhospitality.

"Sit down, Danny," Grandma said. "Rebecca, I asked him to join us. He's already had his dinner, but he'll keep us company and have evening tea with us."

"That's fine." Mother let out a sigh and pulled produce from the bag.

Beth set the sandwiches on the table, folded and stowed the bag, and took the chair next to Danny.

Mother cleaned the carrots and radishes at the sink. "I ran into Judy Martin today," she said loudly to no one in particular as though fishing for a reaction.

"You mean Judy Paikkala," Grandma said.

"Is that her name? Hard to keep track."

"Her new husband's a great guy," Danny said. "Her last husband left her for a woman who shared his passion for booze and gambling. He left her after she spent over thirty years with him as a homemaker. He doesn't want to pay alimony, so he only works for cash." Danny's long explanation countered the dismissive tone in Mother's voice.

Mother turned off the tap. "It sounds like you know her well."

"Mother." Beth didn't like the direction of the conversation.

"Yes," Danny said, "she's my ex-girlfriend's aunt."

Beth inwardly cheered him on.

"That's what I heard." Mother rummaged in the second drawer down on the left of the sink. "Heh, the carrot peeler's in the same place it was when I grew up." She changed the subject, as if sensing she wasn't going to win the battle.

Beth touched Danny's knee underneath the table. She approved of his verbal jousting skills, respectful yet firm.

"What did you get me?" Grandma asked.

"I got you turkey pesto on sourdough," Mother said.

Beth pushed the sandwich toward Grandma.

"Thank you." Grandma tried to peel back the sticker that held the wrapper in place.

Danny reached over and tore the sandwich open.

"Thank you." Grandma sighed.

Mother brought a plate of vegetables to the table. "And here are some carrots and radishes."

The ceramic teakettle whistled, and Danny stood. He inserted the stainless steel tea ball stuffed with chamomile flowers and set the kettle on the edge of the old wood stove.

"Have you heard the news, Danny?" Mother asked with an air of superiority.

Danny nodded. "Beth texted me shortly after she heard," he said somberly.

"So what was all the laughter about?"

"We were talking about Grandpa Sam," Danny said. "Old memories."

"You called him Grandpa?" Mother picked up her sub.

"And he calls me Grandma." Grandma laid her hand on his. "He's family."

Mother arched her eyebrows, looking first at Danny and then at Beth. "You're like cousins."

"No," they exclaimed in unison.

Chapter 36

*H*earing unfamiliar voices the next morning, Beth crept downstairs. As she quietly stood in the doorframe, Mak stirred a pot at the kitchen range. Grandma rested her forehead on arms crossed on the table. Standing behind her, a woman with gray, braided hair lifted the edge of her red tunic and pulled a vial out of her front jeans pocket. After dabbing a substance on her finger, she rubbed it on the back of Grandma's neck and behind her ears.

"Thank you, Lorna." With a pleasant smile, Grandma straightened and sniffed the air. "Is that pine?"

"Yes, and you're welcome." The woman moved around Grandma. "Hello," she said, noticing Beth.

Mak cranked his head around. "*Hyvää päivää.*"

"*Hyvää päivää,*" she replied. "And you must be Lorna."

"It's a pleasure to meet you." Lorna slipped the vial back in her pocket.

"It smells wonderful in here." Beth inhaled deeply.

"Essential oils. This blend has pine and frankincense." Lorna said. "They have healing properties. Perhaps you can help your grandma put a few drops on her shoulders and neck each day."

"Would you like that, Grandma?" Beth asked.

"I wouldn't mind it," Grandma said.

"Or when yous guys sauna, put a couple drops in da water bucket." Mak set the spoon on a plate.

"I used to be a distributor." Lorna stood next to her husband. "I guess I still am, although I don't put much effort into it anymore. They want everybody to be a distributor. I prefer to find a niche in the market."

"Like gluten-free cupcakes?" Beth asked.

"Yes." Lorna's eyes sparkled. "You wouldn't believe how many people are gluten intolerant these days."

"It seems the Internet does that." Mak snorted a laugh.

Lorna slapped his belly with the back of her hand and shook her head.

"*Puuroa*'s on da stove here. Tea is on da old stove there." Mak gave the pot one last stir and shut off the burner.

He had started a fire and made breakfast for them. How sweet. Beth smiled. "Thank you, Mak."

"If it's okay with yous, I'll install this." Mak faced Grandma as he held up a cardboard box. "It's a mechanical bidet. We have a few extras around the house from when Lorna was selling them."

"It's surprising more people aren't willing to try them." Resignation filled Lorna's voice.

"They're helpful, Lou, for everybody," Mak said.

"Okay, Mak." Grandma nodded. "That'll be fine."

Mak stepped into the bathroom, and Beth asked Lorna, "Would you like breakfast? Tea?"

"No, thank you. It won't take Mak long." Lorna sat with Grandma. "Mak has installed a few for the business already. I'm not just sales. I offer service, too."

Pouring cups of peppermint tea for herself and Grandma, Beth heard her mother say, "Excuse me," from outside the bathroom door.

"*Hyvää päivää*," Mak said.

Mother snickered. "Plowing and plumbing." She entered the kitchen. "Oh, hi," she said to Lorna.

Grandma introduced the two and explained the plumbing project. Within a few minutes, Mak returned to the kitchen. "It's all done. Yous can try it. Make sure you're sitting down when you do." He let out another belly laugh. "Well, we should be going and leave yous to your breakfast."

After Lorna and Mak left, Mother stretched her arms and yawned.

Grandma laughed. "I'm glad you slept in."

"It took me a long time to fall asleep last night. I was thinking about options." She hugged Grandma. "I wish I could stay longer, Mom. I can come back early next month and help you pack up, and then the three of us can drive back to California in Beth's car."

Grandma faced the window.

"Think about it." Mother looked to Beth for support, but Beth averted her eyes.

Grandma didn't acknowledge Mother's words.

"Mom, I will go to church with you tomorrow." Mother made a peace offering. "But I'm going to sit in the back... and wear a hat and glasses." She grimaced.

Grandma chuckled. "Maybe a fake mustache, too."

"Now if you'll excuse me." Mother walked to the bathroom.

While Mother took her morning shower, Beth and Grandma ate oatmeal sweetened with the Johnsons' maple syrup. Grandma struggled to bring her spoon to her face, so instead bent over to bring her face to her spoon.

Beth finished her oatmeal and pushed the bowl aside. "I don't understand why God would let this happen to you." She watched the chickadees at the bird feeder. "It doesn't seem fair."

"Beth, when you're young, you have expectations for life. You don't expect to suffer, but this is how life is. This is how it's been since disease and death entered the world. Disease and death weren't part of the original design, so they feel wrong, but one day..." Grandma's voice trailed off and she stared out the window.

"Are you okay?" Beth asked after a few moments.

"Yes. I was thinking of something Rebecca said when she was a child. Once she found a caterpillar and put it in a jar with some grass. A few weeks later, it had spun a cocoon. The jar sat on that windowsill for weeks. One day a moth hatched, and Rebecca was so excited. She told me, 'I thought it was dead, but it was part of the process.'" Grandma's eyes brightened. "This disease is not the final chapter."

The front door opened. "Louisa?"

Beth got up to greet the guests. "What a nice surprise." She bit her lip to keep her face impassive as she led Pastor Chip and Bella down the hall to the kitchen. How would Mother react?

"Hello, Louisa." Bella hugged Grandma.

"Thank you for stopping by. What a blessing."

Pastor Chip placed a hand on her shoulder. "How are you feeling, Lou?"

"I feel fine. I still can't quite believe this is Lou Gehrig's disease."

"We'll pray it's not, and that if it is, God will heal you." Pastor Chip squeezed Grandma's shoulder.

"Thank you," said Grandma. "Would you like tea? Have a seat and we can visit."

"We would love tea," Bella said.

Beth pulled cups from the cupboard, placed them on the table, and filled them with tea from the kettle.

"I heard Becky was in town." Chip sat and took a drink. "I haven't seen her in thirty-five years. Where is she?"

On cue, the bathroom door opened and Mother entered the kitchen. "Wow, that bidet will wake you up. It's invigorating." Her eyes widened, her jaw dropped, and blood drained from her face.

"There you are." Chip stood and extended his hand.

Mother kept hers at her side.

Bella moved around Chip, grabbed Mother's right hand, and shook it. "Chip told me that when he met Beth at Pinehurst a couple of months ago, it was like seeing a ghost. You two look so much alike. Both of you are so beautiful."

Mother's face softened momentarily, and then she frowned and looked at the floor. "I'm really not feeling well. Please excuse me." She left the room and went upstairs.

Chapter 37

*B*eth slid into the third pew next to Senja. Mother sat rigidly next to Grandma. At least she wasn't in the back.

Senja leaned across Beth and squeezed Grandma's arm. "I called the prayer chain yesterday after I talked to you. I hope that's okay."

"Of course," Grandma said, "I need prayer more than I need privacy."

After the song time and announcements, Pastor Chip walked to the podium. "Are there any prayer requests today?"

Senja faced Grandma. "May I?"

Grandma nodded.

Senja stood and shared the news of the diagnosis. A collective gasp filled the sanctuary, and tears came to many eyes.

Beth had thought she was through crying, but, sensing the compassion of the congregation, a lump rose in her throat, and her eyes stung. She felt a hand on her shoulder and turned.

Danny sat in the pew behind them.

Pastor Chip prayed for various concerns of the church and then concluded, "Strengthen and uphold Louisa. Heal her. Comfort her and her family. God, if you don't choose to heal Louisa in this life, we pray her suffering will not be wasted."

Beth peeked at her mother, who looked as puzzled as she felt.

During the sermon, Beth pondered Pastor Chip's prayer. He had prayed that the suffering would not be wasted. How would one use ALS, or not waste it? Something about that just felt wrong. God had made sense in Bible school, but in real life, things were not so clear. Why would God let this happen to Grandma? She felt anger rising within her and she clenched her teeth.

After the service, many people hugged Louisa and offered their sympathy. Beth stepped away and sat a few pews back, watching the outpouring of love. Danny slid in next to her and put his arm around her shoulders. She leaned against him, feeling the stubble on his chin through her hair. "Call me if you need anything," he said, "even if you just want company."

She lost track of time as she sat there next to him feeling protected—loved even?

"I'm ready to leave now." Grandma stood in front of them.

"Okay." Beth faced Danny. "Thanks," she whispered.

"You're welcome." He stood and offered his hand, helping her to her feet. "You hang in there." He gave her a tight squeeze and then moved to hug Grandma before leaving.

Beth scanned the almost empty sanctuary, looking for Mother.

"She's probably waiting in the car, dear," Grandma said.

Beth and Grandma exited the church and crossed the parking lot to Mother's rental car.

Sure enough. Mother slouched in the driver's seat. "I'm not feeling well."

"Are you sick?" Beth asked.

"This is a stressful time." Mother sighed. "I just don't feel like myself."

"Untreated wounds have a habit of festering," Grandma said under her breath.

"What's that, Mom?"

"Nothing. We should hurry so you can have lunch before your flight."

"I'm not hungry."

"Then you can watch us eat."

Beth had never seen Mother so ill at ease. She had always seemed in control of her emotions, of life. Maybe it was a façade, behind which she was as human as anyone was. Had she harbored bitterness and resentment for thirty-five years?

After a quick lunch at home, Grandma and Mother said their good-byes in the kitchen. Beth carried her mother's duffel bag out to the rental car, and Mother got in the car. Standing by the open door, Beth listened as Mother again made the case for California, why Grandma should move there, how the weather was so awful in the UP. The mother Beth knew was back.

Beth didn't respond. She had learned from Grandma.

"Elizabeth, I'm glad you're here, but I can't wait until you're home. The kids miss you. Tate keeps talking about the picture of you snowmobiling. Did you really drive it or was the photo staged?"

"I drove it—just a little ways, but I drove it."

"Be careful. You shouldn't—"

"They're not dangerous," Beth interjected, "if you drive them safely."

"Not that. With Danny. Guard your heart. People aren't always what they seem. Don't forget you need to summer and winter a man to truly know his character. Dr. Benley said that."

Beth smiled, remaining silent.

"And don't forget what Dr. Benley said about making sure your physical and emotional intimacy doesn't get ahead of your commitment level. You're vulnerable right now having so many emotions with the situations with Alan and Grandma. Don't jump into anything until you know you can trust him."

"Mother, I trust him."

"Elizabeth, you are in no state to be objective. Come home and figure out your next steps. And Ashley's baby is due soon. You'll want to meet your new niece."

"Good-bye, Mother." Beth reached into the car and gave her a quick hug before returning to the house.

Chapter 38

*I*n the weeks after the diagnosis, Beth helped Grandma welcome a steady stream of visitors—church folks brought meals, the Johnsons brought flowers and another bottle of maple syrup, and Lorna brought custom blends of essential oils, and herbs, too, "for a parasite cleanse." Uncle Scott flew up from Chicago, taking a rare weekend off from his duties as an executive for an advertising firm.

Sam and Robin Clinton stopped by to chat. Sam empathized with Grandma, sharing the story of his own close call with death. He was stricken with Ewing's Sarcoma, a bone cancer, when he was nineteen years old. The doctors caught the disease early, so he survived, but he had to have part of his femur removed. He never walked quite right thereafter.

"It was a reminder of life's fragility," Sam said. "Now, I live every day like Lazarus after he came out of the tomb."

"Is that why you have such a positive disposition?" Grandma's face crinkled into a smile.

"That's right." Sam nodded. "Life's a gift."

Gradually, life returned to normal. Mak plowed, Danny filled the wood hopper, and Beth and Grandma visited at the kitchen table, drinking tea and watching the birds. Mother called every day. Beth heard Grandma's end of many of those conversations in which she said, "Thank you for the offer, dear. It's good to have options."

Grandma seemed so excited about spring coming. "I can't wait to see this dreary world come back to life," she enthused. "I want to hear the rushing waters of the snowmelt, see apple trees blossom, and taste fresh-picked blueberries—perhaps one last time."

Beth was determined to help her desires come to fruition, so she picked up Grandma's line when Mother argued for them to come back to California—"Thank you, Mother. It's good to have options."

Mother seemed exasperated by the line, probably because it wasn't defiance or agreement. She sighed audibly and said "good grief" or "for crying out loud."

The disease progressed. Grandma's arms continued to weaken and she became fatigued. She napped every afternoon.

By the end of February, she didn't have the energy to attend Senja's prayer group but encouraged Beth to go without her, so Beth did. The ladies missed their prayer warrior, and Aimee said, "If she can't come to us, then I'll go pray with Lou."

Later in the week, Aimee arrived with Russ.

Beth slipped on her boots and greeted them outside. In her old life in California, she never would have imagined stepping outside without a jacket in mid-thirty-degree weather, but there she was in early March, acting like a Yooper, having survived January and February. "Hello, Aimee."

"Beth." Aimee greeted her with a hug.

"You came too, hey, Russ." Beth clapped her hand over her mouth. She sounded like a Yooper.

"Russ is my chauffeur." Aimee flashed him a smile that made Beth wonder if he was more than that.

As they walked to the house, Beth heard barking off in the distance. "Sounds like a pack of stray dogs."

Russ laughed.

"What's so funny?"

"They're not stray dogs, city girl, they're wild dogs—coyotes. They're hunting."

"Hunting what?"

"Probably deer. With the warm weather lately, the snow has a crust on it, and the dogs are chasing the deer out of their bedding areas. The deer don't like to move around in the deep snow, but they'll run from coyotes."

"Those poor deer." Beth frowned and quickened her step.

Aimee followed her into the house, but Russ stayed behind. He pulled a tape measure out of his jacket pocket and measured the porch steps. Aimee stood for a moment watching him out the porch window, a tender look on her face. Russ looked up at Aimee and cast her a wave, a grin spreading across his face.

Beth smiled. She had surmised correctly. He *was* more than Aimee's chauffeur.

One evening, Danny sat next to Beth on the couch. The window behind them framed the rising moon. He caressed her neck with his fingertips, and she shivered.

"I like you," he said softly. He could feel his heart beating wildly.

"I like you, too." She looked up at him, and they locked eyes until she looked down and pulled away.

"What's wrong?" he asked.

"Nothing's wrong."

"You're giving me mixed signals."

"My signals are very clear. We take it slow and stay out of bed. We summer and winter each other. If there are no red flags, then we can move forward." Beth scooted farther away and crossed her arms. "In fact, we've already moved too fast. I need to figure out my next steps."

"Maybe you can't have it all figured out," he said. She was like an igloo with a cold shell but a warm fire burning on the inside. As frustrated as he was, she was worth the pursuit, and he was up for the challenge. In the academy, he had learned to push his body to gain strength and endurance. You don't get anywhere in life if you settle for the way things are. He wanted Beth. No, he needed her. She made him want to be a better man.

"I need to take it day by day and see how Grandma's doing." She sat rigidly.

"I'm concerned about Grandma Lou, too, but how does that affect our relationship?" he asked. He held his breath, waiting for her answer.

"There's too much uncertainty. I've been reading about ALS. The average life expectancy is two to five years, but there are people who die within a year and there are people who live ten or fifteen years with this disease."

"So Grandma Lou could have quite a bit of time."

"Either way, whether the disease progresses quickly or is drawn out, it will be hard. My mother wants Grandma and me to go back to California."

"What do you want, Beth?"

She uncrossed her arms, relaxing, and scooted closer, nestling against him before turning her face toward his. She wanted him to kiss her—he just knew it—but he wasn't going to try that again. "I want to help Grandma do what she wants to do."

"What does she want?"

"She said she wants to stay. She wants one more summer in her house, if that's possible."

"That's good. I've got you at least through the summer." He put his arm around her.

They sat in silence, until Beth asked, "Do you like living here, Danny?"

"I do. The only other place I've ever lived was downstate and there I felt like I had the cold without the fun of the snow."

"Would you ever move somewhere else, somewhere warmer, like California?"

"I'm pretty tied to Michigan with my job. I went to Michigan's police academy. I can't transfer between states." He could feel her stiffen. "And I like living in a small town. People are real, honest."

"I like that. Real and honest." She leaned her head against his shoulder, reached across and grabbed his free hand. "You and I have intimacy."

He let out a burst of laughter. "If you call holding hands intimacy."

She elbowed him in the stomach. "I'm talking about the foundation of our friendship, intimacy from openness and honesty."

He swallowed hard. She liked his openness until she heard too much. Then she shut him down. As disturbed as she was by his past, he couldn't imagine her reaction if she found out he might have a kid. There was a chance AJ wasn't his, but there was a better chance he was. Russ had explained the probabilities. Blue-eyed parents can produce a brown-eyed kid, but it's rare. Would Beth even like him if she knew the real him?

He rested his chin on the top of her head and looked out the window. "Look at the moon."

Beth squeezed his hand. "Last time I saw a moon like that, I had just met you."

He kissed her on the top of the head.

Chapter 39

"*W*inter's far from over," Grandma reminded Beth when, by the middle of March, there were enough warm days to allow Beth to think spring was around the corner. "I could usually cross country ski on my birthday, April 12," Grandma said.

Snow still covered the driveway, but it had melted off Beth's Corolla. How she missed her little car. She liked the all-wheel drive on the Outback, but she didn't like the size of it. Besides, the roads were clear enough. With the sun setting due west, Beth grabbed the keys to the Corolla on her way to pick up a few groceries at the Co-op. "Bye, Grandma. I'll be back with dinner shortly."

The Toyota started right up, not that she would have doubted it, but it did cross her mind a lesser car might not after having sat under the snow for nearly three months. She drove down the county road and turned onto US-41.

It felt good to be back in her car—in her own space. She hardly felt like a guest at Grandma's anymore, but there was something comforting about being in such a familiar personal space. She glanced at the odometer—135,087 miles. She had driven all but 39,000 of those.

As she drove down Quincy Hill, her mind wandered back

to the night she entered town driving fifteen miles per hour down the middle of the street and then being pulled over by Danny. What a way to meet someone. Beth smiled at the memory. A lot had changed since then. Her confidence had grown and she wasn't afraid to drive the speed limit, especially on such a beautiful evening. She wished the trip to the Co-op were longer. Perhaps I'll take a scenic route, she thought, and—

"Aaaaah!" Beth screamed as a deer leapt in front of her car. She hit the brakes narrowly missing it, and then thump—she hit a second deer. She looked out a cracked windshield at a buckled fender.

Imprinted in her mind were the images of the deer. The startling image of the first deer clearing the front of her car followed by the grotesque picture of the second flying into the air, somersaulting, and landing someplace off in the ditch to her side as she came to a stop. The poor majestic creature. What had she done?

She sat motionless, stunned, staring at the crumpled hood in front of her. Thankfully, she'd not been hurt. But the deer and… "Argh. My car!" She hit the steering wheel with the heels of her palms. She took a deep breath. She needed to get off the road. She turned the key in the ignition off and back on. Nothing. She was facing downhill—maybe she could coast to the shoulder. She let her foot off the brake, but the car didn't move. Besides, the steering wheel wouldn't move either.

Her body trembled. Danny. She needed Danny. She dug through her purse. Her phone. With shaking fingers, she found Danny in her contacts and called him.

"Hey, Beth."

"Danny." She sobbed.

"Beth? Are you okay?"

She cried louder.

"Is Grandma Lou okay? Do you need an ambulance?"

Beth sniffled and wiped her eyes. "Do they take animals to the vet?"

"What happened? Where are you?"

"I hit a deer. I'm halfway down the hill."

"I'll be right there."

By the time Danny pulled behind her in his State Police truck, two men had parked their pickups on the shoulder. One man waved traffic around Beth's car while the other tried to pull the driver's door open.

Beth, still in her seat, breathed a sigh of relief when she saw Danny get out of his truck.

"Are you okay?" Danny asked through Beth's open window.

"Yeah." She felt calm come over her—now that he was there. "I saw a deer and I tried to stop as quickly as I could, but then another one came and I hit it. Is it…" She choked out the words, "Is it dead?"

"Yeah."

"I saw the deer crossing signs, but I didn't think they'd know to cross here."

Danny went around to the passenger side and opened the door. "Come out this way. Watch the glass."

She picked shards of glass off her lap and then crawled over the passenger seat and reached up for his hand. He steadied her as she stepped out of the car.

The man who had been working on opening her door came around the car. "You're not gonna take it, hey."

Beth looked at him, confused.

"That was a question," Danny said.

"I know." She faced the man. "What do you mean?"

"Do you want the deer?" he asked gruffly.

Beth frowned, shaking her head. "Why would I want—"

"She'll take it," Danny interrupted.

The man slumped away.

"I'll what?" Beth asked.

"You'll take the deer." He pulled his phone out of his pocket. "I'll call Russ—and a tow truck."

He walked back to his truck while Beth inspected her car. The driver's side fender was crumpled into the door. No wonder it wouldn't open. A flat tire. A cracked windshield.

After a few minutes, Danny got out of his truck. "I'm glad you're okay. Thankfully, the deer didn't go through the windshield. How old is this car?"

"Ten years old."

"How many miles?"

"135,000."

"Yeah, I'm not an expert, but I'm guessing it's going to be totaled."

"No." Tears threatened to spill over. "I like my car."

"Liked." Danny draped his arm over Beth's shoulders and squeezed her. "I'm sorry."

"So what do I do now?" She sighed.

"Clear all your possessions out of the car. Put them in my trooper vehicle and I'll drop you off at the house."

Beth waited in Danny's truck while the tow operator hooked to the front of her car.

Russ pulled up, and she got out to greet him. "Will you bury it?"

"Don't worry about it." Russ dragged the antlerless deer out of the ditch.

"He'll take care of it." Danny handed her a slip of paper. "Here's an incident number in case you need it for your insurance." He grabbed her hand. "Come on. I'll take you home."

The sky was dark by the time they arrived at Grandma's in the State Police vehicle.

"You okay?" Danny asked.

"Yeah. More than anything, I'm mad about my car."

"You'll get a nice check, if you had full coverage."

"I did. My mother works at an insurance agency, so I didn't have a choice in that."

"No doubt. At least you have Grandma's car to drive, and money to replace yours." He got out of the truck and walked around to open her door. He nodded to the darkened windows. "Where's Grandma Lou?"

"Maybe she's napping."

"All right, then tell her 'hey' when she wakes up. And I'll see you tomorrow."

Beth brightened. "Yeah, snowshoeing."

"Hungarian Falls should be beautiful with the snowmelt we've had."

Beth reached up and hugged him. "Thank you."

"Anything for you." He held her, his chin resting on the top of her head. "Besides, it's my job."

After several seconds, Beth broke the moment. "I should go."

Danny climbed back in the truck and waited with his headlights illuminating the house while she made her way inside carrying a bag of stuff she had collected from her car.

As Beth turned on the hall light, she heard weeping coming from the kitchen.

"Are you okay?" Beth rushed down the hall, tossing her bag on the bench as she passed by. She turned on the kitchen light. "Grandma?"

Grandma sat at the kitchen table weeping. On the floor, between the sink and the stove, the ceramic teakettle lay shattered into pieces amidst a pool of water.

Beth came beside her, bent down, and put her arm around Grandma's shoulders. "Are you hurt?"

Grandma sobbed.

"Did you fall?"

"No, no." Grandma choked the words out. "I dropped the blasted thing."

Beth retrieved a dish towel from the drawer. "I'll clean it up."

"Argh, I hate this." Grandma's anguished yell made Beth shudder.

"It's okay. We can replace the teakettle. You got this from The Tea House, right?"

"That's not the point." Grandma's eyes flashed anger.

Stunned, Beth knelt to mop up the water.

Grandma took a deep breath and exhaled slowly. Softening her tone, she said, "I'm sorry. It's not your fault, and I didn't mean to take it out on you. You're a great help, a godsend, a blessing."

"It's okay, Grandma."

"I am so frustrated with the little setbacks—trouble with the car key, trouble turning the pages of a book, trouble lifting my teacup, trouble holding the teakettle. I wasn't even pouring tea. I was just carrying it. At any given point, I think to myself, if it would stop, I could deal with it, but this disease keeps going, keeps robbing me of function, reminding me of the path ahead. This disease will be a death of a thousand cuts. The last cut will be when it takes my breath, but all the cuts before will make me want to die."

Beth didn't know what to say. She collected pieces of broken pottery in her left hand, stacking the smaller pieces inside the largest shard.

"I don't fear death…" Grandma whispered, almost talking to herself. "I dread the process of getting there."

"I'm sorry." Beth threw the shards of clay in the garbage. She wrung out the dish towel in the sink and then mopped up the rest of the water.

Grandma continued, "I was crying out to the Lord, 'What will I do? How will I find meaning when I'm a motionless mass?'"

Tears welled up in Beth's eyes. She tossed the dish towel into the sink and pulled a chair close to Grandma. Beth grabbed her wrinkled hand. "I love you."

"I know, dear. I love you, too." Grandma pulled her hand away and placed her hands in her lap as she straightened. "Okay, that was a good cry. Now I'm hungry. Where are the groceries?"

Chapter 40

Snowshoeing to the top of Hungarian Falls, Danny led Beth through the woods. The soft, white noise of rushing water was suddenly amplified when they came out of the trees. The sun lit the rock face, where water cut between two ice walls into a pool of open water. He stopped short of the ravine and then turned to see her reaction as she approached it.

"Beautiful." Beth's eyes panned from the rocky stream to the plunge pool.

"Yeah, you know it, hey," he said, although he couldn't take his eyes off her. Sparks of sunlight reflected in her blue eyes. "In a month, it'll be twice this with all the melted snow."

After watching her take in the beauty, he led her to a bare rocky outcrop. "Let's have our lunch." He set his backpack on the rock, knelt, and rummaged for a Thermos bottle, a plastic travel mug, two spoons, a box of crackers, and two juice boxes.

"Juice boxes?" Beth grinned. "Yay, I haven't had a juice box since I was in junior high school."

He laughed. "They travel well. Besides, my Thermos is being used for stew."

She grabbed a juice box and pulled the straw off the back. "Do you like to cook, or are you doing this to impress me?"

She punctured the top.

"I have to cook. I have to eat," Danny said. He *was* trying to impress her.

"So if this relationship goes anywhere, are you going to keep cooking?"

"I might have to. I haven't tried your cooking yet." He nudged her shoulder.

She laughed and took a drink.

Never before had he wanted a woman to like him as much as he did now. His other relationships had developed more organically. Really, more physically. But that was not an option with Beth. He'd have to enter her heart through her mind and soul—and stomach.

He shook the bottle, unscrewed the cap, and poured stew into the mug and cap. He gave the mug to Beth. "Let's pray." He grabbed her hand. "Father, thank you for your creation. Thank you for the time Beth and I have together. We pray for Grandma Lou. We thank you for this food. Amen."

"Mmmm, this is good," Beth said, after tasting the stew.

"I'm glad you like it."

"I love beef stew."

"Actually, it's venison."

"Ew." Beth looked into her mug. "I just ate a deer?"

Danny laughed. "No, just part of one, from the back straps." He spooned stew to his mouth.

Beth set the mug down. "I don't know if I can eat venison. I don't like the idea of hunting."

"Why not?"

"I don't even like guns." Beth took a bite of a cracker. "It's a little scary when a half-senile woman greets you with a rifle."

He chuckled. "Unloaded rifle."

"She has her ammo back."

"Yeah, that's a problem," he admitted.

"What are you going to do?"

"There's not much I can do. She has the right to own a gun." He ate another spoonful of stew.

Beth raised her eyebrows.

He shrugged. "I'll keep an eye on her. If there's a problem, any kind of incident, I'll need to get the court involved."

"Do you have guns, other than your cop guns?"

Danny's eyes twinkled. "Other than my service weapons?"

"Yeah."

"Of course, I'm a Yooper."

"Do you hunt?"

"Sure. Russ and I hunt. It's good to manage the deer herd, and I like the meat. We cut the tallow off and give it to Lorna Maki. She makes and sells—well, makes—deer tallow candles and soap."

"Did you catch this one?"

Danny laughed. "First of all, you don't catch deer. You shoot them, or hit them. But I didn't shoot or hit this one. You did."

"This is my deer?"

"Yeah, this is the one that totaled your car."

Beth picked up her mug and took another bite victoriously.

Chapter 41

"*H*e is risen," Pastor Chip greeted his congregation on Easter morning. A smile broke across his face.

"He is risen, indeed," the congregation responded. Someone started clapping. Soon, nearly everyone joined in.

"Hallelujah," Grandma shouted, her hands not cooperating to clap.

Lilies sat on the steps in front of the chancel. Behind the pulpit, a large urn held palm branches children had paraded up the aisle the week before. Resurrection Sunday was a celebration of life, real life in Christ. After the darkness of winter, spring was coming, though it would be a white Easter in the Keweenaw, Beth thought ruefully. In California, Mother would be hiding Easter eggs in the yard for Cora and Tate to find.

Danny's rotating schedule once again made him available on Sunday, and he sat by Beth's side.

The message of resurrection found residence in Beth's heart. *Yes, Lord, yes. Because of you, because of your love, I am filled with love this morning.* She looked to Grandma on her left, and then to Danny on her right. He reached out and squeezed her hand.

All their problems were temporary. Life on earth was temporary. Ultimately, they would be with Christ. New bodies. No more sadness. No more tears. Beth rejoiced in the resurrection that guaranteed her resurrection, Grandma's resurrection.

Later at The Tea House, Danny held Beth's hand under the table as they waited for their food.

Senja unwrapped a straw and placed it in Grandma's teacup. "That was a beautiful Easter service, wasn't it?"

"That sermon so encouraged my soul." Grandma sipped her tea through the straw. "I've been struggling with this diagnosis, worrying about what I'll do when I can't move at all, when I'm paralyzed. This morning the Lord made the answer plain to me." Grandma lifted her chin. "I'll still be able to worship my Savior in a bed, because worship comes from the heart, not from outward actions… and then, in a blink, I'll be in Heaven, raising my hands again." She turned her palms up and rested them on the table.

"What are your plans while you're still with us?" Senja patted Grandma's shoulder.

"I'm taking it one day at a time," Grandma said.

"Is Beth going to stay to help you?" Senja asked.

Grandma smiled lovingly at Beth. "She said she would stay through the summer, bless her heart."

Beth nodded. "That's my purpose here, why God has brought me here."

"I'd hope there were other reasons to stay." Grandma cast a glance in Danny's direction.

He squeezed Beth's hand.

Grandma continued, "For now, I can manage. I need more help with basic chores, but I can still walk, feed myself, bathe myself, and all that. This disease is so unpredictable, affecting each person uniquely. There's no reason to make any rash decisions."

"We'll take care of you, Grandma Lou," Danny said.

Carrying a stand while holding a tray above her shoulder,

Mary came to the table and passed out the entrées. "Is there anything else I can get yous?"

"Yes," Grandma said, "a new teakettle. Please add one to my bill."

Chapter 42

One evening in early April, Beth ate dinner with Danny at the Cornucopia. They laughed at how they first met and recounted their favorite memories of the prior three months.

On the way back to Grandma's, Danny pulled his Jeep into the scenic outlook halfway up Quincy Hill. Snow had buried the pavement for most of the winter but had since melted down to less than a foot, so he could drive up to the guardrail in four-wheel drive.

He reached over and squeezed her arm. "This is it, Beth. This is God knitting our hearts together." He sounded almost giddy.

Beth basked in his touch. Was a relationship with him God's plan for her life? Could it be possible? Maybe? She let out a sigh as she looked out over the valley to the lights of Douglass on the other side of the Portage Canal. "What a view."

"Yeah." His brown eyes scanned her face. They rested on her lips.

She felt flustered, conflicted. She wanted Danny to kiss her, yet hoped he wouldn't—that he wouldn't force her to choose between her heart's desire and her head's disinclination.

His hand slid down her arm to her hand. "Beth, I love you."

She sat silent—blinking. *He loves me?* She searched for words she felt comfortable giving him. "Thank you," she finally said.

"Thank you?" His voice cracked. "I love you." He said the words softly before looking out across the canal and then back at her face. "I know what those words mean to you. I had thought maybe I should wait to say 'I love you' until you're ready to say it, but then I decided I should put myself out there."

She squeezed his hand. She felt honored. Overwhelmed. Conflicted.

He continued, "We love because He first loved us. That's what I'm doing with you. I'm loving you first, waiting for you to accept it and love me back."

"Oh, Danny." Glad tears came to her eyes. "Thank you. Thank you for loving me." She wiped her eyes with the back of her sleeve. "When I say... If I say those words, it will be a commitment, a choice, not a feeling."

"What? Not a feeling?"

"I'll feel it. I already feel it, but I'm talking about love as the verb, not as the noun."

"Is this another grammar lesson?" he teased. "I'm confused."

"You know what I mean."

Danny leaned his head back. "Yeah, I know exactly what you mean. That's what I'm doing, choosing."

"How could you choose now? We've only known each other for three months."

"I know what I need to know. I know your character. I know that you love God, that you love people."

She straightened. "But Danny, we need to make a checklist of the qualities—"

"Come on, Beth. Where do you get this stuff?"

"Dr. Benley said—"

"And you do everything Dr. Benley says?"

"No. Well, maybe, but when it comes to dating, you need to make sure you know all of the problems that could arise.

You need to analyze the situation, make a list of the qualities that you want, use your head not your—"

"Maybe it's more important to know that there will be problems than to know of every problem. Maybe it's enough to have a short list of qualities." He looked out over the valley.

"Danny, I… l—" Beth dragged out the *L* sound.

He looked at her with expectant eyes.

"…like you… a lot." She poked his side.

"Don't, I'm ticklish."

"You're ticklish? What valuable information." She held up both hands ready to pounce.

Danny squirmed and pushed her hands away from his ribs. "Don't do that. Jack tickle-tortured me when I was a kid."

"Okay, I won't tickle you."

"Thank you," he said.

Chapter 43

"*Intimately Yours*," Beth said when she spotted the book among numerous titles on the craftsman-style, quarter-sawn oak bookshelf in the Johnsons' living room. "Did you like it?" she asked Evelyn.

Evelyn nodded. "Oh yes, I like all of Dr. Benley's work." She spoke clearly and precisely, and she looked regal in a blue, Italian wool dress with padded shoulders. "That book was a big help in Dale's and my marriage. Now I'm reading *Still Intimately Yours, A Guide for the Golden Years of Marriage*."

"I've read *Before I'm Intimately Yours*," Beth offered.

"I've read that, too. I bought a copy for Danny and read it before I gave it to him."

"Danny read the book?" Beth raised her eyebrows.

Evelyn laughed. "I hope so."

"He was teasing me, asking if I do everything Dr. Benley says."

"Sometimes Dr. Benley is a bit over the top. He has good suggestions and wisdom, but there's room in the human experience to take different courses, as long as you're seeking direction from God."

Beth felt honored—though a bit out of place—to be included at the celebration of Dale and Evelyn's thirty-fifth wedding anniversary. Dale and Jack lounged on the couch while Danny sat on the floor playing dolls with his niece and stacking blocks for his nephew to knock over. Danny's sister and sister-in-law prepped dinner in the kitchen.

"Come sit with me." Evelyn sat on the loveseat and patted a spot next to her.

Beth stepped over blocks and took a seat.

"Danny told us you're planning to stay awhile longer. I'm so delighted to hear that," Evelyn said warmly.

"That's the plan. I want to give my grandma one more summer in her house, anyway." Beth lifted her feet as blocks tumbled toward them.

Danny swept the blocks together in a pile and rebuilt a tower.

Evelyn touched Beth's shoulder. "I'm so sorry for Louisa. I wish that was not the reason you need to stay, but I am happy for us, for Danny, that you're here."

"I'm glad I came." Beth smiled, but thought Evelyn was getting ahead of herself. At least she seemed to like her. She had not met the approval of Alan's mother, and Beth feared the situation would repeat itself, but many people seemed as excited for her relationship with Danny as she was.

"How are you finding the UP?" Evelyn asked.

Beth leaned back. "It's such a unique place—as strange as it is captivating. There's something genuine about this area."

"Yes, when one is subjugated by the weather, controlled by the environment, one is humbled. The Apostle Paul said that God subjected creation to frustration in hopes that creation itself will be set free from its bondage to decay. What could be more frustrating than living through our harsh winters?"

"Why did you decide to come here?" Beth asked.

"We came for the job at Douglass State. The real question is why we decided to stay. We stayed for the water, the woods, and the people. This is a wonderful place to raise children. One time we got a call from the sheriff telling us our boys were at a party where alcohol was being served. We were waiting for them at the door when they came home. It's easier to keep tabs on children up here than in the city. I love city shopping and cultural events, but one can always travel to do those things. I'm glad to call this place home."

Beth thought about one of her strongest desires—to raise a family. There was likely not a better place to raise kids than the UP.

She watched Danny, engaged in play with his niece and nephew. He'd make an incredible dad. It was becoming much clearer. She had another reason to stay, apart from Grandma— she could stay and allow herself to love this man.

"Beth?" Evelyn said loudly.

"I'm sorry. You were saying?"

"Dinner's ready. Let's go eat."

They ate dinner, and the Johnsons treated Beth as if she were already part of the family. Jack's kids warmed up to Beth quickly, and it wasn't hard for her to imagine being Auntie to the two little children.

After dinner, Danny parked his Jeep in front of Grandma's house and turned his shoulders to face Beth. "They like you."

She cocked her head. "I like them."

"Could you imagine being part of our family?"

"I am warming up to the idea." She smiled. "I had fun tonight."

He grinned. "Good. Because I want this to go someplace." He took a deep breath. "I love you." He waited. Was she going to admit she loved him?

"I..." She twirled a lock of hair around her finger. "Thank you."

"You're welcome."

They laughed, dispelling the tension. The moon brightened patches of snow in the field, and the headlights flooded the front of the gray stucco farmhouse. With lights still on in the house, it looked like Grandma Lou was waiting up for Beth.

"So you're staying awhile, hey." Danny asked.

She stared out the window.

"That was a question."

"I know. No up-speak required. I was thinking. I've been living off savings, but haven't had many expenses with Grandma. I'd like to give her another summer in her house, if I can manage—I'm no nurse. If she goes to a nursing home, I'll need to find a job." Beth sighed. "I'm a ministry worker—and a woman. My chances of finding a job in youth or children's ministry are slim in a rural area. I don't know what else I'm qualified to do."

"We could get married."

She gasped. "Danny. Are you proposing?"

"No, not exactly. I'm saying we can see how things develop over the summer."

"We need to summer and winter before we even think of that. Dr. Benley wrote that in *Before I'm Intimately Yours*."

"I know, I just read it."

"Then wouldn't you agree it's way too soon to even be talking of marriage?"

"Dr. Benley's full of himself. He has opinions, but he states them as if they're the gospel."

"Maybe he's a bit didactic on some things, but I really like what he has to say about intimacy, and that's one thing that we have. Openness and honesty are a good foundation." She looked into his eyes, and he saw longing. Trust. Maybe even love.

He turned away. He couldn't live with the secret forever. She said she didn't want to know any more about his past, but she didn't know what she was refusing to hear. He could keep it from her, but it hurt more to think she was falling in love with a fictitious persona. If she were to love him, she needed to know the real him.

"Beth." He forced himself to spit out the words. "I might have a kid."

"What?" She looked more confused than upset.

"He's probably not mine, and he's only known one father,

but he does look like me."

"What? Who? Who looks like you?"

"When I went to the funeral for my high school girlfriend, I saw her boy. With the timing, maybe he's mine, but there's a chance he's not. He has a good dad, and I have no right to step into his life now. I just thought you needed to know." Shame left his soul, though he realized the revelation may have ended their relationship.

"You should have told me." Her chin quivered. Tears formed in her eyes, and she blinked them away. "I found out Kristine was your high school girlfriend. Why didn't you tell me?"

He leaned forward and ran his fingers through his hair. "I didn't think you'd want to know."

"On our first date, you said you didn't know the woman in the accident. You lied to me."

"It was a long time ago. We were kids." He leaned over the console separating them. "I was going to tell you that night after Scrabble, but you said you didn't want to know any more about my past. I'm sorry." He tried to put his arm around her.

Leaning away from him, she pushed against his chest and scooted closer to the door. "I'd want to know you have a child."

"I would've wanted to know, too, but she never told me. I still don't know if he's mine. That little boy you saw on Facebook the day of the painting party."

"You mean the kid I thought was you? He's beautiful." Her face softened, and she straightened in her seat. "Do you have other kids?"

"Not that I know of." He rested a hand on her shoulder and breathed a sigh of relief when she didn't push him away again.

She dropped her chin "So there might be more of these revelations down the road?"

"It's possible. I don't know."

"I love kids. I'm not upset that you have a child—"

"Might have a child."

"Whatever. I'm just upset you didn't tell me. I thought I

could trust you."

"I was just—intimidated. You're kind of intense about the purity stuff." He pleaded with his eyes for her to understand. "You can trust me. God is knitting our hearts together. This is part of the process."

"This is *not* part of the process." She shrugged his hand off her shoulder. "I'm sure of that."

"You think too much. God's knitting our hearts together, and instead of taking pleasure in his work, you're critiquing his knots."

"You're quite the poet. I am not critiquing his knots. I'm not even sure he's knitting. But I am sure that we've already broken just about every rule."

"Did you follow all the rules with Alan?"

"Yes." She pursed her lips.

"How did that work out?"

Beth's eyes blazed with fury he had never seen. "That's not fair."

Clouds rolled in and covered the moon. Snow fell lightly to the ground, disappearing into the muddy driveway.

"I still love you," he said.

She looked at him, her cheeks red and her eyes glassy. "Thank you." A tear rolled down her cheek.

He pulled a fast food napkin out of the center console and offered it to her.

She blew her nose. "I'll have to think about this."

"I know." He exhaled. "Okay, let's get in there and check on Grandma Lou. I haven't filled her wood hopper for a while now that the weather's warming up." He left the truck running and the headlights on to illuminate their walk up to the front porch.

The wood hopper was still almost full.

"I guess this is goodnight." He felt her relax into his embrace as he pulled her close. He kissed the top of her head.

As Beth opened the front door, sobs came from inside the house.

Chapter 44

*B*eth dashed down the hall and through the kitchen with Danny a step behind.

Grandma lay at the base of the stairs coiled in a fetal position, her face bruised, holding her knee.

"What happened?" Trembling, Beth knelt beside her.

"Let me through." Danny jostled for position, stepping around Beth and crouching down behind Grandma's head. "Okay, don't move."

"If only I could move, I would have by now." Grandma groaned.

Danny stabilized Grandma's neck with his hands. "Can you move your legs?"

"Yes."

Beth stood. "I'll call an ambulance."

"No, I don't need an ambulance." Grandma's voice was firm. "Calm yourselves down. I'm okay."

Beth sat on the floor next to Grandma. "What happened?"

"I missed the last few stairs and came down hard. My arms were too weak to catch myself, and my face hit the door."

Beth pulled hair away from Grandma's cheek, smoothing it back on her forehead.

Grandma winced. "I don't have enough arm strength to push myself up, and my knee hurts."

"How long have you been here?" Danny laid her head gently on the floor, and then scooted around to her side.

"Since about nine. I lost track of time." Grandma tried to raise her head. "What time is it?"

"Almost 10:30," Danny said. "I'm sorry we were out so late."

"You couldn't have known." Grandma patted his hand. "Can you help me up? I'd like to sit in my recliner and put ice on this knee."

Danny reached under her neck and slid his arm down her back as his other arm reached under her knees. He picked her up and carried her through the kitchen.

"Wow." Grandma managed a smile. "I haven't been carried like this since Sam carried me over the threshold of this old house fifty-five years ago."

After grabbing frozen vegetables and towels, Beth caught up with them in the living room, where Danny set Grandma in the recliner. He pulled the lever, raising the footrest, as he used his other hand to recline her back.

Beth set a bag between Grandma's knees and handed the other to Danny. "This is for her cheek." She gently pulled up Grandma's pant leg. "Let's take a look at it." She revealed the bruised, swollen knee. Beth put the bag on her knee and used a dishtowel to hold it in place.

Grandma turned her head to the side, and Danny laid the other frozen pack against her cheek

"Can I get you anything else?" Danny asked.

"Ibuprofen. Look in the cabinet, the one that's next to the door to the staircase. Second from the top shelf," Grandma said.

Danny left the living room.

Beth sat on the floor next to Grandma's feet. "We need to get you a medic alert button, like you see on TV."

Grandma frowned. "I need to call Rebecca. Can you get me the cordless phone—no, can I use your cell phone, with the speaker thing?"

"Of course." Beth reached into the pocket of the jacket she still wore, which reminded her that she was also still wearing her boots and had probably tracked mud into the house.

She called Mother's number, put the phone on speaker, and set it on the recliner back next to Grandma's face.

"Hi, Elizabeth," Mother answered.

"This is Mom. I'm okay," Grandma said.

Beth got up and went to check on the status of the ibuprofen and take off her jacket and boots.

"I had a bit of a fall," Grandma said as Beth left the room.

"Did you find it?" Beth asked Danny, who was rummaging through the medicine cabinet.

"I'm getting close. I have Aleve here. Is that ibuprofen?"

"I don't know, but it should work." Beth walked to the front hallway and slipped off her jacket and boots.

When she returned to the kitchen, Danny stood by the sink, filling a glass of water from the tap.

Beth took the Aleve from the counter. "I'll bring it to her, if you don't mind slipping off your boots and wiping up the mud we tracked in."

"No problem." He handed her the water.

As she returned to the living room, she heard Mother's voice. "It'll be for the best."

"Could I help you take this?" Beth held out the pain reliever and water.

Grandma nodded and sat up, the vegetable pack and phone dropping to her lap.

"Elizabeth? Is that you?" Mother's muffled voice came through the speaker.

Beth righted the phone. "Hi, Mother."

"I need you to help your grandma get out to California." Mother's voice was firm.

Beth looked at Grandma who nodded.

"Will you do that, Elizabeth?" Mother asked. "I'll buy the tickets. Grandma needs your help. She can't travel alone."

"Of course—of course I'll help her."

"I'll book the flights for next week. Now you take care of your grandma. Make sure she drinks enough water."

"Okay, bye, Mother." Beth hung up.

Danny stepped into the living room, kicking a towel across the maple hardwood floor, wiping up the last of the tracked-in mud. "What's going on?" he asked, looking first to Grandma, and then at Beth. "What's wrong?"

"I'm moving to California," Grandma said.

"But you want to stay here." Danny said the words slowly, frowning.

"I want to stay, but I can't." Grandma sighed.

"Yes, you can." He put a hand on her shoulder. "We can make this work."

"I'm afraid I can't. I need more and more help every day."

"Beth is here," Danny said.

Beth glanced at Grandma, who raised her eyebrows. "I'm going with Grandma," she said firmly.

Disappointment filled his eyes as he met Beth's gaze. "Are you coming back?"

"Danny," Grandma interjected, "I need to sleep down here tonight, and I much prefer to sleep in a bed. Could you and Beth get the twin bed from Scott's room and set that up down here?"

"Of course, Grandma Lou. See, we can make this work."

"Until we leave. Knowing my daughter, she's already purchased the tickets." Grandma laid her head back and closed her eyes.

"Come on, Danny." Beth led the way upstairs.

They removed the mattress and box spring and stood them against the wall.

"What does this mean for us?" Danny pulled the bed rails off the headboard.

"I don't know." She had already received the e-mail confirmation—two one-way tickets scheduled to go out the following Tuesday.

"You could come back." Danny leaned the headboard against the wall and turned to take the bed rails off the footboard. "I'll pay for your return flight."

"Maybe it's good this happened, when we've only known each other for a few months."

Danny worked the footboard loose with sharp, jerky movements. He let it drop to the floor with a bang.

"Are you okay?" Grandma's muffled voice came from downstairs.

"We're fine," Beth yelled.

Danny stood, facing Beth, his lips pressed together. Finally, he said, "We can't let this end."

"I'm not opposed to staying in touch, but it won't work for me to move up here." She stared at him, arms crossed.

He shrugged. "Long-distance relationships don't work."

"Absence makes the heart grow fonder." She said the words hopefully, searching his face.

"Absence makes the heart go wander," he countered.

She forced a laugh. "Danny, you don't know that."

"Maybe it's not in a book, but I've seen it. You need to be here, so God can keep knitting our hearts together."

She considered his words for a moment before responding. "Where would I live? What would I do for work?"

"You can live here, at the farmhouse. There will be lots of jobs available in the summer, after the students leave."

"I can't invite myself to live at my grandma's house alone."

"Maybe you could live with Aimee."

"I can't support myself on minimum wage." He was asking too much. It didn't make sense. She didn't even know if she could trust him. "Anyway, I want to help Grandma. You should move to California, if you're serious about winning my heart."

"I can't do that. I'm only qualified to work in the State of Michigan. I'm already years into my career."

"My career is important, too."

"You left it. And you already said one of the things most important to you is to have a family, raise kids. I have nothing against you working, but are you going to choose your work over a family?"

"You're not the only man who could give me a family," she said with an air of challenge.

Danny's face flashed frustration. He bundled up the bed rails and carried them out of the room.

Beth pulled her smart phone out of her pocket and opened up the messaging app. *Jules, coming home on Tuesday.*

As Beth waited for a response, Danny came back and grabbed the footboard and laid it against the headboard, picked them both up, and carried them out of the room.

A few minutes later her phone dinged. *Yay.*

She smiled. It would be good to see her best friend. She typed a reply. *Grandma's coming too.*

A ding. *That's good. What about Dan the Man?*

Beth sighed ruefully and typed a reply. *It was fun while it lasted.*

Danny reentered the room. "Could you help me with this?" He picked up one end of the box spring, leading the way backward as Beth carried the other end. "I'm sorry for that dig about Alan."

She took a breath and exhaled. "I forgive you."

They worked their way down the hall and around a bend to the staircase.

"We could work on Grandma's house, make it handicap accessible." He slowly backed down the stairs.

"That's up to Grandma."

They carried the box spring through the kitchen and into the living room.

"Grandma Lou, we can make your home accessible." Danny propped the box spring against a bookshelf on one end of the living room.

Grandma shook her head. "I don't know if that would make sense."

"I could frame in a wall here, where we're putting the bed, and give you privacy. I've already asked Russ to take measurements to make a ramp for you, for when you need that. He can get going on it right away—he has time."

"That could work." Beth held the side rails of the bed in

place while Danny attached the footboard.

Grandma sighed. "If this disease progresses quickly, it doesn't make any sense to put money into modifying this old house."

"At least think about it." Danny said.

"Thank you, Danny. It's good to have options."

"Beth and I will get your mattress." Danny led the way back upstairs. "So you do want to stay, hey." He glanced over his shoulder at her.

"Yeah, I'd like to. I don't want the discussion we had today to be the end of our relationship." She lifted her chin. "But it takes time to build trust."

In the bedroom, he faced her. "I'm getting mixed signals."

"I would like to stay, but maybe this isn't God's plan."

"Is that how you make decisions in life? If things fall into place, it's God's plan? If things don't fall in place, then it's not God's plan?"

"I want to help Grandma," she said. "Some things in life are more important than—"

"I know Grandma's important," he snapped. "I love her, too. I don't want to see her go, and I don't think she wants to go." He grabbed one end of the mattress and pulled it away from the wall. "She's talking out of fear."

She moved around him and grabbed the other end. "She has a lot to be fearful of."

They carried the mattress carefully down the stairs.

"Grandma Lou," Danny said, as he entered the living room backward. "I don't want to see you go."

"It's for the best. Rebecca was right, as much as I hate to admit it. This disease is progressing faster than I thought it would."

"All your friends are here," Danny said.

"Friends are not family. I couldn't ask them to do what I would ask my family to do."

Beth saw sadness in Danny's face. Defeat.

"I also want to see my great-grandkids," Grandma continued, perhaps also sensing his sorrow. "I've only seen them once, when Tate was a baby, and I'm about to have another grandbaby. Ashley is due next month."

"So you're coming back?" His voice held hope.

Grandma looked down and mumbled, "I don't know. I'll have to take one day at a time."

As Beth helped Danny lift the box spring and mattress onto the bed frame, she glanced out the window. The headlights of Danny's SUV illuminated white streaks of snow that fell from the black sky. "The snow's really coming down out there."

"Winter's far from over," he said. "Grandma Lou, do you think you can get on your feet?"

"I think so."

"Let Beth help you get ready for bed, while I'm still here, and I'll boil water for your bedtime tea," he said.

Grandma managed to get to her feet and hobble around the house, although she grimaced in pain when she put pressure on her knee.

Maybe the fall was due to fast progression of the disease, or maybe it was a freak accident. Either way, the decision was made. They were going to California.

Chapter 45

By Saturday morning, six inches of snow had fallen, and Mak had the driveway plowed before Beth woke. She came downstairs expecting to see Grandma at the kitchen table, but Grandma had for once slept longer than she had.

When Grandma eventually came out of the living room, Beth asked, "Did you sleep okay?"

"Just fine." The bruise on Grandma's face was still purple, but the swelling had gone down.

Grandma sat facing the window. "The chickadees are glad to have the birdseed, now that the ground is covered again."

"Look at the birds of the air. They don't sow or reap or store away in barns, yet God feeds them," Beth quoted Jesus.

"You're feeding them, Beth."

Beth set a cup of peppermint tea in front of Grandma with a straw.

Flurries continued throughout the day, but the snow melted into a mist as it approached the ground, and fog rose from the fields, fighting for spring. By Sunday morning another couple of inches had fallen, not enough to plow, but enough to make a person wonder if spring would ever come.

Beth took Grandma to Pinehurst Church, and, for a moment, it seemed as if life was normal, and everything would be okay. However, Danny wasn't there, and Beth couldn't remember if his rotational schedule had him off or not. She decided against texting him. She didn't want to send him mixed signals, so it was best to give him none.

After Mike Rogers made announcements, instructing everybody to let Senja know if they could bring an entrée, side dish, or dessert to the upcoming International Dinner, Pastor Chip moved to the podium. "Does anybody have prayer requests today?"

"I do." Grandma stood.

"Go ahead, Lou."

"As you already know, we found the answer to my weak arms," she said calmly. "First, I want to let you know how blessed I have been by the fellowship I've had at Pinehurst. You have all loved me so well, and I love you. I want you to keep praying for me. Pray for healing on this side of heaven and pray for my spirit, that I would find joy no matter what. I am going to miss you all so much."

The congregation murmured.

"I decided to go to California to live with my daughter."

Senja and several other congregants gasped.

"It's for the best." Grandma sat down.

For the best? Beth's stomach tightened. Those were Mother's words. This is what Mother wanted, but was it really what Grandma desired?

Beth spent the next day cleaning the house, getting it ready for an indefinite vacancy. She didn't have much to pack for herself aside from clothes she had brought and the couple things she had picked up along the way—her *Torn for You* CD and her *Hope* journal.

With more difficulty, she packed for Grandma, trying to anticipate her needs, because Grandma wasn't interested in bringing anything in particular. "Undergarments and a few outfits, and that'll be enough," Grandma said.

Beth made herself busy whenever her thoughts turned to Danny. She asked Grandma to tell stories of her childhood to fill her mind with something other than him. When Grandma couldn't think of another story, Beth asked her to talk about one of her favorite books. Still, late in the evening, Beth peered across the field to see the lights on in Danny's little house.

On Monday evening, before the Tuesday morning flight, visitors came.

Mak and Lorna stopped in.

Lorna hugged Louisa. "Let me get your daughter's address and I'll send another bidet."

"How's the book coming along?" Beth asked Mak.

"You know, it's funny how that's become da first thing people ask when they see me. Anyways, I figured out my character's fatal flaw. Now I have to find out if it'll be da ruin of her or if she'll be redeemed. That's what makes books interesting—finding out if da flaw is truly fatal."

"I can't wait to read it." Beth hugged him.

Sam Clinton and Robin came by.

Sam squeezed Grandma's shoulder. "Louisa, live every day like it's a gift."

Ladies from the prayer group visited, including Aimee, who was accompanied by Russ. He sat next to her on the couch as they chatted with Grandma. Aimee thanked her for being there for her family, herself and her aunts, Senja and Lorna. "We didn't come from a Christian family, so you were our spiritual mentor."

Late in the evening, after the commotion died down and Beth thought she'd seen the last of the visitors, Danny stopped in.

She avoided looking him in the face, because it took everything she had to hide her emotions. Though she feared he might interpret it as disinterest, she didn't want to hurt him more by pulling the bandage off slowly.

"I'll keep an eye on everything for you, Grandma Lou," he said.

"You're a good man," Grandma said. "A woman couldn't

ask for better grandson."

He gave Grandma a hug.

Later, Danny stood in the porch with Beth a step above on the threshold of the front door. "I guess this is good-bye." His voice cracked as he said the words.

"If our flight can get out. It's snowing again."

"This fluff?" Danny chuckled. "It'll get out."

"Danny, for what it's worth, I liked you—a lot."

"For what it's worth, I love you—still."

"Thank you," she said.

He hugged her, pulling her in tight to his body.

"We can stay in touch," she said hopefully.

He released her. "You need to make a decision first. I'd love to stay in touch if you have any intention to come back here, but staying in touch for the sake of staying in touch will make this more painful."

"Danny, sometimes things don't work out. The timing wasn't right."

"Sometimes you have to go with your heart, take a chance—throw the rule book out the window."

Beth turned her head. "I can't."

"You won't." He gave her one last hug and kissed her on the neck, right below her ear.

She felt a shiver down her spine and she momentarily hated him for making her love him so much.

Chapter 46

*B*eth pulled her new-to-her Mazda 6 into the driveway of Julie's townhouse.

Julie ran out of the house barefoot, her blonde hair trailing behind her. "Beth!" She squeezed Beth's arm through the window. "I missed you." Julie bounced around to the passenger side and climbed in. "Leather seats. This is nice. You just got it? "

"I drove it off the lot today. Almost got hit coming out of the parking lot. I forgot how crazy the traffic is out here."

"I'm sorry things didn't work out with Dan the man, but I admit, I'm not too sorry. I'm glad you're back. The kids are napping. Come on in and we'll get caught up."

Inside the house, Beth stood in the kitchen. Cold, conditioned air blew on the back of her calves.

Julie opened the fridge. "Can I get you something to drink? Water, juice, iced tea?"

"Do you have hot tea?"

"Sure, I'll heat water."

"Thank you."

Julie put a mug of water in the microwave and pressed a single button. It wasn't as if Beth really thought it would make a difference, but she did wonder if tea truly tastes better when heated on a wood stove.

Julie leaned against the counter. "So you're going back to the Resource Center?"

"Yes. Carmen, who took over my job, still has classes this summer, so they can use my help. Gary's going to ask the board if there's money in the budget for another full-time staff in the fall, maybe not with the tutoring program exactly, but still working with the youth."

Julie sat at the kitchen table and waved Beth over. "You get your old life back."

"I guess so, but with a better car." Beth joined her.

"Did you miss California?"

With her legs crossed, Beth rested an elbow on the table and her chin in her hand. "Of course I missed people. You. My family. The kids at the Resource Center. I didn't miss the traffic, but driving in the UP is harrowing for different reasons. I missed the shopping, especially the thrift stores. It's strange, because I didn't feel a need to shop when I was there—I didn't have a desire to have things, except for an expensive journal and pen."

"Sounds like you miss the UP."

"I try not to think about it." Beth looked out the window. A green hedge blocked the view, providing privacy and security. She felt a twinge of longing for the countryside she had left behind.

"How's your grandma doing?"

"She seems to be okay. It's a lot easier for her to walk in and out of my parent's house, and she's already spent time with Jeremy, Ashley, and the kids. Her arms are very weak, but other than that the disease hasn't progressed much."

The microwave beeped and Julie got up and crossed the room. "Are you staying in touch with Danny?" She pulled the mug out.

Beth shrugged sadly. "He doesn't want a long-distance relationship."

"What do you want?" Julie set the mug in front of Beth

along with a Lipton selection box.

Beth looked down at the box of teas in front of her. I want loose-leaf tea, she thought, but she didn't say it. "I can't wait to see your kids." She put a berry hibiscus tea bag in her water.

At home that evening, after a family dinner of lasagna and fresh peach cobbler, Beth played Legos with Cora and Tate on the carpeted living room floor. Ashley, eight months pregnant, sat with Jeremy on the couch, and Mother and Dad sat in two matching armchairs separated by a small table piled with books.

Grandma reclined back in a chair. "It's nice to have the family together."

"I knew you'd like being here," Mother said.

Beth glanced up at her and noticed a familiar title among a stack of books on the table next to her. "Mother, did you read *Still Intimately Yours*?"

Mother sniffed. "Your father and I are both reading it. Our small group at church wanted to go through it."

"Do you like it?"

"Not really."

"I thought you loved everything Dr. Benley said."

"He makes a few good points."

"He has many good points." Dad picked up the book and opened it. "We're only halfway through, and we've already learned a lot."

Mother huffed. "Not all of his advice works in real life."

"But you like everything he said in *Before I'm Intimately Yours*," Beth pressed.

Mother bristled. "That's different."

"Because it was advice for me and not you?"

Mother stood. "You were in the UP too long." She walked toward the kitchen.

Beth faced Cora and Tate. Without up-speak and loud enough for her mother to hear, she asked, "Yous guys want to see how high we can build the tower, hey."

"Yous? Humph." Mother left the room.

Beth's phone rang. It was Aimee. "I'll be right back," she said to the kids as she stood and put the phone to her ear. "Hi, Aimee." She opened the sliding door and stepped onto a cement patio behind the house, which sat at the base of a hill with a much more expensive neighborhood.

"I miss you," Aimee said. "I'm calling to see how you and Louisa are doing."

"She's doing okay. Her legs are holding up. She was worried they were going fast, but she thinks maybe her fall was just a fluke." Beth wanted to ask about Danny, but resisted. "Is it still snowing there?"

Aimee laughed. "No, the last snowfall was that day you left. The snow's melting fast."

"How's Russ?"

"Good. Thanks for asking."

"And Senja? Lorna?"

"Good. They're both good. Beth, are you beating around the bush?"

"What?"

"You want to know how he's doing, don't you?"

Beth took a deep breath of the city air and exhaled slowly.

"He misses you," Aimee said.

"I'm sure he'll forget about me soon enough," Beth said.

"Don't be so sure. How are *you* doing?"

"I'm okay. I forgot how crazy the traffic was out here. The weather's nice, I have to admit, but it seems like I spend most of my time inside buildings anyhow."

"I'd be outside all the time if I lived there."

"It doesn't work like that once you're out here. Everything's crazy-busy. Everybody's busy. I spend my time at work or in my car. When I stop someplace to shop, I don't see people I know, never have any of those special conversations in the aisles."

"Sounds like you're homesick."

"I am home. I guess I wish I were still on vacation."

"He asked me if I heard from you. Danny did."

Not what she wanted to hear. Beth wanted… no, she *needed* to close that chapter of her life.

"You want me to tell him anything?" Aimee continued.

She thought for a moment. "Tell him I'm settling in and that Grandma's doing fine," she finally said.

"That's it?"

"Aimee, sometimes things don't work out."

"Tell me about it. I was after that man for years, and it took you coming along to make me realize it wasn't going to happen. It's for the best, because I would've never noticed Russ if Danny hadn't fallen in love with you."

"I'm glad I could be so useful."

Chapter 47

$\mathcal{B}$eth sat in the resource room at the Center under a banner printed with the words *Go for the Gold*, the theme of the summer program designed to encourage kids to reach reading and math goals. She sketched out an idea for a bulletin board to go along with the theme.

Emma, one of the junior staff, sharpened pencils.

Carmen, the new tutoring coordinator, sat at Beth's old desk. "How should we track the kids' progress?"

"The form from the Shoot for the Moon summer from two years ago should work." Beth crossed the room to a file cabinet and thumbed through folders. "Here." She handed the page to Carmen. "Make something that looks like this."

"Thanks." Carmen turned back to her computer.

Beth returned to her chair at a table. She drew a three-tiered awards platform. The whirring of the pencil sharpener stopped and Beth looked across the room at the teenager. "Emma, can you get a few sheets of yellow construction paper? You can help me stencil and cut out letters."

"Sure." Emma went to the supply closet.

Beth pondered how effortlessly she had resumed her work. She had left the Center in good hands.

"Where is it?" Emma called.

"It should be on the left, a third of the way down from the top." Beth sketched a trophy.

"I can't find it," Emma said.

"Below orange and above the green."

It was unlike Emma to need hand-holding. The teen had been a part of the Resource Center job skills program for over a year.

"I can't find orange and green."

Beth looked up. "Do you see the construction paper?"

"Yeah."

Beth went to the supply closet and found stacks of construction paper in seemingly random order, not in the rainbow order she had left them in last December. "Carmen?" she called from the closet.

"Yes?" Carmen replied.

"Where is the yellow?"

"It's at the bottom. I filed under *Y*, for yellow. I alphabetized them."

Beth laughed. She would have to let it go. She was no longer in charge. She grabbed a couple sheets of yellow paper and handed them to Emma.

When she stepped out of the closet, she heard a distinct, high-pitched squeal. She looked to the door.

"Maritza." Beth hurried to give the young, olive-skinned woman a hug. "It's great to see you."

"I didn't think you were coming back. I missed you."

"How's college life?" It still seemed a miracle that her once-struggling mentee was now a sophomore at Apollos College, her alma mater.

"It's going okay. I'm learning a lot. But let me tell you, for a Christian college, some of the girls aren't very Christian, and my roommate, well, I think they put us together because we're both Mexican." Maritza sighed, blowing air through pursed lips. "She's like third-generation and thinks being Mexican means you eat tacos on *Cinco de Mayo* and she gets mad at me when I play my music. She's a PK so I think she should have a little more grace. But the guys—well, the guys have been very friendly."

"That doesn't surprise me." Beth stepped back. The shy, awkward teen was gone. Maritza stood tall and met Beth's gaze as she flipped her long, silky, black hair behind her slim shoulders. "Is there anyone special?"

"Well…" Maritza's face softened. "I like this guy Phillip. We eat at the same table in the SDR, but we're just friends. He was an MK in Brazil and he speaks Portuguese, and he understands Spanish."

"Look at you. You have the lingo down. Student dining room, pastor's kid, missionary kid."

"Yeah." Maritza laughed. "It's like learning a whole new language, which by the way, I'm learning Portuguese. I'm joining Phillip in São Paulo this summer. I'll stay at his parent's apartment with him and we'll see how it goes. We'll be back in the fall because he still has one more year, but, who knows, he's already asked my ring size, and…"

"Whoa, girl, slow down."

"I know. Phillip teases me for talking too fast, too, but at least I don't talk too fast in Portuguese."

"Ha. I'm not talking about you talking fast, which you do. I'm talking about moving too fast with this boy."

"He's not a boy. He's like two years older than me."

"This man. You should date at least a year, summer and winter him. You need to think rationally, and not let your heart get ahead of your head."

"Yeah, I'm glad I did that with my boyfriends in high school, because I sure wouldn't want to be married to any of them, but Phillip and I don't need that rule. It's different with us. We're such good friends, and he's a great guy. What about you? Are you back for good?"

Beth looked at her feet. "That's the plan, I guess." She sighed and then lifted her chin. "It's good to be back, but we'll see what happens. Gary has a spot for me this summer, but Carmen will be full time after she finishes summer classes, so he's going to ask the board if he can bring on another staff full time. If it doesn't work out, I might stay on part time and go to grad school, back at Apollos College with you."

"Why do you look so sad? You don't look like you're happy to be back." Maritza studied Beth's face. "You met someone in Michigan, didn't you?"

Beth turned away.

"You did. Fess up."

"He's a cop. He's a nice guy, but he's in Michigan and I'm here, so…"

Maritza sighed. "How come there's always complications?" She brightened. "But there's texting, Facebook. There are planes."

"Neither of us wants a long-distance relationship, and he's tied to Michigan with his job as a State Trooper."

"You can make it work if you want," Maritza said enthusiastically. "Like with me and Phillip. Any two Christians can make it work if they're committed to God and to each other."

Beth furrowed her brow.

Concern rose in Maritza's eyes. "Right, Beth? You said that once."

"I don't know, Maritza. I have life less figured out than I used to. Alan broke my heart. My grandma's sick. I'm back in California, and Danny's in Michigan."

"That's his name? Danny?"

"Yes."

"You love him, don't you?"

Beth shook her head. "I…"

"You do love him."

"Maritza, love's a choice."

"You could choose to love him then, couldn't you?"

"Well… Maybe."

"Love will find a way," Maritza said cheerily. "Love never fails."

"You watch too many movies."

"I do. But that one's in the Bible, 1 Corinthians 13:8. I learned something my first two years of Bible college."

After work, Beth took the long way home. She sang along to the radio as she drove on Lincoln Boulevard, past Marina del Rey. She turned up the volume and let the stereo drown out her thoughts of Danny. She exited on Venice Beach Boulevard and drove toward the ocean, where she parked in a lot next to the beach. Couples walked by hand-in-hand, and bare-chested men and bikini-topped women whizzed by on bicycles and in-line skates. Men lifted weights in a fenced-in area, and pairs of women played beach volleyball.

Though she was raised in Los Angeles, it seemed foreign to her. Then she heard through the car speakers a voice from Michigan, "We met at the cross and found grace for each other. We met at the cross and found hope to carry on. We met at the cross and found healing to repair all the broken pieces in our lives." She softly sang along with Allie Nantuck as she stared off into the ocean.

At home, she sat next to Grandma on the couch in the living room.

Beth hugged a throw pillow. "I got my old life back, but I don't feel like my old self. I'm not sure I believe all the things I used to tell the teens. I thought I had God all figured out, but now I'm not so sure."

"'Methinks that in looking at things spiritual, we are too much like oysters observing the sun through the water, and thinking that thick water the thinnest of air.'"

"Melville?"

"Aye." Grandma smiled.

Beth tossed the pillow aside. "How can I work in ministry when I know so little?"

Grandma placed her wrinkled hand over Beth's. "When you realize how little you know, you become more qualified."

Chapter 48

*A*s weeks passed into mid-July, Beth fell into a routine. She worked at the Resource Center, spent time with Grandma, and babysat Cora and Tate so Ashley could rest after being up at night with Annalee, Beth's new niece.

She thought of Danny often. Had she made the right decision? She was tempted to text him, because she missed him, but resisted. She wished they were still in touch, but she respected him and didn't want to lead him on. If she did not intend to return to the UP, it was better to leave things as they were.

Each night before she went to bed, she prayed for him and for guidance, since she still didn't have concrete plans for the fall.

Beth was cleaning the resource room one afternoon when Gary, her boss, poked his head in. "Stop by my office before you leave today."

Her stomach tightened. She knew the board had just met. Gary had such a poker face that she had no idea what the outcome of the meeting had been.

She walked slowly down the hall to his office.

He waited until she sat. "They approved it." He smiled.

"The budget is tight, but they decided to make the open IT position part time."

Beth felt her shoulders relax.

"You don't seem too excited. This means I can offer you a full-time position and even a three percent increase in salary." He leaned forward. "I know you had talked about possibly going back to grad school. If you want to do that, you can still work part time."

"Thank you, Gary. I do love working with the kids. I'm praying about my future. I don't know if God's even calling me to ministry."

"You're a Christian, so we know he has called you to ministry. The question is where."

Beth nodded. Her ministry at the Resource Center was worthwhile. Would it be wrong to leave? Would it be selfish to go back to Michigan and see if God really was knitting her and Danny's hearts together?

"Let me know within a few weeks. Now that the money's in the budget, if you decide you're not interested, I want to post the position and hire someone before we start up again in the fall."

"Thank you, Gary. I'll let you know soon."

Beth prayed as she drove home after work. *God, I need to make a decision. What do you want for me?*

At home, she sat with Grandma on the back patio below a sliver of gray sky between palm trees and a hill with houses, decks, and pools hanging over the edges of terraces. Chain-link fences running down the steep hill marked private property. In one fenced-in area, workers slashed, bundled, and carried brush up the slope.

"Grandma," Beth said, "I don't feel at home here, not like I used to."

"There's something special about the UP. It's God's country. I miss it dearly." Longing filled Grandma's voice. "I love spending time with the family, but I miss my friends, the fresh air."

"I do, too." Beth lay back in her chair and looked up at the haze.

"You miss Danny, don't you?" Grandma looked at her knowingly. "I hoped you would end up together. I thought you and he had something special."

Beth took a deep breath and exhaled. "Grandma, how can I know what God wants for my life?"

"It's pretty simple. He tells us to love him and love others."

Beth straightened in her chair. "I know, but how do I decide if I should take this job at the Resource Center?"

"Do you want it?" Grandma asked.

Beth ran her fingers through her hair. "I'm torn. It seems like everything is falling into place for it. God has aligned everything to make it work."

"Is that how you make decisions? You only decide to do something if it falls into place?"

Beth shrugged, pondering the challenge in Grandma's question. "Everything happens for a reason. That's why God ended my engagement. So I could help you."

"Nonsense," Grandma said sharply. "Alan ended your engagement because he's a weasel."

Beth giggled as Grandma continued, her voice softening, "But once you ended up in the UP, God certainly used you to bless me. I think God would be okay with you planning your own way on this one. God's hand is in our circumstances, but he doesn't micromanage our lives. I didn't mean to drag you apart from Danny."

"It didn't work out, with the timing. It wasn't meant to be." Even as Beth said the words, she wondered if she believed them.

"Hmmm." Grandma cocked her head, studying Beth.

Later that evening, Beth found herself on the family laptop computer. She scrolled through a webpage for Douglass State University's employment opportunities with a number of postings—International Student Counselor, Financial Aid Specialist, Student Services Coordinator. She read the job descriptions and qualifications, and she could see herself doing any one of the jobs and living in the UP. Before she started work on her résumé, she sent a text message to Aimee. *You need a roommate?*

A minute later, her phone dinged. *You coming back?*

Opposing answers volleyed inside Beth's head. *Don't know.*

A message from Aimee. *It would be tight, but we can make it work for a while.*

Maybe she should give Michigan—give Danny a chance.

Another ding. *Should I tell Danny?*

Beth's heart raced as she quickly replied. *NO.*

He misses you.

Really? Beth blinked back tears as she typed. *Then why hasn't he contacted me?*

He said you left him. Isn't the ball in your court?

Chapter 49

*B*eth found Mother and Grandma drinking iced tea at the kitchen table. Looking at Mother's stony face and Grandma's drooping head, she knew she had walked in on the middle of something tense.

Beth took a glass out of the cupboard and filled it with water from the dispenser on the fridge.

"This has been a nice vacation," Grandma said, "but I'm—"

"We can talk about this later." Mother nodded in Beth's direction.

"She can hear this." Grandma lifted her chin. "I'm ready to go back to Michigan. I'm not dying. After the tumble I took, I thought the disease was progressing fast, but I still have time. I want to go home."

"Grandma." Beth sat at the table. "Do you really want to go home?"

Grandma's eyes held a faraway look. "If I go home now, I'll be there in time for blueberry season."

"We can buy blueberries at Trader Joe's, Mom." Mother folded her arms.

"Not fresh blueberries picked from the sands of Big Traverse Bay. I appreciate your hospitality, Rebecca. It's time for me to get back."

"That house is too much for you." Mother shook her head.

Beth squared her shoulders and faced Mother. "I can—"

Grandma cleared her throat. "I'm moving into High Cliff. After my diagnosis, I put myself on the wait list. I've been calling every week, and yesterday they told me they have an opening. I would enjoy being with my friends instead of sitting in this house every day watching TV while you're all at work."

"But that would work only for a while. You'll eventually need full-time care, here at home, or a nursing home," Mother said.

"It's a lot to ask you to take care of me—you all have jobs, busy lives—and if I have to go to a nursing home, I want it to be there, in Quincy."

Mother frowned as Beth smiled.

"There's a level of accountability there that you don't have in the city. I may not know the CNAs or the nurses, but I probably know their mothers and grandmothers." Grandma set her chin. "I've made up my mind. There isn't much I have control over anymore, but I can make this decision."

"I won't allow it."

"Rebecca, it's not your choice."

Mother leaned back in her chair and looked up to the ceiling. After a few moments, she sighed and brought her head down. "Okay, Mom, if that's what you want, I can take time off at the end of August and fly out there with you."

Beth swallowed hard. "I can fly her out."

"Elizabeth, I don't want you going back to the UP."

"I wasn't going to say anything in case it didn't work out, but I'm going anyway. I have job interviews at the university.

"What?" Mother stiffened. "Elizabeth, that's enough. You can leave."

Reflexively, Beth stood and took a step away from the table. She paused. *Enough.* She had to take a stand. Pivoting on her heels, she squeezed the air out of her palms. "I will *not* leave." Maybe she had misunderstood. Giving her mother the benefit of the doubt, she asked, "Did you mean I could leave

California or leave the room?"

"You can leave the room."

"That's what I thought. And I won't. But I *will* leave California."

Grandma's eyes twinkled.

"But what about the Resource Center?" Mother asked.

"Gary doesn't need an answer from me until after I get back." Beth placed a hand on Grandma's shoulder.

Mother stalked out of the room.

"You're planning your way, Beth," Grandma said.

"Yes, I am."

"Elizabeth, could you make a vegetable tray?" Mother opened a bag of fresh green beans. "There are cucumbers and carrots in the fridge."

"Sure." Beth opened the fridge and took out the vegetables. She rinsed them off and set them on a cutting board. She took a plate out of the cupboard, pulled a knife from the drawer, and proceeded to slice a cucumber into coins.

"Peel the cucumbers first and then slice them in quarters the long way and then cut the quarters in half," Mother ordered.

"Certainly, Mother." Beth dug in a drawer for a vegetable peeler.

One last dinner together. The rest of the family gathered on the back patio while she helped get dinner on. She and Mother had settled into an unspoken truce.

Mother snapped the ends off green beans. "Elizabeth, you're not going to get back together with that boy."

Or maybe what Beth thought was a truce was Mother gathering ammunition. Irritation bubbled. "Was that a question? Because there was no up-speak."

"No, that was a statement. I up-speak all of my questions."

"I don't know if I'll see him on this trip, but I will if I get one of the jobs." She found the peeler and closed the drawer with a bang.

"There's something I should tell you. When we were at the Co-op last spring and I ran into Judy Paikkala, she told me her niece used to live with Danny. He has a sexual past, Elizabeth."

"I know, Mother." Beth vigorously peeled a cucumber. "Danny told me."

"He told you that, and you're still interested in him?" Mother huffed. "Remember your list. Sexual purity is on your list. I don't think it's a good match."

"I have a much shorter list these days. He repented, and he's walking with God." Beth wiped the peelings into a paper towel.

"He's got baggage," Mother said sharply.

Beth threw the paper towel of peelings into the garbage can. "We're all broken."

"He's slept with one woman. He's probably slept with more."

"It's in the past."

"Who knows how many kids he has."

Beth slashed the knife through the cucumber and set the pieces on the plate. She turned on her heels. "You're being hypocritical."

"What?"

"You had a past before Dad, with Chip."

Mother's eyes widened.

"You could have another kid out there."

"No, Elizabeth, I would know if I had another kid. And don't bring me into this. We're talking about you and your future. Past behavior is the best predictor of future behavior."

"It didn't predict your future behavior."

"That's different, because I—"

"Became legalistic?" Beth suggested.

Mother gasped and her eyes became steely.

Beth faced off against her mother across the peninsula counter. "It's the truth."

"I am *not* legalistic. Christ said, 'If you love me, obey my commandments.'"

"We should obey Christ's commandments, but we don't

have to obey all of Dr. Benley's commandments."

"I just want what's best for you." Mother pushed the un-snapped green beans aside.

"You want what's best for you—to show the world you raised a pure, virgin daughter who's too good to date anybody but a spiritual giant."

"Don't tell me you've given yourself to that man."

"No, but that's not the point. I'm a sinner, too. I'm full of pride. I'm unforgiving. I'm judgmental."

"Has he kissed you?"

"Mother," Beth snapped.

Mother turned her attention to a glass baking pan. She splashed olive oil on top of raw chicken and seasoned it with salt and pepper.

Beth took a deep breath. "Danny knows he's a sinner, and he's honest about it. He's full of grace and love because he knows he's been forgiven. And he's following Christ now."

"Even so, I don't want you in the UP. Everybody knows everybody's business."

"The only thing that bothers you is that somebody might know yours."

Mother turned away.

"Mother, honesty and grace are God's principles. He doesn't want rule followers. He wants people with changed hearts who love him and love others."

"I don't want you to make the same mistakes I made." Mother's voice cracked.

"I won't. I'll make my own."

Mother's shoulders shook as she cried.

Beth's heart softened, and at last she felt empathy for her. Beth came around the peninsula and put her arm around her. "Mom, we can't control everything in life. Alan was a Boy Scout, met every requirement on my list and yours, and look how that turned out."

Mother wiped tears off her cheek.

Beth searched her face. "Do you understand what Dr. Benley means when he talks about intimacy? God knows us, he knows our sin, and he loves us anyway. When we see others for who they really are, and we accept them, then we can find real intimacy in relationships."

"I don't want to talk about this. I'll put the chicken on the grill. Finish snapping the beans and set them to boil. And you can just cut the carrots in half, the long way. But peel them first." Mother grabbed the pan of raw chicken and, before stepping out, said, "Not a word of this to your father."

After finishing the vegetable tray, Beth pulled her phone from her pocket and tapped the messages icon. She reread the old text messages from Danny, including the first one.

Sorry couldn't do lunch. Get back 2 me re concert. Now u have my #. Danny

Beth texted him. *Miss you.* She waited for a reply. It would be past ten o'clock in Michigan. Would he see it? She set her phone down and snapped ends off the remaining green beans.

After checking her phone throughout the evening, she finally turned it off and went to bed. Maybe he was working—or maybe he had moved on.

Chapter 50

*T*he commuter jet flew over green, rolling hills and out over the greatest of lakes. It made a broad sweeping turn and landed at the airport on top of Quincy Hill. Grandma sat by Beth's side with her head rested against the seat back and her eyes closed until the jet came to a complete stop at the one-gate terminal. The ground crew rolled a staircase up to the plane.

Grandma cautiously stepped down the stairs. She put her right foot out and used her stronger left leg to lower herself down to the next step. After her right leg landed securely, she brought her left foot down to meet it. Beth climbed down ahead of her, turned sideways so she could steady Grandma if needed.

The July sky was blue with a scattering of cumulus clouds, and the temperature was in the mid-seventies with low humidity. Perfect, Beth thought. Like the summers she remembered.

She toted her and Grandma's carry-on bags. A continual stream of deplaning passengers held the door open as they entered the terminal. It was a small airport. It shouldn't be hard to see him, if he cared enough to meet her there. Her heart sank as she searched the room. "Is there a taxi service here,

Grandma?"

"Yeah, right over there." Grandma nodded toward the entrance.

As the crowd moved to the baggage claim area, Beth saw him. A smile spread across his face as she caught his eye. She dropped the bags and ran into his outstretched arms, jumping up and hugging him around the neck.

Danny let her down, but held her close. "Hey, Beth."

She reached up and kissed him, long and slow. "Danny, I love you."

"Thank you." His eyes sparkled as he laughed.

Beth poked him in the side.

He flinched. "I love you, too." He rested his chin on the top of her head as she pressed the side of her face against his chest. "Beth, what happens if you don't get the job?"

She shrugged. "I can't control that, but I can choose to love you."

"*Hyvää päivää*," a voice boomed, and Beth opened her eyes to Mak and Lorna. "We heard yous was coming." Mak gave Grandma a hug. "Beth, I knew you'd have enough *sisu* to come back."

"How's the book coming along?" Beth winked.

Mak snorted. "Almost done. I'm working on a H.E.A. ending."

"What's that?"

"Happily Ever After."

Danny squeezed Beth tighter.

"Mak, is that realistic?" She relaxed in Danny's embrace.

Mak gave a belly laugh. "Life's got its ups and downs, but I'm endin' it on an up note. We'll call it Happy for Now."

Epilogue

𝒜 fifteen-foot balsam fir stood in the front right corner of the nave on Christmas Eve day, ornamented with white, glittery cutouts of angels and the Star of Bethlehem at the top. Regular attendees filled the pews along with several guests.

Mother sat in the front pew next to Grandma. On the chancel, Pastor Chip faced the congregation, holding an open Bible. To his left, Danny stood looking toward the entrance, with Jack and Russ standing on the stairs below him, opposite Julie and Aimee. Below the women, Cora held a basket she had emptied of flower petals.

A pianist sounded the first notes of Pachelbel's Canon in D, accompanied by Chip's granddaughter, Reina, on violin. Mother rose and turned, and the rest of the congregation stood except for Grandma who remained seated in a wheelchair.

Standing on the threshold to the sanctuary, the bride looked through an archway made of bended birch bows, with her father on her side and Senja, the wedding planner, behind her. Senja nudged her and mouthed, "Now."

Holding a bouquet of red roses, Beth looked up at her father, and he pecked her on the forehead. With slow, deliberate steps, they walked down the aisle, past birch bark heart decorations hung on the side of each pew. Heads popped out in the aisle, snapping pictures and taking video on smart phones.

When they reached the front of the nave, Pastor Chip asked, "Who gives this woman to be married to this man?"

"Her mother and I do," Dad said, and Danny descended the three steps. Dad placed Beth's hand in Danny's.

Danny clasped her hand as they stepped up to the chancel and stood facing Pastor Chip.

"'Dear friends, let us love one another for love comes from God.'" Pastor Chip's voice rang out as he read from First John.

After a prayer and a hymn, the pastor clarified the charge, the responsibility of marriage, and asked for the pledge. Beth and Danny each said, "I do accept this responsibility." Danny's hand trembled as he squeezed Beth's fingers.

Jack passed the rings to Pastor Chip who handed them to Beth and Danny.

Facing each other, they repeated their vows, "...to have and to hold, from this day forward, for better, for worse, for richer, for poorer, in sickness and in health, to love you as Christ loved the church, for as long as we both shall live. As a token of my faithfulness I give you this ring."

Hand in hand, they walked to a wooden stand where they lit a deer-tallow unity candle made especially for the wedding as a song played through the church's sound system. Beth closed her eyes and listened as Allie Nantuck's rich voice filled the sanctuary. "We met at the cross and found grace for each other. We met at the cross and found hope to carry on. We met at the cross and found healing to repair all the broken pieces in our lives." So much had changed in a year. "We met at the cross and found love for one another because we're filled with love from up above."

"Now that Danny and Beth have given themselves to each other by their vows," Pastor Chip said when the song concluded and the couple stood facing each other, "I pronounce them to be husband and wife, in the name of the Father, and of the Son, and of the Holy Spirit. Amen." He nodded to Danny. "You may kiss your bride."

Danny wrapped his arms around Beth, pulling her in close, and their lips met in a gentle kiss.

When he released his embrace, they faced the congregation.

"I now present you Mr. Daniel and Mrs. Elizabeth Johnson," Pastor Chip said.

Danny and Beth made their way down the aisle, followed by the best man Jack and the matron of honor Julie. Holding hands, Russ and Aimee followed behind.

A line formed leading into the fellowship hall, past Maribel's old dresser with a red bow draped over the vanity mirror and stacked with gifts. Guests inserted cards into a copper-topped bird feeder.

The bride and groom, along with the Dawson and Johnson parents, greeted each of their guests. There were handshakes, hugs, and congratulations.

Mother, when meeting Danny's friends, asked, "And how do you know my son-in-law?" She had definitely warmed up to him, Beth thought.

Mak had dressed up for the occasion in a burgundy, button-up shirt, which still showed creases from having been folded on the store rack. He wore brown, Carhartt, duck fabric pants with suspenders and swampers. "*Onneksi olkoon.*" Mak shook Danny's hand.

"Thank you, I think," Danny said.

"That's congratulations. Lorna wants to thank yous. She's back in da kitchen. Yous were her first big customer, with da birch bark decorations, deer candles, and pasties—and da gluten-free cupcakes." Mak motioned toward a table that held a multi-tier display with cupcakes cascading below a small wedding cake.

"Tell her she's most welcome." Beth hugged him.

When all had gone through the line, Beth and Danny took a seat at a table with the wedding party. At a nearby table, Dad draped his arm around Mother, who leaned her head against his shoulder. He bent and kissed her on the cheek. Beth smiled. She had not often seen such simple expressions of affection between them until they arrived a few days before the wedding.

Mak bounded to the wedding party table. "I got it. Da last line of my book came to me, and I had to run out to my truck to grab my journal before da idea escaped me."

"Well, let's hear it," Beth said eagerly.

Mak set the journal on the table and donned his reading glasses. "And that was da wedding between two young lovers who overlooked da other's faults, accepted with grace each other's broken pasts, and chose to love each other even when life's circumstances got in da way, not following da myriad of rules made by man, but a few precepts set down by God." Mak peered over his glasses. "Yous think it's too flowery?"

"It's beautiful." Tears filled Beth's eyes as she grabbed Danny's hand and squeezed.

Aimee stood in a cluster of single women on the sidewalk as Danny held the door of his Jeep open for his bride. Beth smiled at the crowd, and then turned her back and tossed the bouquet. It bounced off Senja's fingertips toward Aimee, who grabbed it and held it close to her chest. Aimee looked at Russ, their eyes met, and he winked.

Explore Copper Island and
find discussion questions at

KristinNeva.com

Aimee and Russ's Story
Available Summer 2017

KRISTIN NEVA

COPPER
COUNTRY

A Copper Island Novel
Two

Made in the USA
Lexington, KY
09 March 2018